"Excuse me, Miss, I need to have a few words with you," a thunderous voice boomed from behind Kimara, commanding her attention.

Kimara looked up from the sink and into the mirror above it. Her eyes met those of a male police officer.

"Right," Kimara hissed as she walked out of the restroom and dropped onto the nearest stool.

"Look, Miss Hamilton. You can either cooperate and be done with me in a matter of minutes, or you can keep up the attitude and spend the next hour answering my questions," Officer Porter said, his tone even and serious.

"As I've already said a million times, I have no idea what happened. Are we done?" Kimara asked.

She hopped off the stool and tilted her head back to get a better look at him, meeting his fiery gaze with one of her own. Almond shaped brown eyes stared down at her, their liquid depth like warm pools.

"For now," he answered, unwilling to break the connection their eyes had made.

Jared remained immobile as Kimara snatched the card from him and stomped away in the direction of the ladies room. He watched her retreating figure, the delicious curve of her behind sashaying to an unheard rhythmic drumbeat.

Kim Shaw

Free Verse

BET Publications, LLC
http://www.bet.com
http://www.arabesquebooks.com

ARABESQUE BOOKS are published by

BET Publications, LLC
c/o BET Books
One BET Plaza
1900 W Place NE
Washington, DC 20018-1211

All Kensington Titles, Imprints, and Distributed Lines are available at special quantity discounts for bulk purchases for sales promotions, premiums, fund-raising, and educational or institutional use. Special book excerpts or customized printings can also be created to fit specific needs. For details, write or phone the office of the Kensington special sales manager: Kensington Publishing Corp., 850 Third Avenue, New York, NY 10022, attn: Special Sales Department, Phone: 1-800-221-2647.

First Printing: August 2005

10 9 8 7 6 5 4 3 2 1

Printed in the United States of America

This book is dedicated to writers, poets, rappers and lyricists. You give the gift of words freely and soulfully. Continue making us laugh, cry, sing, dance, grow and think because it is you who keep the world spinning.

Acknowledgments

Thank you readers for making my debut novel, *Pack Light*, a success. Thank you for appreciating the story I had to tell through Vic and Maya.

Thank you to my family for being so patient with me during this writing endeavor. The process is difficult and time consuming, but because you respect my love of writing, you give me the space I need to perfect my craft.

Thank you to the staff at BET for holding my hand as I navigate a new career in my life. I appreciate your support, expertise and your commitment to bringing my words to life.

To my sisters and brothers in writing, from FDCAC, on-line and elsewhere, thank you for the encouragement you give. I can't wait to see your names in print as well.

The poems "You Win" and "Apology" appear courtesy of Kyron Sumpter. Readers, keep your eyes peeled for more from this talented artist.

Chapter 1

Kimara paused momentarily at the bottom step of the landing. She looked behind her at the two steep flights of stairs which she'd already climbed, then leaned over the railing to look up ahead at the dimly lit remaining two flights. She shook her head, letting her long dark hair snap from side to side as she cursed Jimmy Choo for not having considered that she might have a best girlfriend who lived in a fourth-floor walkup. He obviously couldn't relate to her struggle.

"You've got to be joking," Kimara spewed as she stood in front of Jasmine's open apartment door.

Jasmine lived in a quiet Queens neighborhood not far from where they'd grown up together. Queens Village was a small, tight-knit community comprised of working-class, single, and two-parent families. Everyone seemed to know everyone else and it was not uncommon for a child to be chastised by an elder from the community who was unrelated to them.

The tawny-skinned woman standing before her had been her best girlfriend for the past two decades. Jasmine, clad in a yellow terry cloth bathrobe and matching Tweety Bird slippers, shrugged her shoulders. She stepped aside to allow a perturbed Kimara to enter.

"Why aren't you dressed yet, Jasmine?" Kimara demanded, craning her neck upwards, her chestnut colored eyes narrowed. At five-feet-eight Jasmine towered above the petite Kimara, despite the three-inch heels the latter wore.

"Well, uh, see . . ." Jasmine stammered. She offered a weak smile which was met by a drawn-out sucking of teeth by Kimara.

"Come on Kimara. I really was planning to go—"

"No. No, no, no," Kimara bellowed. "I am not even trying to hear this." She let her Prada bag slide from her shoulder, barely catching the straps in her hand before it hit the floor.

"Kimara, please don't be like that. You know Rick's been working a lot of overtime lately and, when he called a few minutes ago to say that he was getting off early, I . . . well," Jasmine hesitated.

"So you're gonna kick me to the curb to stay home with old what's his face? Unbelievable!" Kimara spat.

She stomped across the living room's hardwood floors, plopped down on the brushed-cotton sectional and tossed her handbag onto the cushion next to her. She threw her head back against the fluffy sofa and closed her eyes.

"Don't act like such a baby Kimara," Jasmine ordered.

Kimara inhaled a deep cleansing breath, for the first time becoming aware of the scented candles which were placed strategically around the tiny living room. She opened her eyes and took in the scene of seduction set out before her—wine chilling in a bucket of ice, candlelight which bathed the room in softness and a bowl of fresh strawberries, bright red and still wet from washing. She rolled her eyes and dropped her head back onto the sofa as Jasmine switched the compact disc player to the OFF position, silencing Meli'sa Morgan's "Do Me Baby."

Kimara greedily sucked in another lungful of air, the

combined scents of eucalyptus and sweet cyclamen penetrating her senses. She willed her lips to stay shut before she said something that would cause irreparable damage to her relationship with Jasmine. Although it wouldn't be the first time she'd unleashed a vicious tongue, it could very well be the final straw.

The past year had been a turbulent roller-coaster ride for them. Ever since Jasmine married Frederick Wright, Kimara seemed unable to say or do the correct thing. It was no secret that she didn't like Rick. Everybody on the East coast knew that. But Rick was the man Jasmine had chosen and in her heart, Kimara knew that she had no choice but to accept it. However, try as she might, she couldn't stop the derogatory digs aimed at him from rolling off her wicked tongue every now and again. Especially on the increasingly frequent occasions when his big head seemed to be wedging its way between her and her best girlfriend. Tonight was yet another unwelcome intrusion.

"I'm not acting like a baby," Kimara retorted. "You're a flat-leaver," she added, glaring at Jasmine.

"Oh yeah, real mature Kimara. Look, I'm sorry to do this at the last minute. I tried to reach you, but you'd already left home and, as usual, your cell phone is off."

"My money was a little funny this month, that's all," Kimara defended. She took mental notice of the chiding tone in Jasmine's remark, letting her know once again that Jasmine disapproved of something she had done or failed to do.

"Whatever," Jasmine dismissed with a wave of her hand. "Point is, I'm sorry that you got all dressed up and came over here. But I'm not sorry about wanting to spend some time with my husband," Jasmine said as she struck a match and lit a purple candle which she'd missed.

"Come on Jazz, this party is going to be off the hook. Everybody's going to be there," Kimara pleaded.

"Everybody 'cept me," Jasmine answered.

Kimara gave Jasmine a final beseeching look, but realized from the determined set of her chin that the conversation was useless. If there was one thing Kimara had learned about Jasmine, it was that once this girl made a decision, nothing would change her mind.

She remembered vividly the day they'd met. They were in the second grade in Mrs. Berger's colorfully decorated classroom located on the third floor of P.S. 188. The teacher was introducing Kimara to the roomful of snot-nosed seven-year-olds. She had been beyond excited about beginning at a new school and the chance to make new friends. She'd worn her black Lee jeans with the permanent creases down the legs and a bright yellow sweatshirt. The kids giggled and pointed at her, openly ridiculing her. Who knew that Lees were no longer in style?

The image of standing there that day had remained one of Kimara's worst childhood memories. She'd squeezed her eyes shut tightly, wishing that either the ground would open up and swallow her or that the monster in her bedroom closet would eat the entire class. Her eyes grew watery and her cheeks burned with embarrassment. She hung her head low, two long twisted ponytails with yellow barrettes on the ends dangling in her face as the teacher tried to regain control over the unruly class. All of a sudden she felt cool, slender fingers covering her own. She looked up to find a tall, brown-skinned girl smiling down at her.

"Don't worry about these dummies," the girl said. She pulled Kimara by the hand toward the desks lining the room's windows. "You can sit next to me."

As Kimara followed her, the girl rolled her eyes and stuck her tongue out at the few students who continued to snicker, silencing them. Kimara was too shocked by this girl's brazen act to speak. But she later learned that the girl's name was Jasmine Mitchell and, as the tallest student in the class, even taller than the boys, nobody messed with her. She also learned that Jasmine was the most determined person in the world. She set her mind on being Kimara's friend and no matter what anybody else had to say about it, she remained dedicated.

"Well, I guess that's it, huh?" Kimara asked.

"Yeah girl. But maybe we can do something tomorrow. There's an independent movie opening up at the Angelika," Jasmine offered.

"I don't know . . ." Kimara hesitated, not wanting to give in or up so easily.

"Come on. You know you love those indies. What do you say? I'll buy the popcorn," Jasmine enticed.

"Yeah sure, whatever," Kimara answered softly. She didn't feel like trying to hide her disappointment. Jasmine was her best friend. They had been through everything together—from training bras to unplanned pregnancy scares. They had come of age when Run DMC and LL Cool J were burning up the microphones at local house parties that they were too young to frequent, but did anyway. They had taught one another all the latest dances like the Whop and the Pee Wee Herman. They'd experimented with boys, learned about life and evolved into womanhood together.

Now it was beginning to seem to Kimara as if their season had passed. The demanding roles of wife and school teacher had changed Jasmine, made her very critical and even more uptight. Sometimes it was as if Kimara didn't know her anymore. They didn't talk as much as they used to and when they did, the conversations almost always ended with Jasmine chastising Kimara for one thing or another.

Although their lives had traversed into different directions, the space Jasmine occupied in Kimara's heart was unchanged. She had, however, grown considerably weary of the put-downs. When Jasmine had agreed to attend tonight's label-launch party, Kimara was excited, even more than she was about the party itself. It would be an opportunity to spend time with the old Jasmine. The one with whom she used to juice guys and close down clubs for the night.

"I'm really sorry Kimara," Jasmine said, softening suddenly as if she were reading Kimara's mind.

Jasmine could not love Kimara more if they were blood sisters. She hated to disappoint her, and although she loved a good party just as much as the next person, she also loved her husband. Rick had brought a certain calm to her life and quiet nights alone with him had become more enticing than smoke-filled rooms, gyrating bodies and rainbow colored cocktails with little umbrellas in them. She knew that Kimara didn't like Rick and she hoped that one day that would change. If only Kimara could see Rick the way she saw him—as a warm, supportive, caring man who loved her more than life itself. Jasmine knew this would be a stretch, to say the least, because until Kimara was ready to move into the responsible adult world, she would not be able to understand that Rick was precisely the type of man Jasmine wanted and needed.

A key turned in the lock, drawing both women's attention to the door.

"There'd better be a sexy, naked woman waiting for me behind this—" Rick's voice preceded him into the apartment. He stopped midsentence when he saw Kimara standing next to his wife.

"Oh, Kimara. I wasn't expecting to see you," Rick said.

"Rick," Kimara responded dryly.

"Hi sweetie. Wow, you made good time getting here," Jasmine said as she moved toward him. She kissed him lightly on the lips, taking his work bag and stashing it in the coat closet.

Kimara watched them, the sensation of being a fifth wheel descending instantaneously upon her as usual. In spite of all of her misgivings about Rick, she had to admit that so far, he'd treated Jasmine well. At six-feet-three-inches, he was a lean, athletic looking man. Surely, many women would agree that his sleepy eyes and wide, toothy smile were attractive. Personally, Kimara thought that his head full of locks and full grown beard and mustache made him look even older than his thirty-six years. Add to that the fact that she found his mannerisms even more dated than his look.

When Jasmine first introduced him, having met him one day at the Flushing Station on the number seven train, his speech was peppered with phrases like *word up* and *that's the bomb*. It was all Kimara could do not to burst out laughing in his face. The minute they were alone, she jumped on Jasmine.

"He is so corny! You can't be serious."

"He's not corny. Okay, maybe he's a little behind the times, but—"

"Behind the times? Girl please. My dad is cooler than him. If he said 'word up' one more time, I swear I was gonna scream," Kimara laughed, choking and gasping for air.

"You are mean. I don't care what you say," Jasmine cried. "I think he's cute and nice, and I'm going out with him again."

"Whatever Jasmine. At least he's got a decent job with Transit. Make sure he takes you someplace nicer than Red Lobster."

Kimara didn't think too much more about Mr. Rick Wright until Jasmine started canceling their plans together to be with him and slipping away for extended weekends in Virginia with his family. About five months after they'd met, it became obvious to Kimara that the pesky little fly wasn't going to buzz off. Things had become serious. She thought it was too much too soon and she told Jasmine so.

"Jazz, don't you think things are moving a little fast? I mean, what do you really know about this guy? With a

name like Rick Wright, that's a hint and a half that
something has to be *wrong* with him."

"Stop being so paranoid. I know all about him. I've
even met his family, including his grandmother, Mabel.
Let me tell you, she is a trip. One time—"

"Jasmine, spare me the details about Grandma Mabel.
You've still only just gotten to know him."

"He's a great guy Kimara. He's stable, dependable—"

"Old," Kimara interjected.

"He's not old. He's only a few years older than us."

"Jasmine, a few is four or five. He's ten years older.
That's a decade. That's a whole hell of a lot more than
a few."

"Okay, so he's older. What's wrong with that? I mean
think about it. We spend all of our time running behind
these young guys who don't have anything going on and
ain't trying to put down roots. I'm not like you Kimara.
I don't want to be wined and dined, and I certainly
don't want to keep having to fend off guys who think
buying me a meal entitles them to hit it and quit it. I'm
not going to spend my life playing games with little
boys. I want to settle down. I want kids, a house . . .
damn, can I have the white picket fence and the happily
ever after?"

"Nobody says you can't have all that Jasmine, but you
don't have to settle," Kimara admonished.

"Why do you think I'm settling? Is it that far-fetched
to believe that Rick is the guy for me?"

Kimara was stumped. She couldn't think of a logical
argument for why Jasmine shouldn't see Rick other
than his age, so she shut up and tried to see for herself
what Jasmine saw in him. They went on a couple of
double dates, hung out at Jasmine's place together, but
the more time she spent around him, the more she
grew to dislike and eventually despise him.

Rick always seemed to talk down to everyone, especially Jasmine, like he was Albert Einstein sent back

from the grave to school the youngsters. He was an authority on every subject, or so he thought, and he had an annoying habit of correcting people when they spoke. Kimara took to making constant jokes about his age, in his presence and behind his back.

"Do you want to go to the movies tonight or do you and Father Time have plans?" she would ask.

Jasmine grew increasingly insulted, but Kimara didn't care. Almost a year to the day that Jasmine and Rick had met, they were gathered at Jasmine's place for her mother's birthday celebration. After having made goo-goo eyes at each other all night, they finally announced their engagement. Kimara bit her tongue and sulked quietly all evening until she had an opportunity to be alone with Jasmine.

"Are you crazy?" she shrieked.

"No, I'm not. I'm just in love," Jasmine giggled.

They were in the kitchen and Jasmine was refilling an ice bucket.

"Grab a bottle of grapefruit juice from the fridge. My Aunt Mary can't drink her vodka without it," Jasmine said.

Kimara didn't budge. "Jasmine really, you can't be serious. You cannot marry him."

"I can, and I am," Jasmine protested.

"Jazz, if you marry him, you are going to be bored shitless inside of a year. Mark my words."

"You know Kimara, you are the most selfish person I know. Instead of being happy that I've found a man who treats me well and who will take care of me and love me forever, no matter what, you want to throw stones. I thought you were my friend."

"And I thought you'd gotten over your daddy leaving you," Kimara said pointedly.

"What?" Jasmine asked, moving in close to Kimara, her chin jutting out just inches from Kimara's determined face.

"You heard me," Kimara added, refusing to back down as she looked up at Jasmine. "It's obvious you're looking for a father figure, but I hate to break it to you—old Daddy Daycare in there is a poor replacement."

Jasmine stared at Kimara in disbelief, rendered speechless, before shaking her head and walking away. Kimara knew she'd gone too far and immediately wanted to take the words back. She reached out to grab Jasmine's arm, but Jasmine shrugged her away so hard Kimara fell backward into the wall behind her. It was two weeks before Jasmine would answer Kimara's calls and even though Kimara apologized, it was a long time before things were truly cool between them. Actually, the relationship never did quite return to what it was before, both women feeling a new sense of hesitancy whenever they had to present an idea or scenario to each other. One more reason for Kimara to hate Rick.

"Yep, I was . . . uh, a little anxious to get here," he smiled, his eyes ravaging every inch of Jasmine's slim modelesque frame.

Kimara cleared her throat, snatching Rick back from the jaws of the inferno his imagination had built within him.

"Uh, babe, I'm gonna go and take a shower," Rick growled. He didn't know what he had ever done to make Kimara hate him, besides marry her best friend. Honestly, he was quite tired of trying to be nice to her despite her apparent disdain for him. No matter how much he expressed to Jasmine that Kimara's attitude made him uncomfortable, there was no way that Jasmine would ever completely turn her back on Kimara. They had some inexplicable bond that held like it had been crazy-glued together. He knew that he would just have to deal with the woman, like it or not.

"Good night Kimara," he grunted as he made his way toward the rear of the apartment. He didn't wait for the response that he knew would never come.

Jasmine shook her head. "You two are worse than my five-year-olds at school."

"What?" Kimara asked innocently.

Jasmine narrowed her eyes but did not immediately respond. "Anyway, I'll check the movie schedule and give you a call in the morning," she said, placing an arm around Kimara's waist and walking her to the door.

"Okay, but don't call me too early—depending on how banging this party is, I might not get in 'til the roosters start crowing!"

"One of these days your partying is going to catch up with you," Jasmine joked.

Chapter 2

"What can I get you," Kimara asked as she snapped her fingers and shook her hips to rapper Ludacris' "Stand Up."

"I'll take some of that in a glass, straight up," the customer said, flashing a toothy, platinum covered smile as he surveyed the slender curve of Kimara's behind.

"Not on the menu, partner. What else can I get you?" Kimara retorted, never missing a beat.

Club Silhouette was jumping, the twenty-three and over crowd getting thicker by the minute. D.J. Shock was putting it down—serving up all the latest cuts with a few choice hits from back in the day. He had the dance floor covered with sweaty bodies getting their work-outs on. Kimara spent the evening serving customers, bopping her head to the throbbing bass, and sharing laughs with her co-workers. The time passed quickly, as it did every night. This was precisely the reason why Kimara didn't mind working days as a telephone equipment salesclerk and three nights a week at the club. While neither job could be called challenging, the electrically charged atmosphere of Silhouette was invigorating. She never felt tired from her night shift there and, in fact, didn't really consider it work. And, as

was the case every other night at Club Silhouette, the
night ran smoothly, with everyone having a good, clean
time. Tonight, however, pandemonium broke loose,
turning a peaceful night upside down. It was shortly
before three o'clock in the morning, just a little over an
hour before quitting time.

Although the club didn't close until five, the bar was
always shut down promptly at four. It was the owner,
Gino Stepanov's, desire to sober his patrons up before
unleashing them into the slumbering city. Kimara had
just returned from the stockroom where she'd gotten a
fresh bottle of Triple Sec when the commotion started.
A crowd formed around two tousling bodies a few feet
away from the bar. Suddenly, a shot glass flew across the
room, crashing into the mirrored wall behind Kimara
and shattering it. Shards of glass scattered around her
as she ducked beneath the bar, her heart racing. The
deejay cut the music and suddenly the club was flooded
with bright lights.

While her fellow bartenders ran from behind the bar,
either fleeing with the patrons or running to assist the
club's bouncers, Kimara was unable to move. From her
hiding place she heard screams and shouts, running
feet and more sounds of breaking glass. It seemed like
an eternity but was actually only a matter of minutes
before the bouncers were able to disperse the crowd.

When silence fell, Kimara stood on trembling legs
and peered over the counter. Her skin felt suddenly
cold as goose bumps rose up and down her arms and icy
droplets of sweat formed in her armpits and slid down
the sides of her torso. The shiny parquet dance floor
was vacant with the exception of a young man who lay
immobile in the center. Kimara moved slowly from
behind the bar and stood over the guy. His creamy off-
white silk shirt clung to his sweaty body, a slow red stain
radiating from the wound in his abdomen. The culprit,
a broken Heineken bottle, lay next to him. She kneeled

beside him and used the hand towel hanging from her waist to cover his wound.

"Somebody call an ambulance," Kimara screamed in the direction of the bouncers at the far left side of the club.

"They're on the way," one of them responded as he held the remaining crowd back from the scene.

Kimara looked down into the face of the bleeding young man. His eyes were closed but his lips were moving, opening and closing. He reminded her of a goldfish, its lips pursing and puckering as if it were practicing for its first kiss.

"It's okay. Hang in there man. Help is on the way," she said reassuringly.

He didn't open his eyes, but he nodded his head slightly, letting her know that he was still with her. She pressed down on the wound firmly, as her eyes roamed his face. *Definitely a cutie.* She took in the pain knotting in his brows, the ashy pallor of his lips. He looked younger than the required age for entrance into the club. His smooth skin was devoid of the tell-tale signs of manhood—no stubble, no razor bumps or coarseness. Maybe it was true what they say about dying—just as you approach death's door, you return to innocence, shedding the years like a coat or a second skin.

Kimara shook her head, willing the thought of death from her mind. The possibility that this young man could die, with her beside him no less, was more than she could handle, she knew. Tension coupled with the awkward position in which she was crouched made it seem as if she had aged considerably. Yet it was only minutes before she heard the shrill sound of sirens approaching the club. As they drew nearer and their characteristic screeching grew louder, Kimara began to relax.

Two burly white cops were the first to enter. They kneeled beside her and attempted to talk to the victim, who save for a couple of head shakes, was unresponsive. They asked Kimara what had happened and seemed annoyed when she told them that she didn't know anything. She stayed with the young man until the paramedics took over. She held his hand as they strapped his violated body to a gurney and let go only when they reached the exit door. As the ambulance peeled off, Kimara stared after it until the red-yellow glow cast by its spinning lights blended into the distance. She looked up into the dark lavender sky of a brand new day and melancholy fragments of verse took shape in her frazzled mind.

Soldier strong, shoulders wide
Lift the burdens, carry in stride
A million souls on you depend
Solider fallen, war's inevitable end

Kimara pulled herself away from the exit, where onlookers still lingered and were held back by police officers and the club's bouncers. Back inside, she surveyed the mess of broken glass and discarded clothing. The stench of spilled liquor penetrated her nostrils, coupling with the smell of blood which had caught in her throat and remained from the moment she first approached the injured man. She walked along the outskirts of the dance floor to avoid the debris—blood soaked gauze, a shoe discarded in the haste to flee—and carefully made her way to the bathroom.

The starkness of the room's high-wattage light bulbs surprised her as if she hadn't entered that bathroom over a hundred times before. She took a few deep breaths, then engaged the stopper in one of the sinks, allowing cold water to fill the bowl. She submersed her blood-stained hands into the frigid water and closed her eyes.

"Excuse me, Miss, I need to have a few words with

you," a thunderous voice boomed from behind her, commanding her immediate attention.

Kimara looked up from the sink where she had been washing her hands and into the mirror above it. Her eyes met those of a male police officer. He struck an arresting pose, his dark, ebony brown skin clad in a neatly starched uniform of indigo blue shirt and navy blue pants. The requisite octagonal hat sat perched on a clean-shaven head. Thin, smooth lips were surrounded by a neatly trimmed silky-black mustache and goatee.

Kimara smashed the soap dispenser with the heel of her right hand, causing the cleanser to spit into her palm. She was annoyed by his intrusion. Here she was, covered in some man's blood and the cops didn't have the decency to give her time to clean up before they interrogated her about something she'd already told them she knew nothing about. She glanced down to find that the blood had soaked into the knees of her white DKNY pants as well.

"Great," she muttered. To the cop, she snapped, "You think you can give me a minute?" She snatched a few paper towels from the holder on the wall.

"I'm sorry, but I really need to get as much information about what happened here as quickly as possible," he answered.

"Right," Kimara hissed as she turned the water off and stormed past the officer. She walked out of the restroom and back out into the dance area, dropping onto the nearest bar stool.

"May I have your name please?" he asked.

"Look, Officer . . ." Kimara read the name on the badge affixed to the solid chest which threatened to tear through the thin cotton material covering it. "Porter. I've already told you guys, I don't know what happened."

"Your name please," Officer Porter insisted.

"Kimara Hamilton," she replied through tight lips.

"Your address please," he continued.

"What could you possibly need my address for?" Kimara asked. She had moved past annoyance into hot anger aimed at this cop and his barrage of questions.

"Regulations require me to obtain the name and address of all witnesses to an incident."

"I'm not a witness to anything," she retorted.

"Look, Miss Hamilton. You can either cooperate and be done with me in a matter of minutes, or you can keep up the attitude and spend the next hour answering my questions. Perhaps you'd be more comfortable talking to me down at the station? Let me know how you want to play it," Officer Porter said, his tone even and serious.

He had grown weary of the attitude this woman was piping out. It was bad enough that she had the most startling eyes he had ever seen, their color that of roasted chestnuts, and that her petite, shapely body was making it difficult to concentrate. Her dicey tongue was enough to propel an already long night into an unbearable one. He watched her as she tossed her long thick mane back over her left shoulder, regarded him carefully up and down before letting out an exasperated breath. She folded her arms across full breasts clearly defined in a yellow midriff top, and rattled off her address with evident disdain.

"Can you tell me what happened?" Officer Porter asked pointedly.

"As I've already said a million times, I have no idea what happened. One minute I was serving drinks, close to shutting the bar down for the night, the next minute, glasses were flying, people were yelling and running around the place like it was on fire. I hit the deck and stayed there until the commotion ended."

"And the victim?" he continued.

"What about him?"

"Did you see who stabbed him?"

"No, I did not. He was lying there bleeding when I came from behind the bar. I put a towel on his injury and held it there until you guys arrived. Are we done?" Kimara asked.

She hopped off the stool, impatient to get as far away as possible from the arrogant, condescending, flatfoot standing before her. She tilted her head back to get a better look at him, meeting his fiery gaze with one of her own. Almond-shaped brown eyes stared down at her, their liquid depth like warm pools.

"For now," he answered, unwilling to break the connection their eyes had made. "If you should think of anything else, anything at all, please call the number on this card and ask for me, Officer Jared Porter."

Jared remained immobile as Kimara snatched the card from his fingers, slid it into her back pocket and stomped away in the direction of the ladies room. He watched her retreating figure, the delicious curve of her behind sashaying to an unheard rhythmic drumbeat. Once she was out of sight, he blinked several times as if to dissolve the residual image of her. He knew from painful past experiences that a woman like Kimara was trouble with a capital T. He also knew that more trouble was the last thing he needed in his life.

Chapter 3

"Kimara, telephone," Gena Hamilton yelled through the closed door of her daughter's bedroom as she rapped loudly with her knuckles.

"Take a message," Kimara moaned, covering her head with an oversized, fluffy, down pillow. A heavy milk-white comforter disguised the rest of her diminutive figure as she lay in a ball on the edge of her queen-sized platform bed. The room was dark, thick vertical blinds beating back the bright sun as it attempted to shine through the room's three windows.

Kimara's sparsely decorated bedroom possessed a warm and fresh aura. The walls were painted a pale buttery yellow and a matching scatter rug covered the center of the room's brightly polished laminate floors. An oak rocking chair sat in one corner and was filled with stuffed animals of varying shapes and sizes. On top of the upright chest of drawers were a few cosmetics and grooming items, neatly lined up side by side. On a small side table rested a clock and a large candle in a jar of sage and citrus scent.

The only items adorning the walls were a framed photograph of Kimara at her senior prom and an oil painting of a sunset over the ocean. The orderliness of the room seemed, in some respects, contradictory to the young woman in the bed. However, quite like the room itself, Kimara did lead an orderly life, free from many of the day-to-day complications that others faced. She never felt rushed or harried, never felt like she was doing the wrong thing or in the wrong place because she did only the things that she found pleasing to do. Lying in bed until late in the afternoon was not out of the ordinary for her, although after all these years her mother still hadn't gotten used to it.

"I'm not your secretary. Get up and answer the phone," she snapped.

"Arrgh!" Kimara groaned as she tossed the pillow across the room. She kicked the comforter off and the tangled lemon sheets, rose and stomped to the door. Snatching it open, she was greeted by her frowning mother who held a cordless telephone.

"You should tell your friends not to call you before sunset, Sleeping Beauty."

Kimara rolled her eyes at her mother's retreating back, at the same time kicking the door shut with her bare foot.

"Are you still in bed Kimara? It's two o'clock in the afternoon," Jasmine asked incredulously.

"So what? Dang, can't a girl get her beauty rest around here without everybody having a fit?"

"Uh-oh, somebody took an ugly pill this morning," Jasmine joked. "What time do you think you'll be ready to climb out of the bat cave?"

"For what?" Kimara asked purposely.

"Don't play with me Kimara. Aren't we going to the Schomburg today?" Jasmine snapped.

"I don't know, are we?"

"Look, I am not about to sit here and deal with your funky attitude. Either we're going or we're not."

"All right, all right. What are we going to see again?" Kimara asked.

"It's a traveling exhibition dealing with the African-American's triumph over slavery. I heard it's awesome. And I'd like to pick up some materials for my students too," Jasmine breathed excitedly.

"Yeah well, I guess since it's for the kids."

"Be ready in an hour," Jasmine commanded.

"I had this scandalous dream last night," Kimara snickered.

"Ooh, I like scandalous. Tell me, tell me," Jasmine giggled. They were seated at an outside table at a Mexican restaurant in Manhattan's upper sixties. Jasmine had recently developed an unrelenting craving for burritos.

It was after eight o'clock and the sun was making its descent. They had spent over three hours at the Schomburg and were now enjoying dinner outdoors. They had both been moved at different moments during the day to the point of tears at the numerous poignant photographs, centuries-old written parchments and other articles of the collection. It was an impressive reminder of where they had been as a people, how far they had come since slavery and yet how far they had to go. Jasmine gathered as much material as she could to bring back to school, although Kimara warned that much of it would be over the heads of the five-year-olds Jasmine taught. It was with renewed awe of the accomplishments of their forefathers that the ladies left the Schomburg and headed downtown for dinner.

Kimara took a dramatic sip from the over-sized raspberry frozen margarita in front of her, peering at Jasmine over the salted rim of the glass. "Well . . ." She paused for effect. "Remember what happened at the club the other night?"

"Yeah, and I don't know why you wanna keep working at that place. You could get killed in there with all those ecstasy-addicted clubheads," Jasmine admonished. "But no, don't listen to me. Just go ahead being hard-headed. You'll be the one who ends up with the soft behind."

"Oh would you stop being so dramatic and listen to my story," Kimara huffed.

"My bad," Jasmine replied, although she had every intention at some point of getting back on Kimara's case about working at the club.

"Now, as I was saying. So you remember what I told you about how the cops came at me with fifty million questions and how much they got on my nerves?"

"Uh-huh, yeah," Jasmine answered. Her head was cocked to one side and she held a huge tortilla chip dripping with spicy red salsa poised in midair.

"Well, the one cop—"

"The black one?"

"Yeah, the black one."

"The fine black one?"

"Yes, the fine black one," Kimara said through clenched teeth.

"What precinct in Manhattan does he work out of?" Jasmine asked.

"Why on Earth would you need to know that?"

"See, you don't listen to me. I told you the other day I'm putting together a career day program at school next month, and I need to organize folks to speak. If your cop friend is as fine as you say he is, maybe I could get him to come out and speak to the kiddies. Plus, it would sure pep up the female teachers' day to be able peep at some nice eye candy while we work," Jasmine giggled. "Kill two birds with one stone."

Kimara stared in disbelief at her friend, before shaking her head.

"You ought to be ashamed of yourself!" Kimara chided. "Would you please let me tell the damn story?"

"Okay, okay. So the fine black one . . . with the strapping chest and chiseled chin—"

Kimara swatted the air in a mock showing of slapping Jasmine, who got the point and stopped talking. Salsa sauce dripped from Jasmine's chip as she waited impatiently for Kimara to get to the juice of the matter.

"Yes, damn it. Strapping chest, chiseled chin and long, curly eyelashes. Yes him. Now, as I was saying . . . I dreamed about him last night. I don't know where this outrageous dream came from. But anyway, we were in the woods, camping or something, which is crazy because I don't camp, and I hate bugs and creepy crawly stuff—"

"What happened?" snapped a frustrated Jasmine. She hated to be kept waiting, always so anxious to get to the end of the story that sometimes she read the last chapter of a book before the first. She bit forcefully into the chip, licking the salsa sauce that dangled on her bottom lip.

"Okay so, we're lost and he's chopping up some wood for a fire . . . because it's cold. And it's nighttime," Kimara recited as the memory of the steamy dream infected her.

"So he's chopping the wood," Jasmine baited. "What are you doing?"

"I'm sitting on a tree stump. He's chopping the wood and he's got on a white wife-beater—"

"Wife-beater?" Jasmine gasped.

"It's a T-shirt Jasmine," Kimara answered, having forgotten momentarily that Jasmine had become as much of a square as her husband was, so far from being up on current slang it was embarrassing.

"Anyway, we hear a noise, like an animal or something . . . it was hissing and growling like it was about to burst through the bushes and eat the first living thing it saw. I jump up, and I run over to where he's standing with the axe."

"Oooh."

"And I'm scared to death and I'm shaking all over. So

he puts one of those thick, beefy arms of his around me and pulls me close."

"All right now."

"And he whispers in my ear that it's all good and that he won't let anything happen to me." Kimara shuddered as she was pulled back into a moment which had seemed real enough in her sleep that she'd awoken to find her own arms wrapped tightly around her body.

"He smelled so good, like soap and woodchips and I'm breathing him in and . . ."

"And then you start doing a whole other kind of shaking," Jasmine said laughing.

The women slapped five as they broke up into laughter. Some of the other diners glanced at them, but their attempts to quiet down just caused them to erupt in another round of cackling.

"Didn't he give you his number? You should call him," Jasmine managed finally.

"Hell, no. He might have been sexy as hell, but he was an arrogant son of a gun. I wouldn't call him if he were the last man on Earth."

"Hmph, if he's as fine as he sounds, I wouldn't care if he was deaf, dumb and blind—I'd hit that."

"Listen to Old Mother Hubbard, talking about hitting something. Jasmine please, you forget who you're talking to."

"I'm talking to my bestest girlfriend in the whole wide world, who by her own admission has not had a quality date in over six months," Jasmine reminded her.

"I've had dates," Kimara defended as she held a large stuffed potato skin with her fork and sliced it into three pieces with her knife. "Just haven't had my world rocked properly in a while." She paused, pointing her knife in Jasmine's direction. "What makes you so sure this guy could do any better?"

"Because the last time you had a glow like that in your

eyes when you talked about a man was . . ." Jasmine frowned. "Well, it was . . . never."

Kimara chomped on a piece of potato skin vigorously, as if she could grind the taste of Jared away with her molars.

"You know what I hate? Well, I'll tell you. I hate when you share your heartfelt secrets and desires with your girlfriend and she turns around and throws them back in your face," Kimara pouted.

"Then you should stop telling me your business 'cause throwing things back in your face is what I do best," Jasmine laughed. "Are you going to eat your black beans?"

Jared winced as his sparring partner caught him on the left side of his head with a sharp right jab. He cursed and shook his head, aware that that was the third hit he'd taken in less than three minutes in the ring. He couldn't seem to find his rhythm today, and his form and carriage were sloppy at best.

"What's up with you, my man? Did you come to box today or what?" the guy remarked.

"Come on," Jared growled through teeth that were clenched around a thick white mouthpiece.

He had been wired when he checked out of the station at seven o'clock that morning. He'd had to go back to Club Silhouette because they'd received a tip that the perpetrator of last week's stabbing was spotted at the club, along with a rough looking group of men. The detectives on the case had called him and his partner in as backup. It turned out to be a false lead and a big waste of time. Jared had scanned the club, hoping to get a glimpse of Kimara. His pulse raced as he discreetly searched for her and found himself disappointed when he didn't spot her. Apparently, it was her night off.

Finding himself too wired to go to sleep when his shift

ended this morning, he headed over to Big Will's, a little gym in Bedford Stuyvesant where he worked out several times a week. Griffin, a former middle-weight contender who was now a paid sparring partner, was there and offered to work Jared out a bit in the ring. Jared thought it would be a good way to relieve some of the stress he'd been carrying around and also help clear his mind. Now, he realized that it was a mistake to get into the ring as pre-occupied as he was.

The source of his inability to focus could be summed up in two words: Kimara Hamilton. He couldn't deny it even if he tried. The girl was a dime, with a body and face that screamed for attention. And attitude oozed from every pore. But there was something else, something so pure in her essence that showed through her icy surface like buried treasure. Her voice was creamy velvet and in spite of her harsh words, the tone grabbed a piece of Jared's heart and squeezed.

It was unprofessional of him to be checking her out at the scene of a crime the way he had. This he readily admitted. There was one thing he prided himself on and that was being professional at all times. He had to carry himself differently than his fellow officers because as an African-American male, there was always someone out there waiting to see him get busted down.

Jared's mind quickly flashed back to the time, three years earlier, when he had found himself two seconds away from quitting the force altogether. Those early days had been pressure and no matter how hard he tried, he could never get used to the double standards which existed between himself and his white counter-parts. Everything he did was under scrutiny. If he went easy on a black kid, he was showing favoritism. If he roughed up a white guy, he was overly aggressive and prejudiced. The race card got shuffled around so much in his presence he was beginning to think that he had gotten American history all wrong. That his people were not the oppressed, but the oppressors.

The day he came close to quitting was a couple of days after he'd shot an Hispanic youth in the South Bronx. The kid was only seventeen years old, and looked about two or three years younger. There had been a robbery at a local bodega and the owner had been pistol whipped by one in a gang of three young Hispanic men. Jared and his partner at the time, a big burly redneck named Duke Bradshaw, had answered the call. When they arrived on the scene, witnesses indicated that the youths had walked nonchalantly into an abandoned building about a half a block away from the incident. Duke didn't wait for the backup that Jared had called for. He insisted that they check it out themselves. Jared voiced his disagreement, but followed his partner into the building as was the expectation. They confronted the kids as they were sitting on milk crates in an empty apartment on the first floor. They were getting high on angel dust and didn't even respond when Jared and Duke entered. Jared subdued and cuffed the first kid, an older menacing looking guy, while Duke did the same to one of the others, the kid with the baby face.

The third kid had been staring at them the entire time laughing like he was watching Saturday morning cartoons on television. Duke grabbed the kid by his shirt and threw him up against the wall. That made the kid laugh even harder, which pissed Duke off more than he already was. He slapped the kid with an open hand real hard a couple of times, drawing blood from the boy's nose and lip. He curled his hand into a fist and was just about to hit him again when Jared intervened, grabbing the kid away from Duke and cuffing him himself.

Duke got in Jared's face about it, his chest all puffed out like he had every intention of whipping somebody's ass that day and if Jared wanted to be the fall guy, he'd gladly oblige. All of a sudden a single shot rang out.

Jared pulled his gun and whirled around to where the two suspects had lain handcuffed on the floor. Unfortunately, one of them had gotten up and was no longer cuffed. It seemed that in his haste, Duke had not properly secured the handcuffs and the suspect had freed himself, retrieved a gun from beneath one of the milk crates and fired. The gun was aimed levelly at Jared and without hesitating, Jared pulled his trigger, hitting the center of the boy's chest like an expert marksmen.

The suspect dropped to the floor and Jared got his gun, handcuffed him and then checked the cuffs on the other boy. He checked the restraints on the one who had been Duke's punching bag and ordered him to lie down as well. Both of the young men lay on the ground laughing like hyenas. The shrill cackling sound they made, while two men lay bleeding, their futures growing bleaker by the second, stayed with Jared for a very long time after that day. He remembered screaming at them to shut up, to no avail.

At that point, Jared turned toward Duke, who was leaning against a wall with a surprised, pained look on his face. The bullet had hit him squarely, entering his abdomen. His face was ashen, gone was the cocky wild man of seconds before. Jared called again for backup, entering the code which signaled that an officer was in distress. He lay Duke on the floor and checked his airway and pulse. Jared began CPR, alternating between pumping his partner's chest and breathing air into his lungs. He counted out loud between each action and kept going until help arrived. By the time the paramedics took over, Duke had already lost consciousness and his breathing had grown steadily more labored.

Both Duke and the suspect pulled through and while Jared should have been considered a hero, there were never-ending inquiries instead and Jared found himself having to defend his every action. The brass wanted to cite him for failing to follow proper procedure by entering the building in the first place. Then Duke began telling people that it was Jared's suspect who was not cuffed properly. To make matters worse, the public claimed police brutality after suspect number three's black eye, courtesy of Duke, made the papers. The one whom Jared shot ended up with partial paralysis.

While Jared wasn't surprised that Duke held him out to dry, he was dumbstruck at how reluctant the powers to be were to believe that he, in fact, had done the right thing from start to finish. Adding salt to the wound, when he was finally vindicated of all wrongdoing, they didn't even apologize. It was as if he and Duke wore the same uniform, just in a different shade of blue.

This was a difficult lesson for Jared to learn, but one that he soaked up like a sponge. As a child, he had already been made painfully aware of the unfairness of the world, which was one of the reasons he had become a cop in the first place. The weeks surrounding that incident were tough on him and many of his friends couldn't understand what he was going through. His girlfriend at the time grew impatient with his moodiness, his brooding demeanor and the anger that lived inside of him for days at a time. Millicent turned out to be what his mother would call a fair-weather friend.

During that ordeal, Jared found out who was really in his corner and, later on, was able to view it as an opportunity to lose the dead weight in his life. Finally, it was his mother who convinced him to hang in there and remain on the force. Because of her, he realized that he couldn't give in so easily, this situation being precisely why he was needed on the police force. A diverse nation and multicultural communities needed a police department that was representative of them. He couldn't, with a clear conscious, not represent his people and make sure that at least while he was on the beat, they got a fair shake. He rationalized that no matter what profession he chose, there would always be ignorance and double standards.

He had to choose whether to face it lying down or standing up.

Shortly afterward, Jared transferred precincts, partnered up with a guy who respected him as a partner and as a man. His belief that his actions would continue to be held up to standards different from his fellow white officers never changed. He just accepted that as one of the hazards of the job and, that being said, always acted with decorum and respect, especially while on duty. Never before had a woman he encountered caused him to waver. On the other hand, he'd never come across a woman quite like Kimara Hamilton.

But she was trouble. Way more than he could handle, of this he was sure. She would bring drama back into his life so soon after he had cleared some of it out. It was stupid of him to think about her and even stupider for him to consider contacting her under the guise of needing to ask more questions as he had been contemplating doing all morning.

Jared bit hard into the mouthpiece, hunched his shoulders and raised his gloves. With a determined right uppercut, charged with heavy ammunition, he made contact with Griffin's ribs. Griffin grunted, almost in appreciation that Jared finally seemed to be ready to get it on. Jared steadied his legs and his heart, equally as determined to protect himself from Griffin's next jab as well as from the likes of Kimara Hamilton.

Chapter 4

"Class, attention please. I'd like you all to meet Officers Porter and Jamison. Say good morning to our Career Day guests," Jasmine said, standing before a class of thirty kindergarten students.

"Good morning Officer Porter and Officer Jamison," they recited in unison, faces beaming. The students were on their best we-have-company behavior, seated behind their desks with their hands clasped before them.

"Good morning guys," Jared answered. "We're here today to talk to you about the job we do. Can anyone tell me what a police officer's job is?"

Several students raised their hands and engaged Jared in a spirited conversation. While Jared talked, Officer Jamison passed out materials to the students, demonstrated the use of handcuffs and how to properly hold a nightstick. Jasmine couldn't have hoped for a better presentation. The students were extremely inquisitive and animated, and the officers laughed and played with them as well as instructed them. Several other teachers and office staff came in to watch and a thunderous applause came at the end of their hour-long session.

Jasmine dismissed her class to lunch with the aide and walked the officers to the door. She could not believe how understated Kimara's description of Jared was. He was incredibly good-looking, with enough sex appeal to stop a train. All morning the female teachers had been falling all over themselves to get a better look at him. She had every intention of smacking the daylights out of Kimara the next time she saw her.

"Again, officers, on behalf of the students and the faculty here at P.S. 188, I'd like to thank you for taking time out of your busy schedules to spend the morning with us. The kids absolutely loved you. In fact, I think you guys just recruited a few future peace officers." Jasmine smiled, shaking hands with her departing guests.

Jared smiled at Jasmine. "It was our pleasure. This is actually one of the better parts of the job for us and your students are a spunky little bunch—very smart for their age. I'm sure that's because they've got such a great teacher."

"Ooh, she didn't tell me you were such a flatterer," Jasmine responded.

"Excuse me?" Jared asked, confusion knotting his brow.

"I'm sorry, I was thinking out loud. You see, you and I have a mutual acquaintance," she explained.

"We do?"

"Yes. A couple of weeks ago you responded to a call at Club Silhouette—over on 14th Street."

"That's right," Jared answered slowly, unsure of where this conversation was going.

"Yeah, well, my girlfriend tends the bar there. Kimara Hamilton?"

Bolts of electricity seemed to shoot through Jared's brain at the mention of the name he'd been trying with all of his might to forget. His noticeable reaction was not lost on Jasmine. She smiled as she realized that her girl had apparently left as indelible a mark on Officer Jared Porter as he had on her.

"Yes, I remember her. So, she's a . . . a friend of yours?" Jared stammered.

"Yep. Best friend, in fact. She mentioned the disturbance . . . and you."

"I'm sure she had a mouthful to say about me," Jared commented, raising his eyebrows.

A momentary silence was followed by laughter which erupted from both Jasmine and Jared.

"Yeah well, I won't lie. She wasn't very complimentary. But don't worry, she's all bark and no bite."

"Nah, that girl's definitely got some bite," Jared answered.

"I guess I can't argue that. But she's a beautiful spirit, once you get through the gravelly surface."

"Yeah, right. Well, I think I'll just take your word for that. I don't think she and I should ever be allowed within ten feet of one another."

No sooner than Jared had spoken these words did the front door to the school swing open. With a burst of breezy springtime air, in walked Kimara.

"Hey Jazz, sorry I'm late. It started raining and I had a time catching a cab. Ready?" Kimara huffed, shaking her wet umbrella on the ground. Kimara took another step toward Jasmine and her companions and then froze midstride.

"Kimara, you remember Officer Porter, don't you?" Jasmine oozed sweetly.

Kimara was rendered speechless. For the first time in all the years that Jasmine had known her, the girl could not open her mouth. She just stood there, staring in disbelief. Her gaze shifted from Jasmine to Jared and back to Jasmine. Finally, it was Jared who broke the silence.

"Good to see you again, Ms. Hamilton." He turned to face Jasmine. "It was a pleasure spending time with your class today. Any time you want us to come back, you know the number."

Jared chanced a parting look at Kimara, whose head was down, eyes glued to the floor. He motioned for his partner and they stepped around Kimara and out of the front door.

"What's wrong with you girl? Cat got your tongue?" Jasmine scolded.

"What the hell was he doing here?" Kimara finally managed.

"Watch your mouth Kimara," Jasmine said, glancing around them to make sure there were no kids in sight. "Let's go up to my room."

Kimara followed Jasmine down the hallway and up a flight of stairs to her second-floor classroom. Once inside the empty room, with the door shut securely behind them, she broke. "Before you even try to tell me that it's just a coincidence that he was here today, the very day you invited me over here to have lunch with you, don't. You are the most conniving wench I know," Kimara bellowed.

"Calm down. See, it didn't happen like it looks. The principal approved my Career Day program and gave me the name of the desk sergeant at the precinct in the school's district. So I went over to the ninth precinct last week and told them about my plans for the program and while I was talking to the desk sergeant, Jared's partner just happened to walk by, although I didn't know he was Jared's partner at the time because I didn't even know Jared."

Jasmine was talking with the speed of the already condemned trying to convince a jury of his peers of his innocence. Kimara folded her arms across her chest, lips pursed, not buying one minute of Jasmine's explanation.

"And then, what happened was the desk sergeant stopped Officer Jamison and asked him if he and his partner could help me out. Jamison said he'd love to do it and that he'd check with his partner. He called upstairs and asked Jared to come down to meet me. It wasn't until Jared came downstairs, looking like an Adonis dipped in chocolate, that I knew that he was your Jared. Honestly, Kimara, I did not go there trying to find that man."

"First of all Jasmine, he's not *my* Jared. Second of all, even if I bought that cock-and-bull story of yours, none of this explains why you invited me to lunch today, knowing he would be here."

Kimara was furious, tapping her foot angrily as she glared at Jasmine. Jasmine opened her mouth to protest, but suddenly thought better of it. She plopped down into her chair and hung her head in shame.

"All right, all right. You got me. I'm sorry Kimara. It seemed like a good idea at the time." Jasmine looked up with woeful eyes.

"A good idea? Are you crazy? That's it—my best friend has finally gone and lost her damned mind!" Kimara ranted.

"Wait a minute Bumblebee," Jasmine said, calling Kimara by the nickname she'd given her when they were kids because Kimara's favorite color was yellow. "I really didn't seek him out the way it seems. I swear I didn't. But everything sort of fell into place and then you even mentioned that we hadn't had lunch together in a while, so . . ."

"So you stuck your big nose in my business and tried to hook me up with that balloon-headed jackass. Well, I hope you're happy with yourself. That one blew up in your face, big time, didn't it?"

"Yeah, that was bad. Man, I thought you were going to punch the man or something. You had, like, a whole Carrie look on your face, like you were going to start spitting flames or something."

Kimara broke up laughing at that, realizing that she must have really looked a sight. "I couldn't help it; I was so shocked to see him standing there. I felt like I had just stepped into the *Twilight Zone* or something," Kimara laughed.

"I know K, but you could have at least said something. Hello, maybe. That poor man," Jasmine lamented.

"Bunk that *poor man*. He's lucky I didn't tell his behind off for the way he treated me the other night."

"By the other night do you mean the real other night or in your dreams, the other night?" Jasmine teased.

"Later for you, Jasmine," Kimara replied. "You're not completely off the hook you know? I should tell your husband that you've been matchmaking again. You do remember what he told you when you hooked his sister up with your mailman?" Kimara threatened.

"Okay, I'll stop. Scouts honor," Jasmine said, holding up three fingers which was the Girl Scout symbol of pledging one's word. The last thing Jasmine wanted was to have to listen to Rick condemn her actions. He hadn't quite gotten over the fiasco of his big sister and Postmaster Herman Hitchcock, even though Jasmine swore she didn't know the man had ten kids and three ex-wives.

Outside, Jared laughed aloud nervously as he slid into the driver's seat of the patrol vehicle.

"What's so funny?" Jamison asked.

"Women," Jared remarked without elaborating.

When Kimara entered that school, Jared had been certain he was seeing things. He thought for sure his fevered imagination had gone into overdrive. The way Kimara had breezed in, bringing with her an energy that was inexplicably alluring, made him lose whatever composure he had been fighting to hold on to since Jasmine had clued him in to their mutual acquaintance. One look at those fiery eyes and supple lips, and he was trembling inside. She wore a faded denim jacket over a white tank top and a short khaki skirt that served up toned legs luscious enough to make him want to reach out and touch. He didn't miss the flash of a look that he could only interpret as vulnerability that appeared when her eyes met his. In an instant, it was gone and the familiar steely gaze took its place. It was all he could do to get out of there before he said or did something stupid.

The fact that she did not utter one word to him reminded him of his original impression of her, and he fought to maintain his resolve not to allow himself to fall any deeper for a woman he believed could do nothing for him but break his heart.

Chapter 5

"Dad, I'm so sorry. I must have left my keys in my friend's car," Kimara apologized.

She slithered past her father, cowering under the annoyance which was written all over his sleepy face.

"Kimara, do you have any idea what time it is?" her mother asked from the shadows.

Kimara hadn't realized her mother was standing there, but now that she had made her presence known, Kimara knew she was in for it. "I know it's late Mom. I'm sorry. I don't know where I left my—"

"Yeah, I heard. You don't know where your keys are." Gena Hamilton snapped a switch, flooding the living room with light.

Kimara squinted, the glare from the bright lights making her feel like a prisoner of war under military interrogation. She dropped the high-heeled sandals she'd been carrying to the floor, and shifted from one bare foot to the other.

"Young lady, this is ridiculous. The older you get, the more irresponsible you become," she said.

"Come on Mom, it's not that serious. I said I was sorry."

"And so you think that's enough? You think it's okay

to wake your father and me up in the middle of the night when we both have to get up and go to work in the morning and all you have to say . . . all you have to do is apologize? You think that makes it okay?"

Kimara didn't respond. The four Dirty Martinis she'd consumed that night had her feeling no pain and the last thing she needed right now was a fight with her mother.

Kimara sighed and looked around the neat living room. An overstuffed armchair where her father sat to watch the nightly news and ESPN on his new thirty-six-inch Sony flatscreen was tucked in one corner of the room. A matching sofa, covered with rust-colored corduroy fabric faced the chair. The drapes were the same color and the entertainment center was filled with the many knickknacks and photographs collected over the years. Somehow, this was the first time that Kimara had noticed that this room hadn't changed one bit since she was a little girl. She also realized that neither had her mother.

"I can't believe how irresponsible you've become Kimara," Gena said, slapping her palm on the dining table as if to draw her daughter's wandering attention.

"All right now, Gena, there's no need to get so upset," William interrupted, raising his hand in an attempt to stay his wife's anger.

"Oh no, William. I'm past upset. This girl hangs out all damn night long, till three, four o'clock in the morning. She comes and goes as she pleases and it's disruptive to us and it is downright inconsiderate. I've had enough of this."

"So what do you want me to do?" Kimara snapped, her eyes finally resting on her mother's stern face. "Should I stay home every night and play Scrabble with you and Dad or something?"

"Kimara, lower your voice," her father warned.

Kimara began walking toward her bedroom.

"You get back here young lady," her mother commanded, her voice shaking.

Kimara stopped in her tracks and turned to face her mother. The scene immediately took on the likeness of a showdown in the Wild West. The two women were of matched height, resembling one another more than a little bit. They had the same sparkling eyes the color of burnished wood, the same oval face and in spite of the fact that right now Kimara's lips were pursed in a tight grimace and Gena's were trembling with anger, they shared the same sensuous mouths.

"You may be an adult now, but I'm still the woman of this house. Do you understand me?" Gena Hamilton asked rhetorically.

"Yes, I understand. But I'm still a grown woman and I deserve to be treated as such," Kimara said defiantly.

"Yes you are a grown woman. You're twenty-six years old, and I swear it seems like you never got past your eighteenth birthday. If you want to be a grown-up Kimara, then you're going to need to start acting like one."

"What's that supposed to mean? I go to work every day, and I don't ask you guys for anything."

"It means that it's time for you to take responsibility for yourself. For your life. Your father and have talked about this before and we've decided that the only way you're going to truly grow up is if we force you to."

Kimara turned to her father who stood quietly watching the exchange between mother and daughter. "What is she talking about, Dad?"

"Well baby girl, it's like this—" He paused, placing his hands on Kimara's shoulders. "We think it's time for you to get out on your own."

"What? You're kicking me out?" Kimara yelled, attempting to back away from her father.

"No, no, no. Baby, it's not that way at all. But we just think that it's time you had your own place. Pay your own bills, make your own way. You're a smart, resourceful young lady. You just need some direction, some goals."

William Hamilton held firmly onto Kimara, hating himself for having to say these things to her. At the same time, he recognized that his wife was right. It was time for Kimara to take some steps toward planning her future. They had both been disappointed when she'd announced that she didn't want to go to college. They had been so sure that she would do well in the fields of communications or journalism. Her outgoing personality and bright spirit were undeniable. But Kimara had never been more than an average student, not for lack of intelligence. She just never really applied herself, no matter how much they cajoled, threatened or punished. After high school, she expressed an interest in modeling. For about five minutes they thought that she would really take it seriously and make something of herself. But soon she moved on to being an aerobics instructor. Then there was the massage therapist stint. Nothing held Kimara's attention for long and that didn't seem to faze her one bit.

William gazed at his daughter, his only child, and wondered if there was something he had or hadn't done. He thought they'd provided a solid home. In a day and age where most marriages didn't survive the first three years, he and Gena had been together almost three decades. It hadn't always been easy and there were so many things he wished he could have provided for his girls. But still, he'd done the best he could, which was pretty good by most standards.

Kimara had been a smart, inquisitive child. She was always so sensitive and thoughtful. He had had many expectations of her, believing her capable of far surpassing his meager professional life. He had started off at the age of eighteen, armed only with his high school diploma and a strong back. He took a job in the loading department at Bell Atlantic. Over the years, he'd taken advantage of their in-house training programs and was now a senior installer with their successor. He and Gena had met shortly after he'd started with the phone company. She was a couple of years older than he and worked as a clerk in the engineering department.

The telephone company had provided them with a steady income and a working middle-class lifestyle. They'd given Kimara everything they could and had pinned many of their hopes for a bright future on her. At twenty-six years old it seemed as if she'd never get started. Many of their colleagues had children who'd completed college by now, were either working on graduate degrees or were beginning careers with prominent companies. He didn't expect Kimara to go down the corporate-America track. She was more of a free spirit who needed to be in a creative field. But he certainly didn't expect her to be working as a store clerk and barmaid, partying all night and letting her God-given talents and abilities go to waste.

William sighed. Suddenly he felt every bit of his fifty-two years. He was looking at seven more years before he could accept a decent retirement package from the job and sit back and relax. He hoped to travel a little bit and then maybe make a little change on his favorite pastime of fixing remote-controlled cars. Maybe open a hobby shop or something. He shouldn't have to still be worrying about Kimara.

He didn't want to force his daughter out of his home, but he knew that he had no choice in the matter. Besides the fact that it was time, Gena had reached the end of her rope. She loved their daughter as much as he did, of this he was certain. But having grown up the eldest child in a family of eight, she'd never had time for partying and such. She believed in earning your own way in life and she felt they'd given Kimara more than enough time to find her own way. Yes, it was time for Kimara to get out on her own.

He looked into his daughter's chestnut eyes, almost the same sparkling eyes that had caused him to fall in love with her mother, and saw the fire and vitality of youth. He told himself that she just needed a strong hard push to get going, kissed her lightly on the forehead and went to bed.

Chapter 6

Three weeks had passed since the fight with her parents. Kimara had spent the first week oscillating between sulking and throwing temper tantrums. By week two, it was obvious that her parents weren't going to back down. She half-heartedly began looking through the classified sections of the *Village Voice* and the *Daily News*, checked out a few ads online and was completely disheartened by the end of week three. She shared the Wednesday night shift at Club Silhouette with the owner's daughter, Giselle. Picking up on Kimara's sour mood one night, Giselle asked what was wrong.

"Please tell me it isn't man trouble," Giselle commented during a slow period at the bar.

"What are you talking about?" Kimara asked half-heartedly. She was too preoccupied by the situation with her parents, coupled with nagging fantasies of Officer Porter which crept into her mind unexpectedly, to give her full attention to Giselle.

"You. You've been moping around all night. Normally you're so cheerleader-perky and chipper I want to throw up, but tonight you look like the world's coming to an end. What's up?"

"Nothing much. Just some b.s. with my folks," Kimara answered, focusing on Giselle completely now.

She couldn't help but wonder if she had really been moping noticeably around the club. It was important to her not to wear her heart on her sleeve, a sure way to end up having her business put into the street, so to speak. Kimara considered Giselle who, although she was a nice enough girl, was not someone Kimara could see herself confiding her deep dark secrets to. She didn't really want to get into the topic anyway and have one more person tell her how right her parents were and how childish she was behaving. Sometimes, in spite of what Joe Public liked to think, a person really doesn't want to hear the truth.

"Oooh, parent drama. Been there, done that. That's why I moved into my own apartment the minute I turned seventeen."

"Seventeen? How in the hell did you swing that?" Kimara was already pretty certain how she'd managed that, with her dad being the owner of both Club Silhouette and another spot uptown, but she asked anyway.

"Well, my dad was sick of the catfights between my stepmother and me so he sprung for the whole thing. He even let me furnish it myself, top of the line and everything. It was actually only a studio apartment in the same building where they lived, but trust me, it made all the difference. He got some peace and quiet, and she got to sit around spending his money all day on hundred-dollar manicures and Botox treatments."

"Wow. That seems a little jacked-up to me."

"Maybe. But my dad and I weren't ever really that close, you know, so it was no big deal. Actually, we talk more since I started working here than we ever did before. And living by my own rules, coming and going as I please without anybody bitching is nirvana."

"Now *that* I won't argue with," Kimara grimaced. The

picture of her mother in all her fury still lurked in the recesses of her memory.

"So what bones are your parents picking with you? Is it the staying out too late or the bringing company home trip?"

"Basically, they think I'm a freeloader. They said it's time for me to get my own place. It's not like they support me or anything. I buy my own clothes, pay half the telephone and cable bills, and I'm hardly ever home so I barely eat there. Usually, I don't ask them for a dime."

"My dear Kimara, you've obviously missed lesson number one when it comes to parents; they are never satisfied no matter what you do."

"Tell me about it," Kimara griped.

Just that morning she'd come into the kitchen where her father sat reading the morning paper. Next to the coffee maker was a clipping from the *Times'* Classified Section of an apartment for rent. She sucked her teeth as she pushed the paper aside and poured herself a cup of coffee.

"Did you see that ad your mother left for you?" her father had asked.

"Yeah, and you should tell her it's dangerous to leave flammable items next to heat sources," Kimara had responded dryly.

"So what are you going to do?" Giselle asked.

"I don't know. I've been checking ads and stuff but there's nothing appealing. Either they want you to sleep on a pull-out sofa in the living room, or they've got four cats and two dogs—"

"And a parakeet," Giselle chimed in.

"And if there's one thing I don't do, it's animals. But I guess I've got to keep looking 'cause it doesn't seem like my parents are going to back down on this one."

"What would you say about an apartment on the upper-east side, doorman building with a view of Central Park and your own bedroom with a half bathroom?"

"No pets?"

"Not even a goldfish."

"I'd say hell yes. You know someone who's looking for a roommate?"

"Yep. Me," Giselle answered. "I moved in about a year ago and my dad thought it was overpriced so he only pays half the rent. Between the spending allowance he gives me and what I make here, I could still use a little extra cash."

"Wow. Upper-east side, huh? I don't know if I can afford that."

"I'm sure we can work something out. Besides, you need a place to live and I could use the company. What do you say?"

"I say yes," Kimara cheered, hoping that she was making the right choice but also feeling a sense of relief over the entire situation.

The good-bye was bittersweet as Kimara made the transition from her parents' home to Giselle's. With every step away from home Kimara felt like a weak baby bird taking that first uncertain flight. She stood outside of Giselle's apartment for a full ten minutes before working up the nerve to ring the bell.

"Wow Giselle, your place is really nice. Did you decorate yourself?"

Kimara dropped her garment bag and three-piece luggage set in the middle of the living room as she looked around. It was the first time she had seen Giselle's apartment, having accepted the offer for a room sight unseen.

Now, looking around Giselle's apartment, she was more sure that she'd made a wise decision. The rust colored Italian leather sofa was complemented by a sand colored stone coffee table and off-white granite ceramic tiles. The room's architectural elements included a huge stone fireplace which adorned the wall facing the sofa, and graceful crown moldings. A Persian rug in the center of the room provided a lively splash of color, enhancing the shine of the floor tiles. A low-hung ceiling fan spun at a slow speed, creating a gentle breeze.

"Yep," Giselle answered. "Come on, let me show you around."

Giselle led Kimara from room to room, starting with the spacious living room, continuing on to the elegantly modern kitchen with its stainless steel appliances and decorative pulls on all of the glass cabinets. There was a breakfast nook which led to a terrace from which she could see a large span of Central Park, including one of her favorite landmarks, the Metropolitan Museum of Art. Giselle's bedroom was massive with its own private bath. Finally they stopped at what would be Kimara's bedroom and her heart soared when she discovered that it was twice the size of her old bedroom at home. It had a queen-sized sleigh bed, an oak dresser and vanity table and another ceiling fan hung above the bed.

"Giselle, I really can't thank you enough. And don't worry, I'll be on time with the rent and you won't have to worry about me cramping your style. You'll hardly know I'm here."

"Nonsense, Kimara. I want you to make yourself at home. This is going to be so cool—two sexy, single women with a swinging bachelorette pad. Coordinating outfits is a whole lot easier when you have a second pair of female eyes around," Giselle joked.

Kimara laughed along with her, but in her heart, a nagging sensation of trepidation cast a shadow on what should have been an exciting day for her. For the first time in her life she was on her own; gone was the cushioning support of having someone else to take care of her. Instead of the inherent comfort in knowing that the ultimate responsibilities of everyday life did not rest on her shoulders, she was filled with an overwhelming sense of accountability, which to her seemed a burden. She couldn't help missing home and missing her parents, even though they were just a thirty-minute subway ride away.

Chapter 7

"Oh please, Jasmine. Stop being so damned cheap," Kimara teased.

Jasmine turned her wrist over, moving it first away from her and then closer to her face again, admiring the bracelet. It was really beautiful and she knew that Rick would love it. But diamond-studded, eighteen-karat Gucci link baubles were definitely not in their budget. They had agreed to be very frugal in their spending while they saved for their future together. Their plans included children, a home and seeing the world before arthritis set in.

But on the other hand, Rick had grown up in a household even poorer than Jasmine's. His father's health had always been poor, often putting him out of work for months at a time. There were five children, of which Rick was the oldest, and he had had to take on much of the responsibility of bringing money into the home at an early age. His mother worked long hours as a waitress and Rick did everything from delivering newspapers at twelve years old to loading boxes at a warehouse by age fourteen. He never had the latest sneakers or clothes, never went to parties and concerts as a teen. While he swore that none of those things mattered to him growing up and that all he cared about was making sure his brothers and sisters were okay, Jasmine was certain that the child in him had to, on some level, feel robbed. Even now as an adult, he rarely spent money on himself. Buying him this bracelet, a precious item that he would never consider purchasing on his own, would be a small repayment of all the sacrifices he had made.

However, even as she told herself this, she worried that he would be angry that she'd spent so much money on something that he didn't really need.

As if reading her mind, Kimara added, "Look Jasmine, most of this money is found money. The five hundred bucks you won in the lottery is not coming out of your budget. Add that amount with what you saved for his present, and there you go."

Jasmine frowned.

"I don't know though. It's a little extravagant."

"It's beyond extravagant. It's beautiful. And besides, Jazz, back in the day, if we met a brother rocking a piece like that . . ."

"Exactly. I don't want some *skank* like you trying to make my husband her sugar daddy," Jasmine laughed.

"That you don't have to worry about. Don't nobody want him!" Kimara returned.

"Very funny. But seriously Kimara, I don't know if I should spend this much."

"Aren't you the one always going on, ad nauseam, about how hard your baby works and how good he is to you?"

Kimara haggled with Jasmine while the salesclerk looked on with the eager smile of a person about to earn a fat commission. By the time they had left the store, the exquisite bracelet was artfully gift wrapped and stored inside of Jasmine's purse, Jasmine was excitedly contemplating Rick's reaction, and Kimara was mentally exhausted. Even the salesclerk was worn out from having to keep that cheesy smile frozen on her face for so long. Kimara felt strangely victorious while Jasmine felt somewhat naughty.

The women stopped in the mall's food court, where Kimara wolfed down an order of cheese fries while Jasmine sipped on seltzer water.

"You sure you don't want some of these—they're really cheesy just like you like 'em?" Kimara said, waving a fry at her friend.

"No, my stomach's upset," Jasmine answered with a sour look on her face.

"I bet it is, after you dropped enough money on a bracelet to feed a Rwandan family of ten for two whole months. Girl, you ought to be ashamed of yourself," Kimara joked.

"Stop it. You're the one who talked me into buying it. You think it's too much?" Jasmine asked, doubt once again creeping into her mind.

"I'm just playing with you. It's beautiful and Rick's got to love it. And if he doesn't, give it to me," Kimara answered.

Another hour of window shopping passed before Kimara noticed that Jasmine wasn't her normal chatty self. "Are you okay, Jazz? Don't tell me you're still tripping over the bracelet?" Kimara was concerned now as she noticed how drawn Jasmine's faced looked.

"No, it's not that. I don't know . . . I don't feel right," Jasmine said weakly.

"You don't look too good. Let's go sit down somewhere," Kimara suggested. She scanned the area for a bench or a cluster of chairs.

"No, come on. Let's just get out of here," Jasmine answered.

Kimara look at Jasmine again, noting the sweat beading her hairline and the glassy look in her eyes. She took her by the arm and led her through the throng of shoppers toward the mall's exit doors.

"We'll catch a cab up to my place," Kimara said.

Jasmine nodded. "I feel so hot," she said as they moved through the revolving doors, Kimara in the section directly behind her.

As Kimara stepped out onto the sidewalk a couple of paces behind Jasmine, Jasmine put her hands to her face and her eyes closed. Before Kimara knew what was happening, Jasmine sank like a sack of potatoes, collapsing onto the pavement. Kimara immediately dropped to her side, panic causing her to lose all sensibility.

"Jasmine," she screamed. "Jasmine, Jasmine!"

A group of gawkers formed around them, but no one stepped forward to help. Kimara's heart began racing and she grew more frantic with each passing second. Suddenly, a strong voice in the crowd soared above both the noise of the busy street and Kimara's screams. Kimara looked up to find Jared Porter approaching, pushing his way through the crowd. He kneeled down at Kimara's side. Without a word, he took Jasmine's slender wrist in his hand and expertly felt for a pulse. He then leaned in closely to her chest and listened for breathing sounds.

Kimara raised her voice in protest when Jared sharply slapped Jasmine's cheeks, first one then the other, but stopped when Jasmine began to stir. Her eyes fluttered open, a confused look swimming in them. She lifted her head and questioningly looked from Jared to Kimara. Jared checked her pulse again, asked her to recite her name and the day's date to be certain that she was fully conscious. Slowly, he helped the disoriented Jasmine to her feet. Kimara brushed dirt from Jasmine's back and hair, all while asking her if she was okay.

"I'm fine. I don't know what happened," Jasmine answered, still sounding slightly off to Kimara's worried ears.

Despite Jasmine's protests to the contrary, Kimara insisted that Jasmine go to the nearest hospital. Jared ushered the women down the street to the next corner toward his Ford Expedition which was parked in a tow-away zone. Kimara noticed the police decal in the window, and once again felt a growing irritation threatening her composure. Her concern for her friend's health could not completely overshadow the agitation Jared Porter seemed to invoke in her.

"You know what, Officer Porter, we don't want to impose. I can take Jasmine to the hospital in a taxi," she stated flatly.

"Nonsense," he answered roughly, starting the ignition without another word.

Kimara sank into the backseat next to Jasmine feeling helpless and irritated. In spite of the fact that she knew the polite thing to do was to be appreciative and thankful, having to swallow the guy's take-charge manner left a huge lump in her throat. The way that he didn't even bother to look at her when he spoke was equivalent to a slap in the face. To her it gave testimony to his arrogance, as if she had to do whatever he said just because he'd said it. She didn't know who this guy thought he was or what kind of treatment he was used to receiving from women, but with Kimara, he was well on his way to getting told off.

During the short ride to the hospital, Kimara focused all of her attention on Jasmine, fawning over her like a mother hen. Left to themselves while Jasmine was examined upon arrival, Kimara sulked, vacillating between concern for her friend and being pissed off with Jared. At one point, Jared stepped outside of the E.R.'s waiting room to place a call on his cell phone. Kimara watched him walk away, noting that he possessed a stride that was slow and deliberate, more like a swagger. His bowed legs were accented by the not tight, but fitted blue jeans he wore. A broad back was covered by a blue New Jersey Nets jersey and a matching fitted cap. Kimara continued staring through the glass doors as

Jared talked. When he laughed into the phone, she noticed a wide mouth filled with gleaming white teeth.

All that, housing the personality of a lump of coal, she thought shaking her head.

Jared returned and took his seat next to Kimara again. "Any word?" he asked Kimara, looking at her directly for the first time.

"No. You don't really have to wait around, you know," she responded, meeting his gaze. She looked at that mouth, those lips, and noticed that they held a bemused look, the beginnings of a dazzling smile flirting there. Something softened inside of her then and she found herself wanting to smile.

"Maybe I don't have anything else to do right now," Jared answered.

"What, no bad guys to bust . . . no damsels in distress to save?"

"Lucky for you ladies I'm on vacation this week. You?"

"Just hanging out with my girl today, doing some shopping."

"Oh. How are things at the club?"

"Great."

"You like working there, huh?"

"It's a job," Kimara answered.

As Kimara and Jared continued to chat, their discourse remained superficial yet polite, both too aware of their own discomfort to let go and talk freely. This unease was clearly born of their attraction to one another, a feeling which intensified with each passing moment, although neither of them would willingly acknowledge it.

The conversation lulled and Kimara tried desperately to quiet the frenzy of butterflies in her belly by scratching out a poem on the back of a health pamphlet she'd pulled from a stack on a nearby table. Jared sat quietly contemplating what it was specifically about Kimara that so unnerved him. He watched her from the corner of his eye, taken by her glowing skin bronzed by the summer sun. She crossed her legs, the short denim skirt she wore exposing a well-toned thigh which he could easily envision wrapped around his waist in the throws of passion.

Jared stood, stretching his arms above his head in an effort to rewire his thoughts and was just about to ask her to grab a bite to eat with him in the cafeteria, when a nurse approached. She summoned Kimara into the examination room.

Kimara walked quickly away, leaving her thoughts lying on a vacant chair. Curiosity getting the best of him, Jared picked up the pamphlet and read the lyrics. Her flowery penmanship seemed to contradict her tough-as-nails character, but it was her words which surprised him most. The passion of Kimara's expressive verse immediately enthralled him, as he could almost hear in his head the written words spoken in her melodic tone. He had thought that he had her pegged. From the moment he'd met her with her smart mouth and spitfire attitude, he'd summed her up to be one of those pretty women who thought the sun rose and set around her. All at once, she became much more to him. She now appeared down-to-earth and at the same time mysterious to him, an enigma which was as equally baffling as it was inviting.

A short while later Kimara returned to the waiting room to advise Jared that Jasmine would be fine and that her husband Rick was on his way to pick them up. She assured him that there was no need for him to wait around any longer, curtly thanked him for his help and turned on her heels, eager to put some distance between them. Jared, however, stood mesmerized.

Chapter 8

Kimara dug methodically into the dampened earth, carefully removing the weeds which threatened the delicate azaleas. Pulling weeds had always been her favorite part of gardening, quite possibly because it was her mother's least favorite part. Gena would often leave Kimara to herself while she de-weeded the entire garden. A reprieve from the constant nagging and barrage of questions was always welcome.

The two of them had always seemed to be at odds over one thing or another. Even when Kimara was a little girl her mother had been critical of everything she did. She was always admonishing her to sit up straight, not to say this, don't do that. Kimara felt that nothing she did pleased her mother and as she got older, she purposely did things to upset her mother. Their relationship was strained with her father serving in the capacity of mediator and negotiator.

William Hamilton was the most easygoing person Kimara had ever known. He was a gentle giant who provided comfort to everyone in need, even when they didn't know they needed it. His and Kimara's relationship was special and Kimara could do no wrong in his eyes. She never understood how he could fall for someone like her mother, but they had been together for twenty-eight years and there were no indications that they'd be splitting up anytime soon.

Kimara sighed as she looked around the tiny back-yard. She remembered when they first moved into the house from their apartment in Hollis, Queens. The three bedroom cape-styled house had seemed like a palace to seven-year-old Kimara. Her father had been so proud and for awhile, even her mother had seemed genuinely happy. For a brief time she was less critical of Kimara and more like other moms. It wasn't long, however, before that lackluster look returned to Gena's eyes and she seemed distant and removed again. By the time Kimara was a teenager, she thought she understood her. She was certain that her mother resented being a wife and mother. While Kimara was unsure of the what, she knew that her mother had wanted something else out of life and was bitterly disappointed with what she had. This realization made Kimara angrier with her mother, but at the same time she vowed to herself that she would never end up in the same predicament.

It was only ten-thirty in the morning, but already the heat had risen to an almost suffocating level. Kimara was down on her knees, her light cotton shorts and pink cami sticking to her body. Her hair was done in a sloppy French braid and she was barefoot, having kicked off her flip-flops near the back door. When she came to her parents' apartment that morning, her intention was to get a few of the summer clothes which she'd left in storage bins in the closet and leave. She'd purposely come by when her parents were at work because she didn't want to see them. Having been asked to move out still hurt too much.

As she'd passed the door leading to the small back-yard, she was compelled to open it. Stepping out into the garden, she was greeted with the sweetly familiar scent of flowers in full bloom, their heady odor making her feel even more homesick. Before she knew it, she was down in the dirt, working her fingers through it and contemplating her life.

Working as a clerk at a wireless phone store was hardly her idea of a dream job. It was decent pay for little work, nothing more. Like many of the other jobs she'd held since high school, it required little effort on her part and that had always been fine with her. But lately, in spite of herself, she had begun to feel restless. Usually, when that feeling awakened inside of her and began making its presence known, she would simply quit her job, find something else and give her social life a shot in the arm.

For the first time, she'd begun to wonder how much longer she could go on as she had been. It seemed like everything around her was changing and everyone was moving away from her.

Her thoughts turned to Jasmine, who was doing the whole married thing and now had a baby on the way. At the hospital they confirmed what Jasmine had secretly suspected. She was six weeks pregnant. The fainting episode had been a combination of inadequate eating and a slightly elevated blood pressure. The doctors were certain that with a proper diet and close monitoring by her obstetrician, both Jasmine and the baby would be fine.

Kimara chastised Jasmine for not telling her that she thought she was pregnant, but was still overjoyed for her. When Rick arrived, Kimara excused herself. She watched briefly through the windowed swinging doors of the emergency room as Rick held Jasmine. A jealous pang stabbed her in the heart, changing the tears of joy which had been lining her sockets to tears of something else. She left the hospital and took the subway home, frightened by her own feelings and not sure if she could face Jasmine and all her happiness right now. At the same time, she felt guilty that her friend's joy should be clouded by her own selfish envy.

Kimara realized that she didn't really even have other girlfriends with whom she shared more than an occasional hello and phone call. Her parents didn't want her around. She hadn't met one single guy with whom she wanted to spend a minute of her time in several weeks, if not months—fantasies of the cop not included.

Kimara couldn't figure out when it was that she had stopped dreaming. It was like one day she woke up and realized that she had no plans for tomorrow and as a result, every day was just like the day before. By no means was she unhappy about her life. She enjoyed the sheer act of living, and meeting people and going places provided the excitement that an adrenaline-rush junkie like her craved. But lately it was as if something was missing. She just didn't know what it was.

I don't even want kids, she told herself. But she knew that was a lie even as she thought it. Still, the idea of having children, of being responsible for someone else was too scary for serious thought. Commitment was a dirty word to her, something that was entirely overrated and rarely worked out for the parties involved. It required living a life of selflessness and compromise that she felt incapable of doing. The last thing she wanted to do was end up like her mother. No, that wouldn't be fair to herself nor to any child.

Chapter 9

"You've got a delivery," Gino said, pointing to a large bouquet of tiger lilies on a file cabinet in his office as Kimara walked by on her way in to work.

It was Tuesday night, shortly after nine o'clock. Kimara had just entered the club and was headed to the room which doubled as a locker room and employee lounge, a few feet past Gino's office. At the sound of his voice, Kimara backtracked.

"Are you talking to me Gino?"

"Yeah. You've got some flowers here. New guy?" he asked.

"No, not that I know of," Kimara replied, eyeing the flowers suspiciously. She approached the bouquet, turning the vase slowly around before plucking the card from the center of the arrangement. She peeled the envelope away and silently read the handwritten note. She didn't recognize the neat, tightly-spaced writing, but continued reading anyway.

"Well?" Gino asked as he watched her expression change from wonderment to confusion to surprise.

"Huh?" she asked, looking away from the card. A slow smile spread across her face.

"Uh-huh, just as I suspected . . . a new guy. You girls

are something else." Gino laughed in a burly voice, his grey-green eyes filled with amusement. His dialect still evidenced his Russian ancestry. "You and my Giselle are the kind of girls my mother warned me about. *Krasee-vah*, but heartbreakers for sure."

"We're not that bad," Kimara defended.

Kimara carried the flowers to the lounge, pleased to find the room empty. She placed the flowers in the center of the four-seater oak table and plopped down in one of the chairs. She read the card to herself, still surprised by the signature line.

The mystery of you has haunted me from the moment I first met you. I need to know who you are and why you affect me so much. Have dinner with me? One dinner, my questions will be answered, and I'll leave you alone. Please say yes. Jared.

Beneath Jared's signature was a telephone number. Kimara read the note a half a dozen times until she had memorized every word. She sat perplexed as to what she should do. On impulse she grabbed the handset from the wall and dialed Jasmine's number.

"Hello," Jasmine answered sleepily. Now that they knew that Jasmine was pregnant, it was as if she had taken on the common characteristics and symptoms all at once. She was always sleepy, hungry, nauseous and cranky, and sometimes, these states of being all took hold of her at the same time.

"Did I wake you?" Kimara asked.

"No, no. I was up. I was watching something on Lifetime," Jasmine replied yawning. "What's up?"

"Nothing much. I'm about to start my shift at the club," Kimara answered.

"Humph," Jasmine remarked. It was no secret that she disliked the fact that Kimara worked at a nightclub but for once she held her tongue. The club was one of the many subjects Jasmine and Kimara's parents agreed on when it came to her life. They all thought that she should be doing something better, something more meaningful, or in her mother's words, more respectful. They acted like she was giving lap dances at some seedy T & A bar. All she did was serve drinks. She had grown tired of telling them that Club Silhouette was one of the most upstanding dance clubs and watering holes in the city. With the exception of the stabbing the other night, which turned out to be a lover's quarrel gone too far, there was rarely even an argument between patrons on the premises. It didn't matter what she said to them, all three remained steadfast in their disapproval, with Jasmine being the most vocal about it.

"Anyway, how are you feeling?" Kimara continued, trying to ignore Jasmine's slight.

"Pregnant. But that's not why you called me. What's up?"

"You won't believe in a million years who sent me flowers today."

"Who?" Jasmine asked, her curiosity momentarily surpassing both her fatigue and her disdain for Kimara's job.

"Jared Porter. The cop who helped us out the other day."

"Really, now. Sexy Chocolate?" Jasmine responded with great interest.

"Yeah, ain't that a trip? Listen to the card he wrote." Kimara read the card to Jasmine, hearing Jared's words aloud for the first time. Their rawness filled her with an uneasy excitement.

"Go 'head Mr. Good Bar! Although Kimara, I can't say that I'm surprised."

"What's that supposed to mean?"

"Let's just say that the energy flowing between you two the other day was hotter than the Mississippi Delta in July, mosquitoes and all. Y'all were drumming up enough heat to make me faint again," Jasmine laughed.

"Oh, that is such a big fat lie. There wasn't anything

flowing between us . . . except contempt maybe," Kimara protested.

"Kimara, please spare me. You know you're feeling the brother, just admit it. Shoot, if I wasn't happily married and knocked up, I'd be feeling him too. He's fine. He's Denzel Washington, Morris Chestnut, Boris Kodjoe fine."

"I am not feeling him," Kimara offered weakly, unable to sound convincing even to her own ears.

"Mmm, hmm," Jasmine said, yawning again.

"I'm not . . . okay, well maybe he's got a little somethin' somethin' going on, but that doesn't mean a thing," Kimara conceded.

"At the very least it means you should go out with the man and see what he's all about—other than the facts that he's fine, gainfully employed and a pretty considerate guy."

"You think?" Kimara said doubtfully.

"I think. He could have stepped right over my rusty behind on the sidewalk that day and kept on going. He wasn't on duty and yet he went out of his way for me," Jasmine said admiringly.

"But he's so full of himself."

"There's something the two of you have in common," Jasmine retorted.

"Hardy har-har."

"Seriously Kimara, what have you got to lose?"

When Kimara didn't respond for lack of possessing anything remotely resembling a logical answer, Jasmine continued. "Would you just call him already? And then call me right back. This is better than this tired old movie anyway."

It wasn't until during her break an hour later that Kimara drummed up the nerve to call Jared. She couldn't believe how nervous she was, like some school girl experiencing the agony of her first crush. She had to remind herself that he was just another guy, like any other she'd met. He put his shoes on one foot at a time, same as anyone else. All she had to do was call him and put an end to whatever it was he was stirring up inside of her, end of story.

Their conversation was brief and did nothing to quiet the storm which had begun brewing between them. Kimara thanked him for the flowers, he asked about Jasmine and then they made plans to have dinner the following night. By the time she hung up the phone, Kimara didn't know what to make of it. She wasn't sure if she was excited, anxious or just curious.

Jasmine, however, was bouncing off the walls with glee like she'd just hit the mega-millions lottery or something. One thing Kimara did know for certain was that she'd yet to meet the man who could make her heart do more than skip a beat and she doubted seriously that Jared Porter had enough of what it would take.

Chapter 10

"So, Ms. Hamilton. Seems like every time I see you, there's some sort of crisis going on around you. Is it you?"

"Not hardly. I stay as far away from crisis and drama as I can get."

Jared and Kimara were headed down the Long Island Expressway in Jared's aspen-green Expedition. WBLS' Quiet Storm played softly on the radio filling the cavernous vehicle with a romantic presence. The flint-grey butter-soft leather seats caressed Kimara's legs, which were bare from the middle of her thigh on down. Jared had opened the sunroof and every so often a strong wind blew, rumpling Kimara's hair. He shifted his eyes from the road to Kimara often, surprised to find her more beautiful than the times he'd seen her before.

"I like your hair curly like that. It's cute."

"Thank you Mr. Porter."

"Is that your hair?" Jared blurted.

Quick as a flash, Kimara wrinkled her brow and threw a hand on her hip. "What the hell kind of question is that?" she snapped.

"No . . . I meant . . . well, you know what I meant," Jared stammered, embarrassed by his ineloquence.

"Yes, it's my hair and no, I didn't pay for it," Kimara laughed suddenly at his blunder, easing the moment. Questioning a black woman about her hair was the quickest way to getting your feelings hurt.

"So you were saying," Jared continued recovering, "you're not about crisis and you stay away from drama. What are you about?"

"You're very direct, aren't you?"

Jared shrugged. "Sorry. Job hazard I guess. Skip the preliminaries and get the questions answered."

"Okay. Well then, I'll say this—I believe that more good times equals less worry lines."

"I like that," Jared answered. He smiled that hundred-watt smile of his and Kimara's heart skipped four beats. She shifted in her seat and turned her attention to the road.

"You still haven't told me where we're going."

"We're going on a journey."

"A journey?"

"Yeah, a journey. Are you game?"

"I suppose . . . as long as this journey gets me back in time for work tomorrow."

"Hmm, well that severely limits my options doesn't it?"

"Sorry Charlie, but that's the breaks. Do you mind?" Kimara asked, her hand hovering over the radio dial. She didn't want to just change the station because most brothers would cut your hand off for touching their radios. On the other hand, all this love music was doing things to her. Jared looking so good wasn't helping much either, but there was nothing she could do about that.

"Go ahead," he answered.

Kimara flipped the switch to Power 105. She turned up the volume as Eve's "Gangsta Loving" filled the car. She chimed in, rhyming along with Eve.

Jared listened intently. "You've got a nice voice," he commented.

"Thank you."

He pulled the car off the expressway and merged onto Route 27 East. The daylight had begun to dim slightly. They drove in silence, Kimara staring out of the window as they passed through numerous small villages. There were stretches of road flanked by fields of grass and farmhouses on either side of them. Towns with cute names like Mastic, Shirley and Speonk. Kimara's eyes lit up delightfully at the quaint homes, some of which looked like the gingerbread houses of the childhood fairytales she'd fallen in love with when she was little. She squealed excitedly as a pack of horses galloped in the distance.

"I can't figure you out. One minute you're ready to bite a brother's head off and the next you're like a bashful little girl," Jared commented, thinking aloud.

"When did I bite your head off?" Kimara asked, knowing precisely what he was referring to.

"You know what? Let's not even go there," Jared laughed.

"I smell the ocean," Kimara replied, ignoring his comment. "Where are we?" They had been driving for an hour and a half. Secretly, she hoped there was food involved with wherever they were going because her stomach was beginning to growl.

"We are at Montauk Point. It's one of the harbors on the Long Island Sound."

Jared pulled into a lot and parked in front of a restaurant called *The Crow's Nest*. After exiting the car, he came around to the passenger side and opened the door for Kimara. He held her hand as she stepped out, then led the way into the restaurant as if he owned the place as Kimara looked around soaking in the décor.

They were seated at a lamplit table for two. Built into some of the walls were large tanks housing various types of sea creatures. Mariner paintings adorned the remaining walls. The restaurant was dark with very sparse lighting. Jazz tunes played softly, providing background to the numerous conversing patrons and the clank of dishes could be heard as smiling waiters flowed effortlessly to and from the dining area carrying various heavenly smelling selections from the sea.

Jared ordered the lobster, begging Kimara to order one too. He claimed *The Crow's Nest* had the best lobster he'd ever eaten. Kimara, however, decided on the special which was a large lump of crabmeat, sautéed with vegetables and served over wild rice. She ate slowly, savoring every delicious morsel, but didn't decline a taste of Jared's lobster, which was also divine.

After dinner they strolled along the pier. The conversation flowed incessantly, as Jared was an arsenal of questions and Kimara delighted in providing answers. His manner of speaking, so direct and informal made it easy to share bits of her life with him. She told him about her parents, lingering on details of her close relationship with her father. She was uncustomarily analytical in her description of her mother. He wanted to know what growing up in New York City was like, having been born down South and later raised in Deerwood, Maryland himself. They talked about her job at the club and what she liked about working there.

Jared steered her toward the area where the boats were docked.

"Your chariot awaits you," he beamed, pointing to a striking white keelboat anchored beside them. The blue and white sail billowed in the light wind, flapping and waving as if to welcome them aboard.

"Is this your boat?" Kimara asked, cautiously impressed.

"I wish I could claim her, but I'd be lying. She belongs to a good friend of mine," Jared answered.

He led Kimara down the steps and untied the ropes which secured the boat to the pier. He handed Kimara a life vest and assisted her in fastening it, before donning his own. He retrieved a set of keys from his pocket and turned on the ignition. The engine purred softly as it kicked over. The boat trembled for a few moments and then slowly, with ease and confidence, Jared began inching them backwards.

"So you've got a friend who owns this boat?" Kimara asked skeptically.

She was seated on the cushioned, vinyl-covered bench on the deck of the *Main Lady*. Jared steered the boat expertly away from the dock and around the two dozen other boats in their path.

"Yeah," Jared responded. "He inherited it from his dad last year. Isn't she beautiful?"

"Yeah," Kimara admired. She had gone sailing once while on vacation with her parents in the Bahamas. It had been her first experience with the sea and she had fallen in love with the tranquility sailing evoked.

"And your friend just lets you take his boat out any time you want?"

"Yep. Marco's a cool dude."

One look at Kimara and he added with a laugh, "Man, you are one suspicious lady."

"All I'm saying is, I need a friend or two like that," Kimara quipped.

Once they were sailing into the open water, land slowly disappearing from view, Jared gave Kimara a tour of the vessel. He explained that it was about twenty-four feet long and traveled smoothly at high speeds. The sailing rig consisted of one mast with a triangular sail in the front, which was commonly called a jib and another sail located off of the back of the mast, known as the mainsail. There was a small enclosed cabin below deck which contained a half bathroom, a twin-sized futon, a mini refrigerator and a microwave.

Jared went into great detail, explaining many of the boat's operating mechanisms, the size and ability of the motor and steering system. The more impressed with his knowledge Kimara appeared to be, the more detailed his explanations became. It was obvious that Jared loved sailing and his infatuation with the sport was highly contagious.

As they sailed the length of the Long Island Sound, Jared pointed out various points of interests such as Shinnecock Bay and the Montauk Point Lighthouse. Kimara sipped a glass of Chardonnay from a bottle Jared had discovered in a cabinet. A few miles out from shore, Jared lowered the anchor and joined Kimara on the deck, bringing the bottle of soda he had been drinking.

"Have you been sailing long? You're obviously a professional," Kimara noted.

The night air was warm, even out at sea. Every so often she felt a spray of warm water on her skin. There were a million stars in the sky shining down on them. The moon illuminated the scene. Kimara felt completely relaxed as she sat talking to Jared. It was as if the troubles of everyday life, the current strain between her and her parents were all a million miles away instead of only the few that they had traveled to get there.

"You know something? The first time I ever set foot on a boat is when I met my friend Marco about, two . . . no three years ago."

"Really?"

"Yep. Seems longer though," Jared mused. "I became a certified small boat sailor a few months after I met him. That's like dinghies and day sailers. That was light stuff compared to the bigger boats. Eventually, I took some courses at a keelboat school."

"Stop playing. They actually have keelboat schools?" Kimara laughed.

"Yeah girl, this is serious business. About six months ago I got my keelboat certification and the rest is history. One of these days I'm going to buy myself a boat. Maybe I'll name her after you." Jared smiled.

Kimara blushed but let his compliment go without a response. "So this friend of yours . . . Marco—you guys must be really tight. How did you meet?"

"He and I were in the academy together, but we didn't run in the same circles. We just kinda spoke in passing. It wasn't until a few years after we graduated and ended up at the same house that we became good friends."

"*House.* You talk that cop talk just like they do on television. I've never dated a cop."

"Well then, don't think of it as dating a cop. I'm just a dashing brother who happens to earn a living as a cop," Jared returned.

He tucked his bottom lip into his mouth, giving her an innocent look which only made him look sexier than she'd remembered in her dreams. There were a whole host of words other than *dashing* which she could think of to describe Jared Porter.

"Do you and Marco still work together?" she asked, wanting to keep him talking.

"Nah, Marco was shot by this kid about seven or eight months ago. The bullet lodged in his back . . . too close to his spine to remove. Landed him on permanent disability."

"That's a shame."

"Yeah, but that's the risk. Anyway, he's doing pretty good for himself. He went into the auto business with one of his dad's old contacts and he's happy. They have a huge garage out here on the island."

"How do you go to work each day knowing that you could get hurt like that at any moment?" Kimara asked.

"You don't think about it. You can't. If you did, it would get in the way of doing the job. I like the fact that I'm in a position to help people out. And despite what you see on television, that's what most of my day is about. Helping people out," Jared explained, wanting to dispel the unfortunate, yet common myths which existed about police officers.

"Have you ever had to shoot someone?"

Kimara was curious about how people could voluntarily do such dangerous jobs like policing or military service. She always wondered what kind of person it took to strap on a weapon every day and face all kinds of elements sight unseen.

"Once," Jared answered.

He grew noticeably tense at the memory. Kimara instantly regretted asking the question. "I'm sorry, you don't have to talk about it if you don't want to," she apologized.

"No, it's not that. I just hate that part of the job, you know. When I first joined the force, I only thought about the good parts—helping people, making a difference . . . that sort of stuff. I didn't really allow myself to consider that one day I might have to use my gun, maybe even take a life. I don't think that's something I'll ever be comfortable with," Jared answered honestly. It was a memory that while he just as soon wished to forget, he knew he had to hold onto it, because it was an experience that had changed him. It also continued to shape everything he did in his life.

"Did the person you shot die?"

"No, thank God. He was just some dumb kid trying to prove he was hard. I pray every day that I won't have to hurt anybody out there. That's why I do the job that I do every day. Maybe if some of those kids like the ones I bust see me out there, trying to hold out a hand and show them that life doesn't have to be all about banging and hustling, well, maybe some of them might think twice. I just want to give one kid a chance at a different life."

"That's admirable," Kimara commented.

"What about you?" Jared asked.

"Me? Well let's see, I hate guns and uniforms do nothing for my figure, so I guess that rules out the protecting and serving business for me. I hated school—thought I would die of boredom in high school. I'm not sure what I want to do. My parents and Jasmine think something's wrong with me. It's like, in their eyes if you haven't made a life's plan by the time you're twenty-one, you might as well forget it. Everybody doesn't have the same dreams and aspirations and they certainly aren't on the same timetable," Kimara answered honestly.

"That's true. But what do you dream about, when you dare to dream?" Jared asked openly.

"I like seeing people have fun and being happy. I never told anybody this but sometimes I imagine myself becoming like a party planner. You know that person who plans other people's weddings, anniversary parties and stuff? I could do that, you know. I work well with people and I love to shop and put stuff together."

"So why don't you do it?"

"I don't know. I don't know the first thing about it. And who would hire me?"

"Those aren't very good reasons not to do something you're interested in, if you ask me. But maybe now isn't the time. I'm sure when you're ready, you'll be good at whatever you do."

"Oh yeah? What makes you so sure of that Mr. Porter? You don't even know me."

"Oh, but I do know you. You're smart, caring, fun to be with, feisty and very, very beautiful," Jared complimented.

Kimara blushed. Without responding, she turned her head toward the night sky and watched the stars swaying above them. They'd sailed for hours, oblivious to the time as they talked.

Finally and reluctantly, Jared turned the boat around and headed back to shore. When they arrived, he docked the boat and helped Kimara onto the pier. She stood by watching him as he secured the ropes to the pier before joining her. Jared reached down and took her hand as they stood for a few minutes watching the sun begin to rise. A new day had begun as well as a new beginning for each of them. The past ten hours shared between them had changed them both irrevocably.

"Did you have a good time?" Jared asked as they strolled unhurriedly back to his car.

"Mmm, hmm. You?"

"Very good."

They rode home in comfortable silence and when he dropped her off in front of her building, Jared didn't even attempt to kiss her good night. He held both of her hands in his for a moment, gave them a gentle squeeze and walked back to his car. The look in his eyes and the heat of his touch made her feel like she had been kissed and more.

Chapter 11

"So, who exactly is Officer Jared Marquise Porter?" Kimara asked as she thumbed through a photo album which she'd picked up from Jared's coffee table. Inside, the first few pages were filled with pictures of Jared at his Police Academy graduation ceremony. In some of the pictures he stood next to a younger version of himself. The young man smiling beside him was slightly taller and a shade lighter, but otherwise bore a striking resemblance to Jared. There was another picture of the two of them standing on either side of a petite older woman who Kimara could easily tell was mother to both men.

Jared entered the room wearing a terry cloth bathrobe and carrying a glass of white wine. Kimara stared openly at him, his strong physique appearing trapped by the material. She graciously accepted the glass of wine and waited for his response.

"Oh no. I knew I should have hidden that," Jared said.

"Your brother's a cutie," she said, pointing to one of the pictures.

"Yeah, he thinks he's a playa," Jared laughed.

"What about you? Are you a playa too?" Kimara asked, not entirely serious.

"Nope. I'm a one woman kind of man. Provided the woman is woman enough to hold my attention," he said smugly.

"Provided you're man enough to handle it," she retorted.

"Whatever," Jared laughed, "I'm going to get dressed, *Woman*."

Jared had picked Kimara up from her day job after his double shift ended. They were headed out to dinner and a movie, but Jared wanted to stop at home to shower and change beforehand. Kimara was worried that he would be too tired after having worked so many hours and, despite the fact that she was longing to see him, suggested that they postpone their plans. Jared, however, was adamant about not wanting to cancel. It had been a week since their first and only date. A week full of marathon phone calls and fervent exchanges. He felt like he had gotten to know Kimara so well in a short amount of time, but was hungry to know her even better. His fantasies of her were overshadowing everything else in his life and he was powerless to stop them.

Kimara curiously surveyed Jared's living room. She didn't consider herself nosy, just possessed by an inquiring mind. She firmly believed that looking at a person's belongings and the things he chose to surround himself with provided a window to the soul.

Jared's apartment was small and tastefully furnished. The look was a blend of Ikea and Pier 1 Imports—nothing had come in matched pairs, but the décor was thrown together in a colorful potpourri which gave the place a fresh, modern appeal. On a metal two-tiered desk sat a Dell computer and a stack of textbooks. Kimara thumbed through the scholarly works on the desk and the other dozen which lined a bookshelf in one corner of the room.

When Jared returned to the living room, wearing a striped cotton short-sleeved button-down shirt, denim shorts and sandals, Kimara gave him an appreciative smile. "You sure clean up nicely," she remarked.

"Cute," he responded.

"So, Officer Porter. What's up with all the higher learning? Looks to me like somebody's studying the law," Kimara said, sweeping her hand in the direction of Jared's desk.

"Guilty. I'm in my last year at Brooklyn Law School."

"In all the conversing we've been doing, I don't see how that little tidbit got lost in translation."

"Well, I guess I didn't mention it. Not that it's a secret or anything like that. I just . . . well, I thought you might be a little hesitant to date me if you knew I was in school. You were pretty vocal with your opinions on education."

Kimara felt ashamed to have said all that she had. "You still should have told me. I think school is great, if that's your thing. I didn't mean to knock it like that. It's just that I don't think college and all that jazz is for everyone. It certainly isn't for me."

"I can respect that."

"And I can respect you too," Kimara smiled. Every day it seemed like she was peeling back another layer on this guy, finding more and more surprises as she went along. She wasn't necessarily sure if that was a good or bad thing, but at least, it kept things interesting.

"You never answered my earlier question. Who are you?"

"Just your average Joe. A little country boy from North Carolina."

Jared's candy-sweet smile was almost enough to send Kimara into sugar shock. He didn't smile often, but when he did it was an amazing sight to behold.

"There's got to be more to it than that, but I'll play your little secretive game for now," Kimara remarked.

"I'm an open book. I promise," he told her. He stuffed his wallet into his back pocket. "Ready?"

Kimara nodded as she walked to where Jared stood near the apartment door. When she reached him, the instinct to make physical contact with him so compelled her that she couldn't control it. She allowed the back of her hand to touch his lightly. His fingers responded instantly, wrapping themselves around hers. When their eyes met, it was as if all the thousands of words, thoughts and intimacies shared between them this past week during their telephone interludes had bonded them as completely as if they'd spent every minute of that time in each other's physical presence.

Neither of them wanted to move or speak at first. It was enough to just look into one another's eyes, the magic of what was building between them giving new light to them both. Finally, Jared released the doorknob he was holding and let the door close. He ran two fingers down the side of Kimara's face and she shuddered noticeably. She leaned forward then, unable to resist the urge that had had her trying to climb through the telephone line all week. Her high-heeled mules lessened the difference between their heights, but Jared still had to lower his head to meet her lips, which he did so willingly.

Kimara seductively ran her tongue across Jared's smooth lower lip. His breath caught in his throat as the smell of warm butterscotch escaped her. He covered her mouth with his lips and slowly his tongue made its way between her succulent lips. They explored one another thoroughly, their mouths joined so tightly together it was as if they sought to devour one another whole. Jared pulled Kimara closer to him, his arms encircling her. With a mind of its own, his hand traveled down her back seeking to feel for itself if her rear was as firm and welcoming to the touch as it appeared to be. His satisfaction came in the form of a deep sigh as he squeezed and caressed her behind.

Several pleasurable minutes passed before they parted, albeit unwillingly. The passion, having been awakened the moment they first met that fated night at Club Silhouette, was now elevated to a new height. They both became painfully aware of the level of desire mounting between them and were equally as alarmed as they were excited by it.

A small voice in the back of Kimara's mind cautioned her to hit the brakes. She had a bad habit of rushing into things, allowing the thrill of the moment to over-rule her senses. That was fine when the attraction she shared with a man was purely physical. In that case, it didn't matter if there was no conversation the morning after because she didn't stick around long enough anyway. Jared was different and although she would have hated to have to admit it, she deeply cared about the *after* since everything leading up to it was pro-foundly special. The last thing she wanted was for them to move too quickly and ruin the foreplay.

"I'm starved." Kimara smiled, smoothing her skirt self-consciously.

Jared didn't miss the change in her demeanor.

"You cool?" he asked.

"Very," Kimara insisted. She kissed him quickly on the cheek and reached for the doorknob. "Just hungry," she replied.

Jared followed her out of the door, hoping the evening air would cool the flames burning within. As he watched her walk down the hallway, her body poetry in motion, he doubted it seriously.

Days turned into weeks and the pair became insepa-rable. Ironically, their choices of entertainment varied tremendously. Jared preferred quiet nights, staying at home and renting movies. In addition to sailing, he also liked bowling and Rollerblading. Kimara, who enjoyed noise and crowds, dragged him to comedy clubs, street festivals and amusement parks. Reluctantly, he attended a few dance clubs and even a couple of parties thrown by Giselle and other friends of Kimara's.

It was obvious that he was very uncomfortable in nightclubs and Kimara had a hard time understanding his discomfort. Who could resist a throbbing beat, a bumping base line and a funky guitar thrown in from time to time for good measure? Jared was obviously unmoved by these things. He seemed to be surveying the crowd and sizing everyone up who passed by him. Eventually, Kimara stopped inviting him to certain places, although she didn't stop attending these gatherings herself. It was Jared who, filled with a desire to be with her as often as their schedules permitted and also wary of her partying alone, insisted upon going to functions that he didn't particularly like. Those evenings often ended early, Kimara feeling distracted by Jared's discomfort. They strove to do things that they both liked, but neither could shake the nagging suspicion that their different lifestyles would at some point interfere with their budding relationship.

Jasmine, on the other hand, couldn't have been more thrilled than if Oprah Winfrey had knocked on her front door to surprise her with a makeover, a new house of her dreams and a request to travel with her to Africa to provide books and clothes to needy children. She kindly took credit for the union, citing the matchmaking fiasco on Career Day and fainting spell as the catalyst for bringing the pair together. She purposely forgot about the fact that it was Kimara's job at Club Silhouette— a job that Jasmine despised—that was the place where the initial encounter took place, setting the stage for the entire romantic adventure.

In any event, the more Jasmine learned about Jared,

the more she flipped over him. While Kimara, too, was head over heels, she reminded Jasmine that he was just another man—not the second coming of Christ as Jasmine made him out to be. Kimara did not forget for one second that every man has faults, some worse than others. Only time would tell what Jared's faults were, and, what's more, if she would be able to accept them.

Chapter 12

Kimara's mouth hungrily met Jared's, sending instant ripples of pleasure through her body. The balmy night air paled in comparison to the torrid passion mounting between and within each of them. It was as if they were pantomimes, acting out the words as Prince sang the words of his soul-stirring hit, "Adore," which happened to be Kimara's favorite song.

Jared had surprised Kimara with tickets to Prince's concert in Central Park after learning that he was her all-time favorite artist. Kimara had been a Prince fan all of her life. She knew every lyric to every song, including the ones where all he did was scream and moan.

The days and weeks had flown by as Kimara and Jared spent every possible moment with one another or talking on the telephone. He sent her flowers at the club once a week. She baked him homemade cheesecake, his favorite dessert, and dropped it off at the station house. For the first time, Kimara had taken the time to really get to know a man and, what's more, let him get to know her. She let Jared into places that she had never let anyone else, and she wasn't the least bit hesitant with him. Their love affair was an emotional slow grind that continued long after the music had stopped playing. They made their own music.

Jared was easily aroused by the mere sound of Kimara's voice. When he wasn't with her, images of her shapely calves or lips the color of peaches sent the blood rushing to his groin. He wanted her more than he'd wanted any other woman in his life. But he didn't want to rush her. He could tell that she wanted to take things slowly and he respected that. As difficult as it was, he waited patiently, knowing that when she gave herself to him, it would be well worth the agonizing wait.

The park was jam-packed the night of the concert, Prince's fans spanning every generation and every walk of life. Kimara excitedly pulled Jared through the crowd, eager to get close to the stage.

The forces of the warm summer night air, the crowd, and Prince's cathartic serenade combined to build Kimara to a frenzied arousal. She was more aware of Jared's presence than she'd ever been before. He stood behind her, the strength of him pressed against her body, his arms wrapped tightly around her. His body heat and the sheer smell of him were driving her crazy. Each time his warm breath hit her neck, she shivered. By the midpoint of Prince's act, every inch of Kimara's skin was ablaze with desire. She turned to face Jared and his waiting lips sought hers. Their joining was almost magical, charging the air around them until sparks seemed to shoot out into the night sky.

They parted, the spell remaining intact. Kimara searched Jared's eyes, finding the same wild ardency which rested in her own. No words were necessary and none were spoken. They each knew what the other was thinking and were acutely aware of what the other was feeling. The silent pact made between them filled them with an unparalleled urgency to act.

Jared draped his arm around Kimara's shoulder as they walked, and she slid her hand into his back pocket.

They strolled slowly away from the stage area, as if now that the decision had been made, they had all the time in the world to accomplish their goal. The crowd thinned as they proceeded to the rear of the grassy knoll. As they neared the entrance to the parking lot, Kimara was at first surprised and then flushed with an embarrassing excitement as Jared steered her away and to the left of the gate. Instead of going to his truck as she had thought they would, he moved her along a narrow cobblestone path which led to a cluster of trees. They stepped through the brush where the path ended, and they entered a wooded hideaway. A mere ten or so steps led them into seclusion, where the darkness enveloped them quickly. New York City disappeared and the throng of concert goers ceased to exist. Distant sounds from the show drifted toward them, a faint reminder of the world which continued to revolve without them. None of it seemed real as they felt for each other in the darkness. Once their eyes became accustomed to the pitch-black landscape, the beauty of their private love nest set their bodies aflame.

Jared's mouth found Kimara's again in the darkness and he devoured her with ravenous kisses. The excitement building within her made her breath ragged and her head feel light. If the weeks of foreplay between them, the dinners, the dates, the teasing conversations, could be classified as a dance, it would be a waltz. Tonight's dance was the tango, filled with all the fervent passion that two people could muster.

With her back pressed to a large oak tree for support, Jared unzipped the fitted denim dress Kimara wore and dropped to his knees. He ran his hands slowly from the base of her delicate neck, feeling the wild beating of her heart as it pounded in her chest. He found the softness of her skin remarkable in every place that he touched. The intricate lace of her black bra teased his fingers as he massaged the firm mounds of flesh it restrained. Her nipples became hard engorged peaks as he pinched them, gently at first and then harder between his trembling fingers.

Kimara moaned, placing one of her own fingers in her hot mouth. She bit down hard in an effort to stifle her screams as Jared lapped at her belly button, his nostrils filled with the scent of her, a potent mixture of vanilla musk body spray and sexual arousal. The tantalizing aroma made him feel drunk with impatient desire.

Through her sheer, black panties, he found her spot. Soft tangled curly hair parted for him as his tongue sought out the prize. Kimara grasped the back of Jared's smooth head as he dove in with rabid attention. It was as if his sole mission in life was to take her higher and higher with each lick, each kiss, each suck. She almost couldn't stand the pleasure, but felt that she would die if he stopped. He dined on her love juices as she climaxed again and again, her legs weak as the energy released from her body like rushing waters against a broken dam.

Jared traveled up the length of her body, his tongue revisiting her stomach, breasts and neck. Kimara reached down and unzipped his khaki shorts, releasing his solid pulsating organ. He groaned audibly as she held him in soft hands and massaged him firmly, driven by the intention to please him as thoroughly as he had pleased her. From his back pocket he retrieved a condom which Kimara aided him in putting on.

Jared lifted Kimara off of her feet, entering her slowly as she wrapped both legs around his waist. Moving with the rhythm of a gentle steed, he drove himself into her, reaching the center of her womanhood and once again sending shockwaves of pleasure through her body.

Kimara felt Jared's body tense as he neared his own climax. She held him tightly within her as she whispered sweet words in his ear. She nibbled every part of him that her mouth could reach, tonguing his ear with the same urgency as she had tongued his mouth. He fired, trembling with pleasure and she received him, her own heart bursting with the joyful feeling of being in the throws of the ultimate union. They were quiet afterwards, panting as they reluctantly descended the mountain they'd just climbed.

"You set my soul on fire," Kimara whispered against Jared's chest, a mild blaze still burning within.

He kissed her damp forehead and face repeatedly, as the post-climatic shudders which claimed her body began to subside.

"And you've made mine come alive," he answered honestly. He wanted to tell her that he loved her but held back. His feelings for her were still so raw, so impassioned that he was reluctant to reveal too much too soon for fear of scaring her away. In spite of this new level of intimacy, Kimara remained a mystery to him. So much of her was still out of reach and his biggest fear was that she'd slip away before he had a chance to uncover all of her. He feared that he would awake one day, alone and this would all be a dream. She was, after all, trouble with a capital T.

Chapter 13

Kimara giggled to herself. She was lying in Giselle's over-sized, ball and claw-foot tub surrounded by lavender scented bubbles. The warm water skimmed the rim of the thirty-six-inch-wide cast-iron receptacle. She slid further into the water and blushed unabashedly as she remembered her encounter with Jared in the park a few days before. Jasmine had almost fallen out of her seat when she'd described the risqué interlude to her. Even now, long after it was over, Kimara grew moist at the memory. It was the single most memorable sexual experience she had ever had in her life. Besides being an incredible, gentle lover, she shared a connection with Jared which was unlike anything she'd ever felt. When she'd tried to describe that sensation to Jasmine, unable to label what she was feeling, Jasmine, as quick as a flash told her that it was love.

Love? Kimara had been saying the word over and over again in her mind since, as if she'd never heard it before. Could it really be love? Could a tiny monosyllabic word contain and explain all that she was feeling? She didn't think so, yet there was nothing else that hinted at the magnitude of her want for and need of Jared. He had awakened something deep within—a part of her which she hadn't realized was asleep. It was funny, but all of those qualities which at first disturbed her about him had become endearing. She realized that she had wrongly attributed his self-assured demeanor and the ease with which he slipped into the driver's seat in most situations to arrogance when, in fact, it was his desire to take care of other people which drove him. His even temperament and easy smile often caught her off guard, making her want to reach out and kiss him every chance she got.

That night in the park had filled Kimara's senses to bursting with a robust passion unlike any she'd ever imagined possible. At night her dreams were taken over by him and when her eyes opened each morning, visions of him continued to delight her memory. For the first time in her life Kimara found herself waiting hungrily for a man's phone call, anxious just to hear his voice, to talk about his day and tell him about hers. Part of her warned herself to be wary. After all, didn't someone once say that everything that glitters ain't gold? Despite this knowledge, she couldn't make herself tread carefully. She felt like she had been standing on a boardwalk, looking out at an ocean so blue it hurt her eyes and wanting so desperately to swim in it. The only thing separating her from her goal was a mile of hot sand and finally, after waiting longer than she could stand, she ran blindly across that sand, not caring how badly she got burned, to her ocean. Once there, wrapped in the cool arms of passion, she spitefully turned around and told that sand to kiss her where the sun didn't shine. She was determined to keep this feeling, this thing that Jared had brought into her life for as long as she could. She wouldn't worry about the end, whatever and whenever that may be, because the beginning and middle were just too delicious.

Kimara's head was thrown back, her mind having convinced herself that the liquid pleasure she'd known with

Jared a few nights before was happening now. She was near that critical point of release, the excitement paling in comparison to the real thing, but close enough for now, when the phone rang. The shrill siren brought her back to reality and she cursed the man who'd invented the contraption.

She leaned over the side of the tub and snatched the cordless handset from its perch. *What kind of nut puts a phone in the bathroom anyway?* she thought.

"Hello?"

"Good afternoon. This is Power 105 calling for Kimara Hamilton."

"Who is this?"

"This is the station manager at Power 105. Kimara Hamilton?"

"Speaking."

"Hi there, Ms. Hamilton. I'm calling from Power 105 to tell you that out of over two thousand contestants from the metropolitan area, you are our winner."

"Look, I don't know what you're talking about, but you must have the wrong Kimara Hamilton," she answered, preparing to hang up.

"Wait, Ms. Hamilton. Do you have a friend by the name of Jasmine Wright?"

"Ye . . . yeah," Kimara answered hesitantly.

"Well then we've got the right person. You see, Power 105 hosts an annual poetry contest. We receive entries from our listeners which number in the millions from the tri-state area and beyond."

"Poetry?"

"Yes. Mrs. Wright entered a poem you wrote, "Sugarcane" and we're happy to tell you that a panel of judges has selected your poem as the first place winner."

"She what?"

"Uh, I take it Mrs. Wright failed to inform you about the contest. Well no matter, you've won. Aren't you excited?"

"You can't imagine," Kimara said wryly.

She listened as the exuberant station manager explained the contest's rules and went on to tell her what she had won. By the time she hung up the phone, her bubbles had dissolved and the water was tepid. She released the plug to allow the tub to drain and stepped out onto a fuzzy bath mat, hastily wrapping an oversized towel around her dripping body.

She was flabbergasted, to say the least, by the entire situation. Miss Jasmine had gone too far this time and Kimara aimed to tell her about herself. She was tired of Jasmine trying to run her life as if she were incapable of doing it on her own. Kimara got dressed in record time, slipping into a fuchsia and white tennis dress and a pair of sneaker mules and stomped out of the door. She hailed a yellow taxi and sunk silently into the backseat, fuming and muttering under her breath. The driver glanced at her quizzically in the rearview mirror, but she was too perturbed to notice.

Twenty minutes later, Kimara had ascended the four death-defying flights of stairs at break-neck speed and was banging on Jasmine's door. Rick opened it, dressed in his transit uniform.

"Is your wife here?" she asked without offering a word of greeting.

Rick was used to Kimara's behavior by now. He silently stepped aside and allowed her to enter.

"Babe," he called, "Kimara's here, and I'm leaving. I'll call you tonight on my break."

"Okay, sweetie. See you later. And don't forget to call your sister back before she has a fit."

Rick stole a parting glance at Kimara who was pacing up and down the living room floor. He wasn't sure what her beef was this time, but he didn't want to stick around to see this duel to the deaths play out. Jasmine took a lot of stuff off of Kimara in his opinion. She tolerated her tantrums, her attitudes and her smart mouth. But even Jasmine had her limits as to how much she would take from anyone and based on the way the wicked witch had barged in tonight, it was safe to say that she'd quickly say something that would catapult her well beyond those limits.

Jasmine emerged from the bedroom just as Rick shut the apartment door behind him with a chuckle. She was wearing a purple sleeveless housedress and wore her hair braided in a zillion, auburn-colored micro box braids, which hung past her shoulders. Her midsection seemed to have doubled in size since Kimara had last seen her a few days ago. At the rate she was growing, it looked to Kimara as if she were cooking up triplets in there.

"Hey girl, I didn't know you were coming by here today. Were you out this way visiting your parents?" Jasmine asked.

"Never mind all that. I can't believe you," Kimara yelled hotly.

"What in the world is wrong with you Kimara?" Jasmine answered, stunned by her abruptness.

"Don't try to act all innocent with me. I would think you would have much better things to do with your time . . . what with your perfect life and husband and baby makes three. You shouldn't have time to be constantly interfering in my life."

"Look Kimara, I don't know what you are talking about, but you're going to need to calm down and stop yelling in my house like you're crazy or something."

"How could you take something I wrote specifically for you and share it with the whole free world?" Kimara barked. Her arms were folded across her chest tightly and she was tapping her sneaker clad foot on the floor.

Jasmine stared at her blankly for a moment. Slowly, understanding spread across her newly plump face, followed by a shy smile. "Is that what this is all about? The contest? What, did they call you?" Jasmine asked, expectant excitement rising within.

"Yes they called me. I can't believe you sent them one of my poems without my permission."

"Kimara, first of all I didn't share it with the whole free world—just the folks at Power 105. Besides girl, you're good. You're really, really good. It's about time somebody besides me knows it," Jasmine defended.

"They read it on the damned radio Jasmine. Who told you that was okay with me?"

"Well the way I see it, you gave me the poem, making it my property, and I'm free to do with my property whatever I choose to do. Want some lemonade?" Jasmine asked casually as she sauntered toward the kitchen.

Kimara pounced on her heels in hot pursuit. "No I don't want any of your lemonade. You might take my DNA off the glass and send that to somebody too."

"Okay, now you're being real extra. What is the big freaking deal Kimara?"

"The big *freaking* deal is that you need to stop meddling in my life."

Jasmine filled two glasses with crushed ice and poured lemonade into both. She left one on the counter, sat heavily on one of the stools and quietly sipped her lemonade. Several minutes passed before Kimara picked up the second glass and drank from it.

"Are you going to tell me what they said?" Jasmine asked.

"I'm surprised they didn't just call you themselves and deliver the news."

Patiently, Jasmine waited. She knew that eventually Hurricane Kimara would wind down into maybe just a summer storm and she'd be ready to talk rationally.

"They said I won the contest."

"Yes!" Jasmine exclaimed. "Girl, I knew you would. I just knew it." Jasmine began dancing, doing a lousy

Harlem Shake and coming off looking like Barney the Dinosaur.

"You're stuff is way better than the garbage they usually have on any of those spoken word contests," she continued breathlessly. "You know, I even told the guy—"

"Hello, Earth to Jasmine. Have you heard anything I've said? Has it not penetrated that thick skull of yours that I'm not happy with you right now?"

"Let's forget about that for just one second. Kimara, you won. You won! Don't tell me that doesn't excite you just a tiny little bit."

Jasmine held her hand near Kimara's face, pinching her index and thumb together. Kimara swatted Jasmine's hand away and sighed. It was pointless trying to be angry with this woman.

"Well . . ." she began.

"I knew it, I knew it!" Jasmine squealed, reaching out to tickle Kimara's neck.

"Stop it. And don't get yourself all geeked up. I don't care what they say or what you say, I'm not getting up on anybody's stage and reading my stuff. No way."

"Kimara, you've got to. You won the contest. First prize is one hundred dollars and a spot in the spoken word line-up at Roots and Culture Café in Brooklyn."

"So I've heard. I'm still not doing it."

"You've got to be kidding me. Don't even act like you can't use the hundred bucks." Jasmine arched her eyebrows and pursed her lips, a cut-the-crap look on her face.

"So I'll take the money. That's the least I deserve for having my right to privacy violated by a nosy, meddlesome, overweight—"

"Watch it now," Jasmine warned.

"I'm still not doing the show." Kimara folded her arms across her chest and walked out of the kitchen. She plopped down on the sofa in the living room feeling defeated as she realized that she'd lost yet another battle with Jasmine.

"Why not?" Jasmine followed her into the living room. She sat down next to Kimara, the cushions sagging under her weight.

Kimara covered her face with her hands. Though she loved Jasmine like the sister she'd never had, sometimes the urge to glue her lips together with Gorilla Glue was extremely overwhelming. Kimara worked tirelessly to tune Jasmine out for the next hour as she begged, pleaded, cajoled and threatened Kimara into doing the show.

"I think you should do it," Jared said as he poured a capful of shampoo into his palms and rubbed it into Kimara's hair. They were in his bathtub, bathed by the soft light glowing from a solitary yellow light bulb above the vanity.

"I've never done anything like that before. That's not me."

Jared laughed. "Don't try to tell me you're shy."

"Well, what if I am? What would be so hard to believe about me being shy?" Kimara asked as she stroked Jared's shins beneath the frothy water.

"Babe, you're a lot of things. Shy certainly isn't one of them. You love being the center of attention and you damn sure ain't afraid to open your mouth to people," Jared laughed.

"That's not the point. I still can't believe Jasmine had the nerve to do something like this behind my back. She's lucky I'm even speaking to her."

"I know you're upset with her, but did you ever stop to think that she had your best interests in mind? Jasmine loves you like a sister and I really don't think she was trying to hurt or disrespect your friendship. She only wants good things for you."

"Good things like what? Standing up in front of

strangers and sharing my innermost thoughts?" Kimara asked sarcastically.

"Yeah and like me."

"Who says you're good for me, besides Ms. Know It All?" Kimara leaned her head back against Jared's shoulder. She looked into his liquid brown eyes feeling all of her resolve melting away like butter.

"I do," Jared said, sliding his warm tongue into her smiling mouth. He kissed her deeply.

"This is bribery," Kimara mumbled.

"Is it working?" Jared asked. He reached beneath the water and her fort came tumbling down.

Chapter 14

Kimara squinted, holding one hand across her forehead in an attempt to shade her eyes from the bright spotlight which illuminated her petite figure as she stood on the box stage. As she scanned the dimly lit room, her stomach careened, tightening and relaxing intermittently. The only problem was that this roller coaster ride she was on would last a heck of a lot longer than the usual three minutes offered at most amusement parks.

Suddenly, the halter top the color of lemon meringue she wore felt too bright, the black parachute pants which gathered below her knees seemed all wrong for the occasion, and the Kate Spade stilettos began to wobble beneath her like a bronco trying to dethrone its rider. Now she wished she'd let Jasmine do something different with her hair as offered, feeling like a plain Jane with her usual hairstyle—a wrap, which was parted in the center and hung straight down each side of her face.

The other performers scheduled to take the stage tonight seemed more of what you'd expect on the poetry scene. The guy, who had placed second in the contest, was tall and rail-thin. He had short, ratty locks and a goatee in need of a trim. His wrinkled T-shirt and sweatpants gave him a very artistic look, almost as if he had been holed up in a room somewhere for the past two months working on his master creation and had just been pulled out unwillingly and thrust upon the stage.

The other female, a short Puerto Rican woman, no more than eighteen years old, wore a long floral skirt, sandals and a white tank top. Her hair was tied up in a white head wrap and she had huge hoop silver earrings in each ear and a smaller one in her nose.

Kimara definitely felt out of place and wanted to kick herself for agreeing to do the show. Briefly she reflected on Jared's persuasive argument, which caused a warm fluttering sensation to rise up in her belly. He had been oh-so-very convincing. She'd spent the past week working out her routine. She'd rummaged through a half a dozen shoeboxes in which she kept poems and prose which dated back to junior high school. Finally, when she felt like she'd found a connecting thread to tie it all together, she committed her words to memory, created a rhythm and hoped she wasn't making a big mistake.

She took a deep cleansing breath which did nothing to ease her tension and became aware of the crowd's increasing impatience. She knew that she couldn't keep them waiting much longer. Nervously, she tapped the microphone sharply two times. It was working just fine. There were no more excuses, nor reasons to delay. Silently, she cursed Jasmine for getting her into this predicament in the first place. She cleared her throat and licked her lips. A guy seated just below the stage gave an appreciative grunt at the gesture. Kimara ignored him. She shaded her eyes again and made one more furtive sweep of the room.

On the far side, near an exit door stood Jared. Dressed in the canary short-sleeved button down shirt she'd bought him and a pair of slacks, he was her sexy knight in shining armor. He waved to her, his gesture quick and

eager. Seated at a table near him were Jasmine and
Giselle. Jasmine, who was grinning from ear to ear, gave
her the thumbs-up. Her people, her best girlfriend, her
gorgeous boyfriend and her zany roommate. All of them
wishing her well and having her back. The realization
came that while she was up on that stage alone, they
were right there with her. They had her back. She didn't
doubt that if the crowd started booing, they'd be ready
to kick some poetry-loving butt up in there.

Kimara exhaled and the anxiety flowed from her body.
In its place, a static energy began to fill her. She placed
one hand around the base of the microphone, closed her
eyes and effortlessly, the words began to pour from
her lips.

For fifteen minutes she spoke as though in the comfort of her living room with friends. These hundred or
so people sat enthralled by her, hanging on to her every
word as if it were gospel. She spoke of love and loss; of
loving and hurting; of soul-stirring surrender and heart-
breaking abandon. Her velvety tone and cadence
turned phrases into melodies, sweeping the crowd into
an erotic frenzy, whirling them in circles of delicious
pleasure and finally, delivering them in a satiating
climax. Her body language, once she relaxed, brought
life to the words. Her performance was as musical in
quality as it was poetic. Yet it didn't really feel like she
was performing. It was more like having a conversation
or telling a story in which she became so involved that
she forgot that she didn't know these people from a can
of paint. It didn't matter. They were into her and she,
into them. When she finished, a thin line of sweat had
formed above her lip and on her brow. The room was
silent.

Kimara remained onstage resting as the crowd, too,
rested, spent and exhausted. After a few moments someone at the center of the room recovered and began
clapping a loud echoing clap. Others followed and soon

the entire room was filled with voracious applause. The packed house had been blown away.

Kimara left the stage filled with a feeling of power and intense elation which paralleled no other feeling. She waded through a sea of smiling faces, clapping hands and whistling lips. When she reached her friends, she found them to be ten times louder than the crowd around them.

"That's right ya'll. She's my best friend. My girl," Jasmine screamed as she clapped fanatically.

Kimara blushed. "Ssh girl. You are so loud!"

"I don't care. I want the whole world to know. When you blow up and become a famous poet or something, I want it to be known where you come from," Jasmine yelled, hugging Kimara as much as her big belly would allow.

"Aw baby, you were something else," Jared chimed in. He stuck his pointer and ring fingers into his mouth and let out a shrill whistle.

Kimara gave up trying to quiet the two of them and turned to Giselle. "Did you like it?" she asked.

"Like it? Loved it. Kimara, you were fantastic. You had this crowd by the throat. They didn't even know how to react at first. And—" she paused nodding her head in the direction of the bar. "You see that guy over there? The one in the tan suit?"

"Yeah, what about him?" Kimara asked, sneaking a peak over her shoulder toward the bar.

Leaning against the counter was a tall olive-skinned man wearing a tan designer suit. He was sipping a martini and staring in her direction.

"That's Bill Abrams," Giselle answered.

"Who?" Kimara peered at him again, still having no idea who the man was.

"Bill Abrams. The guy who runs Penchant Records. You have to have heard of him. He's only like one of the richest record label executives in the country. He's always in *Forbes* magazine. He's got an A-list roster of singers in his pocket."

"Oh yeah, isn't that new girl on his label. The one that sounds like Whitney Houston?" Jasmine asked.

"Yep and a whole bunch of other people are too. He is definitely the man. His eyes never left you the whole time you were on stage and as soon as you finished he made a call on his cell phone," Giselle reported.

"So what does that mean?" Jasmine snapped at Giselle. "Maybe he was calling his driver or lining up a booty call for the night."

Jasmine didn't even try to hide her annoyance with Giselle. She didn't like the girl, hated the fact that Kimara was living with her for fear of the negative influence she believed Giselle to be. Kimara made a mental note to talk to her about it later, for the umpteenth time.

"All I'm saying is that he's been staring over here ever since," Giselle said to Kimara, turning away from Jasmine purposely.

"Why would he be interested in me?" Kimara asked. "I'm not a singer."

"I know that's right," Jasmine laughed.

"Well, we're about to find out. He's coming this way," Jared added.

Abrams approached the group with an unreadable face. Jared laced his arm around Kimara's shoulder protectively.

"Folks, hello," he said. "Ms. Hamilton, I'm Bill Abrams, Penchant Records. I just wanted to tell you that you were amazing." He stuck out his hand. Kimara took it, shaking it firmly.

"Thank you, Mr. Abrams."

"They usually only feature newcomers down here, but you've obviously taken the stage before," he complimented.

"Nope. This was my first time."

"Her debut," Jasmine beamed.

"Wow, that's surprising. You seemed like a natural. You totally owned that stage tonight," Abrams said, genuinely impressed.

"Thank you again. I'm glad it appeared that way. I was crazy nervous though," Kimara admitted.

"It didn't show."

"Mr. Abrams, this is my boyfriend Jared Porter, my friends, Jasmine Wright, Giselle Stepanov."

"Please, it's Bill." Abrams shook hands first with Jared, then with each of the ladies.

"Nice to meet you," Jared said as he sized Abrams up with a quick, but not so discreet scan. He couldn't help himself—the cop in him forced him to scrutinize every new face and carefully assess their intentions. Yet there was more to it than just a professional compulsion. Jared felt extremely protective of Kimara and, as much as he hated to admit it, was sometimes jealous of the attention she received. He knew that it was the price one had to pay for having a beautiful, vivacious woman on his arm. However, sometimes, some men could be downright rude when vying for her attention. There had been many a day when Jared had to exercise every bit of restraint he could muster to prevent himself from beating some guy down to the ground for making unwanted, boisterous advances at Kimara.

While he didn't necessarily think that this Bill Abrams guy wasn't on the up and up, he wouldn't put anything past any man. There were plenty of guys who flashed around their credentials and purported to be someone of importance just as a means to an end. He vowed that as long as he was around, he wouldn't let anybody try to play Kimara like that.

The group made small talk for a few minutes more. Bill signaled a waitress and ordered a round of champagne. As he prepared to leave, he removed a business card from his breast pocket and handed it to Kimara.

"Kimara, I know you've said that this was your first time on stage, but I for one don't think it should be your last. Groups like Floetry and The Roots have taken the spoken word art to a whole new level, opening up a branch of music heretofore untapped. I think you'd do well to consider a future in the music business."

"Wow, Mr. Abrams . . . I mean, Bill . . . I'm flattered, but I really don't think that's something I'd be able to do. I'm not a singer you know."

"No one said anything about you singing. Just do me a favor and think about it. Give me a call and we'll talk about it over lunch or something."

Kimara took the card and shook Abrams' hand again. She stared after him as he departed and then looked to her friends for support. Before anyone could respond, they were approached by two other men, both casually dressed in jeans and T-shirts.

"Excuse me, Ms. Hamilton?" one of them asked.

"Yes."

"Hi, I'm Harrell James. This is my man N-tyme. We're down with Smithtown Records."

"Hello, nice to meet you," Kimara responded.

"Listen, we caught your act and just wanted to tell you that it was all that."

"Thank you guys. I appreciate the love I'm getting in here tonight."

"I won't take up any more of your time. I just wanted to let you know that you were great and also, give you my business card. If you're thinking about a future in recording, then give me a call. I think you've got a nice flow and you definitely have the look. Is that all right?"

Kimara nodded, astounded by the attention she was receiving. Harrell handed Kimara his card, slapped five with Jared and smiled at the ladies. He and the silent N-tyme disappeared into the crowd.

"Wow, this is too much," Kimara stated.

"This is fantastic," Jasmine squealed.

Jared noticed a gradual change in Kimara's expression and her mood. She grew silent and appeared disturbed.

"Are you all right?" he asked as he tightened his arm around her shoulder, drawing her closer to him.

"Yeah, I'm fine. I'm just ready to get out of here," she replied. An uneasiness had settled over her, the attention she'd been receiving becoming overwhelming. People in the crowd kept filing past her, smiling and nodding their heads in approval and while it was, on one hand, a nice feeling, it all started to become too much for her to digest.

"We're out of here," Jared announced to their small group, ushering Kimara toward the door.

Jasmine followed, leaving Giselle behind, who stuck around, reluctant to pass on a good party. Jared moved quickly, wading through a hundred or more bodies. He was anxious to get Kimara, who was gripping his waist tightly with her eyes trained to the floor, out of there. After hailing a taxi for Jasmine, Jared tucked Kimara safely into his SUV and drove her back to his apartment. She was silent during the entire ride, staring out of the window at deserted Brooklyn streets.

Later, they lay across his bed sipping bottled beer and still she didn't talk. He gave her the space she obviously needed and just lay next to her, rubbing her back. Finally, she turned on to her side and kissed his cheek.

"I don't know what came over me. That whole scene was surreal. It just kinda bugged me out."

Jared smiled. "That's natural, I'm sure. Those poetry heads are a little intense."

"It was cool though," Kimara mused, "having people hang onto your words like that; actually being moved by what you're saying. I guess I just didn't expect that sort of reception."

"Do you think you might call one of those record guys?" Jared asked.

"I don't know. Think I should?"

"Well, I mean, it couldn't hurt to see what they're talking about. If you don't like what they have to say, then you can just walk away."

"I don't know," Kimara sighed, too tired to give it any more thought that night.

Jared removed the empty bottle from her hands, placed both of them on the nightstand beside the bed and pulled Kimara into his arms. She settled into him and drifted off to sleep instantly. All night long, dreams of cheering crowds and stage lights plagued her, keeping her tossing and turning in her sleep.

Chapter 15

Several nights after the show at Roots and Culture Café, Jared surprised Kimara by dropping by Club Silhouette while she was on duty. It was around midnight, four hours before her shift was scheduled to end. The club was hopping, the norm for a Friday night, and Kimara was already in a good mood. Seeing Jared unexpectedly made her feel even more elated.

"Hey you," she said as Jared slid onto a bar stool. Kimara leaned over the counter and kissed him sweetly. "What are you doing here?"

"Just wanted to see you," Jared answered.

"Playing hooky?" Kimara asked as she poured Jared a glass of cranberry juice over ice. He accepted the drink, taking a grateful swallow from it before answering.

"Yep. Didn't really feel like chasing any bad guys tonight."

Jared sat quietly, watching Kimara do her work as he sipped his juice. A steady stream of patrons floated to and from the bar, many of the men openly flirting with Kimara. She flashed each of them her dazzling smile, was courteous and professional, and sent them on their way drinks in tow. Occasionally, she tossed a quick wink and a smile in Jared's direction, which he

gratefully accepted, knowing that he was getting the
best part of her attention. The light which emanated
from Kimara was so bright that at times he was afraid
that it would blind him. She was the kind of person
people naturally gravitate to, eager to have whatever
it was that made her so vibrant rub off on them.

"So you still haven't called that Abrams guy back have
you?" Jared asked when there was a lull in the flow of
customers and Kimara leaned across the bar and stuck
a maraschino cherry between his lips.

He had been at Kimara's place a couple of days ago
when a hand delivery from Bill Abrams arrived. Inside
was a standard contract and letter in which Penchant offered Kimara a six-album deal with them as a solo artist.
Kimara had tossed the package aside with barely a word.

Jared knew how much Kimara hated to be pressed
about anything, but he could not understand her nonchalant attitude over Penchant's offer. He could not
accept the rationale that she was bashful or afraid to
take the stage again. The Kimara he had come to know
over the past few months was not afraid of anything. She
was a show-stopper, no matter what she was doing.
There had to be more to it than that, but she tacitly
avoided the subject whenever he brought it up.

"Nope, not yet," she answered.

A customer approached the bar and Kimara turned
her attention to him. The guy was already pretty drunk
and loud as he ordered another drink.

"Hey beau–ti–fulll," he slobbered, "How's about you
and me gets tagether some time."

"Sorry brother, but fraternizing with customers is
against club rules."

"S . . . s . . . sorry? Do I look sorry to you sweetheart. I'm
Slick Rob. You better reco . . . recognize. I got sh . . . sh . . .
I got's stuff on lock baby."

"Okay, well Slick Rob, I'm sure you are the man and
all, but—"

"That's right. I am da . . . da man. So baby, you better get with this program. Come on. I'ma take you out . . . take you to my crib and work you out!" Slick Rob reached across the bar and snatched Kimara's wrist.

"Okay partner, that's enough. Take your hands off of her," Jared said, grabbing the drunken man's arm and forcefully shoving him away from Kimara.

"Jared, I got this," Kimara said.

"Say, what's your problem man. Do you know who I am?"

"Yeah, I know. You're Slick Rob, the man," Jared said, moving closer to the man's face. "Look, I don't give a damn who you are. Touch her again and I'm gonna kick your ass all over this place," Jared growled.

Another bartender, who had noticed the commotion, signaled to Ox, one of the club's bouncers. Ox approached the bar just as the drunken patron balled up his fist and took a lazy swing at Jared. Ox grabbed the man by the back of his shirt, lifted him off his feet and disappeared into the crowd before anyone could react. The man was escorted out to the street by Ox and another bouncer with a warning never to return.

"Jared, I cannot believe you did that," Kimara hissed beneath her breath.

The last thing she needed was Jared coming into the club, acting jealous and starting to mess with the customers. Besides, while some women may have been flattered by a man who was willing to draw swords for his woman, violence did not impress Kimara in the least. She was not a woman who needed someone else to fight her battles, certainly not against a half-drunk loser like that.

"What was I supposed to do? Sit here and let him attack you?" Jared answered, miffed that Kimara was angry with him.

"He wasn't attacking me, and I certainly could have

handled it. I handle guys like him every day, without you or anybody else intervening," Kimara snapped.

"Oh, so this kind of crap happens to you every night that you're in this place, does it?"

"I didn't say that. Men approach women, sometimes forcefully, every damn day Jared. It doesn't just happen in clubs. That could have happened in the supermarket or at the mall."

"I doubt seriously drunken perverts leer at you and accost you in the dairy aisle," Jared replied sarcastically.

Kimara noticed that Gino had come out of his office and was looking over toward the bar where the commotion had taken place.

"Look Jared, I can't have this conversation with you here . . . right now."

Gino was not a back-breaker nor was he an unreasonable man. However, the one thing he did ask of his employees was that they keep their personal business out of the club.

"Fine. I'm out," Jared said hotly.

They stared at one another for a moment before another customer approached the bar.

"What can I get for you?" Kimara asked, turning away from Jared.

By the time she finished serving the customer, Jared was gone. She caught a glimpse of his back as he disappeared through the exit door. Sighing heavily, she excused herself, telling her co-workers that she was going to take her break now. In the lounge, she paced the floor, walking back and forth and taking deep breaths until her agitation subsided. Jared's behavior tonight had crossed the line, but as she thought about it, his behavior over the past few weeks had become increasingly overbearing. She was beginning to feel suffocated and wondered what she could do to set things back on the right course between them.

* * *

"I'm not going to sit here and tell you that I don't agree with Jared. Working at a nightclub opens you up to all kinds of unwanted attention Kimara. You are absolutely right, some men bother women anywhere and everywhere, but a nightclub is like a breeding ground for nutcases and sex fiends. A lot of these men think that any woman who is in a club is fair game, even open to being harassed," Jasmine said.

The women were seated side by side in the pedicure station of Heaven Help Us beauty salon in Queens Village. Their legs were immersed in bubble-filled tubs of gurgling water. It was early evening on a Saturday, the day following the scene at Club Silhouette. Kimara had avoided Jared all day, still seething over his behavior. He'd left two messages on her cell phone asking her to call him at the station to talk.

"Jasmine, I'm so tired of having this conversation with you and with everyone else. I never said I was going to make a career out of serving drinks. But the bottom line is this: I like working in the club, I like listening to music, watching people cut up on the dance floor, and I'm not going to apologize for that. What's more, I don't care what everybody thinks about it. That said, none of this has anything to do with Jared's behavior. It doesn't explain it nor does it justify it. Lately, he's been acting too jealous and demanding for my comfort."

"Jealous of you and other men?" Jasmine asked.

"Jealous of me and everything. He doesn't want me to work at the club, is nagging me to no end about this music thing, and oh, get this one—he had the nerve to tell me the other morning that the skirt I was wearing to work that day was too short for a shift at a phone store, to paraphrase."

"Yikes. So he's trying to dress you now. What'd you say to that?" Jasmine asked.

"I told him he must have fallen and bumped his

noggin if he thinks for one minute he can tell me what to wear."

"I know that's right. But listen Kimara, maybe that's just his way of showing how much he cares about you. He doesn't want to see you get into trouble," Jasmine, always the peacemaker, reasoned.

"Jasmine, the last time I checked, I was a grown woman. I'm not about to let Jared run my life. If he doesn't like to party, that's his business. I do. So when I feel the need to shake my booty, he can either come and watch it shake or sit home and sulk."

"It's like that, huh?" Jasmine asked.

"It's like that."

Jasmine was quiet for a while, leaning her head back against the headrest and depressing the keypad on the chair's massager for another round of relaxation. She closed her eyes and allowed the mechanical fingers to mold her flesh and muscles. She had known Kimara for more than half of their lives, yet she had yet to figure out why she always seemed so willing, eager almost, to sabotage her own happiness.

"You know what I was just thinking about?" Jasmine asked as the operator returned and began applying sea salts first to Jasmine's feet and legs and then to Kimara's.

"What's that?" Kimara asked unenthusiastically, certain that a lecture was coming.

"I was thinking about the time when little Stevie Ramirez asked you to go to the sixth-grade spring dance. Remember, we were outside of Jack's Candy store eating caramel-coated apples? After you said yes, he added that he had one condition—that you had to let him lead when y'all danced. I cracked up laughing and you stood there looking at him like he was crazy." Jasmine laughed.

Kimara smiled at the memory of poor little Stevie Ramirez, who she ended up leaving at the dance for Anthony Hodges.

"Kimara," Jasmine said after she'd finished laughing.

"Sometimes it's not a bad idea to let your man lead.
Sometimes, it actually feels good to sit back and let him
run the show."

While she understood the point Jasmine was trying to
make, she did not agree that that was the answer to her
problems with Jared. It seemed that she and Jared had
reached some sort of impasse that would define the
future of their relationship, if they had one.

Chapter 16

Kimara inhaled, careful to take only small amounts of air into her lungs at a time. Her calves were beginning to develop that familiar burning sensation, a heat radiating from the core of the muscles outward to her skin. She loosened her closed fingers, releasing some of the stress in her hands and wrists. Sweat had matted the edges of her hair to her forehead. Her French braid slapped the center of her back with each down step.

She continued running to the imaginary beat pulsing inside of her brain, determined not to quit. She was removed from, but at the same time acutely aware of, all of the activities around her. Prospect Park in Brooklyn was like a potluck dinner—filled with as many languages, smells, sights and sounds as there were nationalities in New York. Children's laughter tickled her ears. Music blared from different locations, coming together in a convoluted concoction of reggae, salsa and rock and roll. The smell of souvlaki on a stick reached out from a vendor's truck on the side of the path and caused water to form in her mouth. She kept going, fighting against everything inside of her that begged her to stop.

Up ahead, a good twenty feet in front of her, Jared

ran undaunted. It was obvious that he had every intention of going the full five miles they'd agreed upon and
while Kimara had been as dedicated at the start, her resolve was slowly beginning to melt. She had been running three and a half miles, twice a week for the past six
months and believed that she could push the envelope
a little bit. Jared's challenge was precisely the fuel she
needed to add to her fire.

His movements seemed effortless, even at the beginning of the fourth mile. His upper back remained erect
as he ran, reminding her of former Olympian Michael
Johnson. His broad shoulders and toned back were carried by a high, tight buttocks and equally impressive
thighs. He was poetry in motion, a statuesque ebony
prince. She smiled at the thought that he was hers.

Kimara had dated fine men before. Most of the guys
she seemed to attract were either drop-dead gorgeous
or, at the very least, pleasing to the eye. And while Jared
definitely belonged in the first category, he had a beauty
which came from within. It was more than facial features which complemented each other, a well defined
body, nice skin. He was just downright sexy—his speech,
his carriage, all of him.

Staring at his form buoyed Kimara's strength, the
promise of an up-close encounter egging her on. She
pulled herself together, fighting to maintain her posture
and rhythm. She focused on Jared, blocking out the nagging sensations of pain which ate at the edges of her
mind.

They ran past the bandshell where a guitarist was
warming up for a set. They continued running, past the
farmer's market whose tables of ripe melons, juicy cher-
ries and a host of other enticing fruit begged for Kimara
to stop, but Jared never even glanced at the delightful
treats and so she kept running behind him. The entrance to the zoo teamed with excited children and at-
tentive parents. Kimara and Jared dodged around them

all, never breaking their stride. The heady fragrance which lingered around the botanical garden as they went by was also inviting. Kimara promised herself that she'd have Jared bring her back to the park, without their running shoes on, so that she could enjoy all that it had to offer instead of whizzing by everything as she fought to keep up with him.

They ended their run near the Grand Army Plaza entrance. Outside of the park the clean streets of renovated brownstones and town houses were teaming with Brooklynites as they strolled by, checking out the wares of vendors who lined the sidewalks. Kimara crumbled at Jared's feet as he cooled down with stretches and jumping jacks on a patch of grass.

"Come on baby. You don't want to get all cramped and tight. You know better," Jared said as he pulled her back to her feet.

The couple stretched and moved about, releasing the tension in their muscles and reducing their elevated body temperatures. After several minutes, Kimara returned to her perch on the grass, exhausted.

"Let's go back to my apartment. I was writing all night long and some of this stuff is actually pretty good, if I must say so myself," she suggested.

"When are you meeting with those guys at Penchant?" Jared asked as he continued to stretch.

"Friday afternoon. I'm bringing a lot of my old pieces but I wanted to have some new material too. I even wrote a piece about you."

"About me? What'd you write about me?"

"Don't be scared!" Kimara laughed. "Seriously though, I want your opinion. I'm not working at the club tonight so we can spend the whole night together," Kimara said.

"Fine, on one condition," Jared answered.

"What's that?"

"We go and get some things from your place, but

we come back to Brooklyn and you spend the night with me."

"Why go all the way to the City and back? That doesn't make sense." Kimara spread her legs wide and leaned forward until her chest touched the grass. She exhaled as she felt the muscles at the back of her thighs release themselves.

"Look Kimara, I . . . I'm just not comfortable in Giselle's apartment," Jared confessed.

"That's my apartment too. I pay rent there."

"Yeah, but I don't really dig her. Her whole vibe is crazy."

Kimara stopped stretching, looking quizzically at Jared. This was the first time he had indicated having any negative feelings toward Giselle. The two of them had never really spent much time together, save for an occasional conversation in passing.

"What do you mean, you don't dig her? Did she say something to you?" Kimara knew what a flirt Giselle could be at times. Maybe she'd said or done something inappropriate when Kimara's back was turned. If that was the case, she had every intention of stepping to her. Look but don't touch—that was one thing she didn't tolerate.

"Nah, it's nothing like that," Jared answered. "She's just a little too rowdy for my tastes. And all those different guys she entertains. What's up with that?"

Kimara had never really given much thought to Giselle's associates. Sure, she often had male company in the apartment. Kimara didn't know for certain who she was hitting skins with and frankly didn't care. As far as roommates go, living with Giselle was pretty comfortable. Giselle slept most of the day and stayed up and out most of the night. When she did have company over, Kimara stayed in her bedroom and let Giselle have the run of the apartment. It was her house, after all. Occasionally, she'd come out and drink with Giselle and her friends. She always declined when they smoked weed, having given that up after high school. She preferred the mellow vibe brought on by a glass or two of alcohol as opposed to the silliness prompted by a marijuana high. All in all, however, while she and Giselle hadn't become the best buddy bachelorettes the latter had predicted, she liked the girl and didn't see anything wrong with her lifestyle.

"I don't know what's up with that. I do know that what Giselle does is none of my business. Why do you care who she's sleeping with?"

"I don't care. I'm just saying, that apartment should have a revolving door on it," Jared countered.

"What Giselle does is *her* business Jared, it's that simple. However, if you're uncomfortable there then fine, we can go to your place."

Kimara stood and began walking toward the park's exit. Jared caught up with her, grabbing her by the waist. "You're upset with me now," he stated.

"No I'm not. I just think you're being silly."

"All right, all right, we can stay at your place."

"No, obviously it's not all right. We're going to pick up a few of my things and we're coming back to Brooklyn. Got it?" Kimara asked, poking Jared in the chest.

"Yes, Ma'am." He kissed Kimara deeply. "Thank you," he added.

It was at times like this that Kimara felt herself dangerously close to the edge with Jared. She was teetering on that treacherous cliff off of which one falls into love. She wanted to pull back. Her sense of self-preservation warned her to pull back, especially when he acted like he disapproved of her or of the things she did. But she'd look into his eyes and at that infectious smile and warm glow that rested there and she'd feel drawn like a moth to a flame. There was no way she could cut those feelings off. Knowing that made her feel, to equal extents, fearful and delighted.

Later that evening, after they'd gone a round of delicious lovemaking and devoured take-out from the neighborhood Chinese restaurant, there was a surprise knock at the door. They were lying on the living room floor, naked as the day they were born, watching a movie on Jared's DVD player. Jared wrapped a sheet around his waist and peered through the peephole.

"This cannot be happening," he muttered.

"Who is it?" Kimara whispered, alarmed.

"My mother."

Mrs. Porter knocked again.

"Just a minute," Jared yelled through the closed door. Kimara jumped up from the floor and scrambled around trying to find her clothes. She and Jared became entangled in each other and the sheets as they tried to restore some order to themselves and to the room. Finally, Kimara made a mad dash to the bathroom as Jared slid into a pair of shorts.

"Ma? What are you doing here," Jared asked as his mother entered. He embraced her quickly and stole a furtive glance over his shoulder. Feeling busted like a high school kid caught making out on his parents' sofa, he stepped aside to let her enter.

"I told you I was coming up this week to see Dottie Saunder's new grandbaby. Don't you remember me telling you that?"

"That was this week? No, I . . . uh, well I've been a little busy lately. I must have forgotten."

"Mmm, hmm. What were you doing?"

The toilet flushed.

"Oh, you've got company?"

"Uh, yeah, uh my friend . . . my girlfriend Kimara is here."

Kimara remained in the bathroom for as long as she possibly could, leaning against the sink and nervously biting her fingernails. Jared had already told her that he wanted her to meet his mother soon and while she was excited by the prospect, she certainly didn't want to meet her like this. She wasn't prepared and feared that his mother would think the worst of her before they even had a chance to get to know one another. She peered into the mirror and began fighting with her wild hair.

Eventually, instead of laying down to die of embarrassment, Kimara pulled herself together and came out of hiding. In spite of the rough start, the evening turned out well after all.

"You're a very pretty young lady," Mrs. Porter stated matter-of-factly as she cut into her steak. After the first few embarrassing minutes during which Jared made the introductions, and Mrs. Porter informed Kimara that her shirt was on backwards, they began to hit it off. Jared took them all out to dinner at The House, a steakhouse in lower Manhattan that he and a lot of other police officers frequented.

"Thank you, Mrs. Porter," Kimara blushed.

"So my son tells me you and he met at the night club where you work."

"Yes, that's right."

"Hmm, that must be something. Working in a club. Bet you meet a lotta fellows. Pretty girl like you."

Inez Porter was a bubbly warm woman, whose voice contained a soothing southern drawl that Kimara found extremely engaging. Contrarily, her direct manner of speaking and unrestricted personality made her surprisingly easy to talk to.

"Well, I don't socialize with the customers. I'm just there to serve drinks," Kimara explained.

"I should get me a job in a club somewhere. I betcha I'll be doing more than serving drinks," Mrs. Porter laughed.

"Ma!" Jared shouted, astonished by his mother's brazen comments.

"Watch out now, Mrs. Porter. I don't think Jared likes the idea of you getting your mack on," Kimara laughed.

"My mother ain't got no mack Kimara. You know what I think? You're a bad influence on her," Jared said.

"Boy, hush up. I like this here girl," Mrs. Porter snapped.

"Yeah, hush up," Kimara added as Jared silently sulked.

It was a lovely evening as Mrs. Porter regaled Kimara with side-splitting stories from Jared's youth. When they returned to Jared's apartment, they found that a message had been left on his answering machine informing him that an officer from his precinct had been shot. As was the custom, Jared made a beeline for the hospital, asking Kimara to entertain his mother until he returned.

Kimara fixed two cups of tea and cut a couple of slices of the sour cream pound cake she'd made the day before. They settled on the sofa and talked some more.

"I probably shouldn't be telling you this honey, and if you repeat it, I'll deny I said it, but Jared seems to have fallen hard for you. You wouldn't be planning on breaking his heart, would you?"

Kimara swallowed hard, trying to dislodge the piece of cake which Mrs. Porter's abrupt question had sent sailing down her windpipe.

"No, uh . . . Mrs. Porter. I assure you, I don't plan to break Jared's heart. I . . . like him a lot too."

"I don't mean to get in ya'lls business and I certainly don't want you to think I run around meddling in my son's private affairs. It's just that Jared has been through a lot in his lifetime and he deserves some happiness now. He's a good man, and I just don't want to see him going through no more bad times."

"I understand."

"After we lost Jared's father, I thought my son wasn't ever going to smile again. You have no idea how heart wrenching it is to see a seven year old lose his smile."

"Seven?" Kimara asked confused. "I thought Jared's father died when he was seventeen?"

"Yes, that's right, he was seventeen when Sean passed. But I guess Jared didn't tell you that we actually lost his father ten years before he passed."

Kimara stared in confusion at Mrs. Porter. She wasn't sure what to make of the conversation thus far, none of it was making much sense. She secretly hoped she wouldn't have to break the news to Jared that his mother had flipped her wig.

"Let me explain," Mrs. Porter said, patting Kimara's hand. "You see, my husband got into a fist fight in a club one night when Jared was just in second grade and my other son, Javon, was in preschool. That night changed our lives forever," Mrs. Porter mused.

Her voice had grown soft. Kimara was unsure if she was going to continue, but was not comfortable enough to ask her to.

"The thugs my husband fought were punks who didn't fight fair. They jumped him and whipped his butt pretty good. But then Sean got ahold of one of them and . . . well, he was defending himself."

Mrs. Porter was a pretty chocolate brown-skinned woman, her silky black hair sprinkled with a small number of gray strands. She wore her hair pulled back into a tight bun at the nape of her neck, giving her a matronly look. Jared's eyes were the same deep-set, brown eyes as his mother's, unshed tears now coating hers. Ironically, even in her sadness there was grace and beauty, a fact which Kimara not only noticed but admired.

"The man he fought with received a head injury, and he died. They convicted Sean of manslaughter, even though he was defending himself," she continued, a solitary tear sliding from her eye onto her cheek. "He was sentenced to a term of seven-to-ten years in the state prison."

"Oh goodness, Mrs. Porter. I'm so sorry you had to go through something so horrible," Kimara said, feeling pretty close to tears herself.

"Yeah well, it was hard on all of us, but especially on Jared. Javon was very young, barely out of diapers. He didn't really know what was going on and besides, he was such an even-tempered little boy that he just accepted not seeing his daddy every day like it was normal. But not Jared. He took everything to heart. Although he never said anything to me, I knew that he hated seeing his father locked up. I could read it all over his sad little face. It got so bad that I stopped making him visit." Mrs. Porter was quiet for a time, her mind obviously replaying events of long ago.

"He was such a good boy," she continued. "Never gave me an ounce of trouble and he took care of his little brother. But he just never seemed really happy again. Those ten years closed out a part of his heart and no matter what I tried, I never seemed to be able to find a way to make him smile."

From that moment Kimara began to see Jared clearly for the first time. She felt like she understood him more from his mother's explanation of his childhood than from anything Jared had ever told her. His quiet reserve, his disdain for nightclubs all made sense now. Even the melancholy moods which from time to time descended on him had a rhyme and a reason. Her heart ached for all that he had lost as a child, but at the same time she felt proud that he had come through it all to be the beautiful, upstanding and honorable man that she had come to know.

"A few months before my husband was scheduled to be released from prison, he suffered a massive brain aneurysm. He died before they could pick up the phone to call me," Mrs. Porter continued.

"Mrs. Porter, how do you go on after something like

that? How do you believe that everything is going to be all right again?"

"You just do, child. You just keep putting one foot in front of the other and before you know it, you've gotten through a day, a month, a year. Jared did that. He just kept it inside and did what he had to do with his life," Mrs. Porter said proudly.

"I know he did, but I'm sure it hurt him deeply and still does," Kimara said.

Mrs. Porter nodded her head in agreement.

"I don't know if he ever cried. He helped me take care of things—the funeral and such. Then we made the move to Maryland where my sisters live and he just went on. He graduated from high school and started taking classes at a local college. A couple of years later he decided to move to New York and join the police force here. I was both happy and sad to see him go. I thought a new start, out on his own, would be good for him."

"I know I haven't known him long, but I want you to know that he seems to be doing just fine now, Mrs. Porter," Kimara reported sincerely.

"Yes, sugar, I'd have to agree with you there. He had a rough few years up here, but I think he's finally found some sunshine." Mrs. Porter took Kimara's hand. "You just keep making my son happy, and I'll keep my butt down in Maryland. No reason for me to be busting up in here interrupting you two lovebirds."

Love. There was that pesky little word again. No matter how fast she ran, how deftly she dodged, it didn't seem like she could shake that word. It hung in the air around her and had definitely penetrated her surfaces. She wondered if she had what it took to love like Mrs. Porter did and to lose, yet to keep on keeping on. In her short life span, she had never had her love tested, and she lacked the confidence to believe she could.

An Important Message From The ARABESQUE Publisher

Dear Arabesque Reader,

I invite you to join the club! The Arabesque book club delivers four novels each month right to your front door! It's easy, and you will never miss a romance by one of our award-winning authors!

With upcoming novels featuring strong, sexy women, and African-American heroes that are charming, loving and true… you won't want to miss a single release. Our authors fill each page with exceptional dialogue, exciting plot twists, and enough sizzling romance to keep you riveted until the satisfying end! To receive novels by bestselling authors such as Gwynne Forster, Janice Sims, Angela Winters and others, I encourage you to join now!

Read about the men we love… in the pages of Arabesque!

Linda Gill
PUBLISHER, ARABESQUE ROMANCE NOVELS

*P.S. Watch out for the next Summer Series **"Ports Of Call"** that will take you to the exotic locales of Venice, Fiji, the Caribbean and Ghana! You won't need a passport to travel, just collect all four novels to enjoy romance around the world! For more details, visit us at www.BET.com.*

A SPECIAL "THANK YOU" FROM ARABESQUE JUST FOR YOU!

Send this card back and you'll receive 4 FREE Arabesque Novels—a $25.96 value—absolutely FREE!

The introductory 4 Arabesque Romance books are yours FREE (plus $1.99 shipping & handling). If you wish to continue to receive 4 books every month, do nothing. Each month, we will send you 4 New Arabesque Romance Novels for your free examination. If you wish to keep them, pay just $18* (plus, $1.99 shipping & handling). If you decide not to continue, you owe nothing!

- Send no money now.
- Never an obligation.
- Books delivered to your door!

We hope that after receiving your FREE books you'll want to remain an Arabesque subscriber, but the choice is yours! So why not take advantage of this Arabesque offer, with no risk of any kind. You'll be glad you did!

In fact, we're so sure you will love your Arabesque novels, that we will send you an Arabesque Tote Bag FREE with your first paid shipment.

* PRICES SUBJECT TO CHANGE.

YOU'LL GET 4 SELECT ROMANCES PLUS THIS FABULOUS TOTE BAG!

Visit us at:
www.BET.com

Chapter 17

The rough beat of Beanie Man's latest hit throbbed like an extra pulse in Kimara's neck. She swayed her hips slowly from side to side, letting the rhythm guide her in a slow groove against Jared's sturdy frame.

They were at the L&K Lounge, a trendy social club deep in the heart of Brooklyn between DeKalb and Nostrand Avenues. Sweaty bodies surrounded them as the deejay delivered track after track of raw reggae music. From the music Dennis Brown created in a shanty in Kingston, Jamaica to the Sean Paul tracks currently burning up the pop charts, from Bob Marley to Barrington Levy and Yellow Man, the groove transcended time and space. They moved their bodies over lyrics of love, of liberation, of struggle, strife and ultimately of blessings bestowed. Wicked songs of love, lust and robust sexuality drew their bodies closer together.

L&K's was small, what most people would call a hole-in-the-wall. The main dance area was a square room where, reminiscent of old skating rinks, the deejay booth was located in the center of the room. Through an archway at the rear of the room was another, smaller room where the walls were fitted with worn sofas and tiny tables for two. A small buffet of oxtails, brown stew chicken, peas and rice and steamed cabbage was set up in one corner of the smaller room and many patrons purchased plates of these delicacies throughout the night.

Kimara looked incredible wearing a green and black silk wrap skirt, black bodysuit and black mules. She'd parted her hair down the center and braided the two halves, making her look like a modern-day Pocahontas. Jared could keep neither eyes nor his hands off of her. He felt like the luckiest man in the world to have a woman as beautiful and as vivacious as Kimara on his arm. The zest for life which radiated from her was almost intimidating and indeed, lesser men than Jared would not be able to handle her. Sometimes Jared feared that he might not be enough for Kimara. Other times, like now, he just held on tight and enjoyed the ride, hoping that it lasted but always aware that tomorrow was not promised.

They had been dancing for close to an hour straight, shrouded in a vacuum of their own intimacy. Jasmine and Rick were seated at the bar, she sipping on virgin piña coladas and swaying her chubby body to the beat.

This double date had been Jasmine's idea. She had gone completely nuts over the idea of Kimara having a *steady* as she liked to call it. For once, she had stopped bugging Kimara about her life, her loves, her jobs. She even went so far as to clip a picture of a wedding gown out of a bridal magazine which she swore Kimara would look amazing in. Kimara didn't say much, figuring she'd let Jasmine have her fun. Secretly, she was actually enjoying the feeling of being *hooked up* too. It was like belonging to an exclusive, respectable club that everyone else wanted desperately to join but failed to meet the requirements for.

They'd had dinner at Ashford and Simpson's Sugar Bar and talked over delectable dishes of catfish meunière with mashed potatoes and collard greens, beef tenderloin with red onions and spinach and Kimara's favorite, grilled pork chops with rice, beans and plantains. Most of the conversation circled around the baby and around Kimara's performance. Jasmine was begging Kimara for a repeat performance, trying to convince her to take the stage at the open-mike night held at a lounge in Queens once a week. To Jasmine's dismay, Kimara was adamant in her refusal.

Jared and Rick seemed to hit it off, although that wasn't saying much because Jared's personality was one that allowed him to pretty much get along with everyone. He and Rick talked about their jobs, having the connection to civil service in common. Kimara tried hard to be cordial to Rick, even when he said something irritating. Jasmine, who was perky and basking in the sheer joy of having them all together, served as the glue which kept the entire evening together.

"Ya'll are burning up the floor out there, dancing to all that baby-making music," Jasmine said as Jared and Kimara returned to the bar.

"Uh, we'll leave the baby making to you guys," Kimara answered, rubbing Jasmine's protruding belly for emphasis.

Jared ordered a Remy Martin straight up for himself and after checking with Kimara, doubled the order. The couples stood around the bar for another hour talking, laughing and drinking. It was well after midnight when Jasmine began yawning, yet protesting that she wasn't tired. The four of them left the club and traveled to Queens in Jared's SUV. By the time they arrived at Rick and Jasmine's apartment building, Jasmine was fast asleep, snuggled against Rick's arm. He helped her sleepy frame from the car and she waved good night.

"I remember when that girl used to out-party me. We'd dance all night, come home for a shower and breakfast and head off to work. Now look at her," Kimara laughed.

"She looks good pregnant. Something about being around a woman carrying a baby that makes the world seem all right to me," Jared mused.

"Yeah, she does look kind of cute, in that bloated, invasion of the body snatchers sort of way," Kimara joked. "But you know something, the idea of Jasmine being a mother . . ."

"What? Don't you think she'll make a good mother?" Jared asked.

"No, no it's not that. Of course I think she'll be a good mother to the baby. It's just freaky. When we were kids, I never thought about us growing up, becoming adults. Getting married and all that jazz just never factored in. Now seeing her . . . I don't know. It's weird."

"You sound like you think growing up is a dirty word or something."

Later on, all thoughts about the complexities of life were temporarily set aside as they made love on the red-wood chaise longue on Jared's terrace. He had screened in the open areas of the terrace completely, converting the small space into a semi-private room. His neighbors who shared the adjoining terrace were an elderly couple, who rarely came out of their apartment, leaving Jared and Kimara to themselves in their secluded haven.

Afterwards, they lay staring up at the night sky, each lost in comfortable reflection. Jared realized that he could no longer hold back. What he was feeling for Kimara had him off center and at all times on edge.

"You're doing something to me Kimara," he said plainly.

"Yeah, what's that?" Kimara asked.

"I don't know, but you're definitely doing something to me. I don't know if I can handle it," he admitted, not looking at her but continuing to stare at the bright stars in his line of vision.

Kimara shifted to face Jared. She ran her palm along the side of his face. "You can handle it," she replied.

Jared placed his hand over the one that continued to rub the side of his face. "I'm falling in love with you." He spoke these words into the palm of her hand.

"I know." Kimara smiled, her eyes shining. "I'm already there," she answered.

Silence fell around them as each thought about the gamble involved in affairs of the heart. While they were both wary of being hurt, each felt buoyed by the mere presence of the other in their lives and by the knowledge that the growing love each held was being returned.

Hours later, Jared awoke with a start. Sweat covered his head, neck and chest.

"What's the matter?" Kimara asked, roused from her sleep.

"Nothing," Jared replied. He was reluctant to tell her that he'd had another nightmare. She'd woken him up from the same dream a few nights before as he thrashed about in his sleep, speaking incoherently. He'd told her he didn't remember what he was dreaming about, which was an outright lie. He'd been dreaming then, as he had tonight and many other nights before, about his father.

Although he had obviously not been present when his father was arrested, he thought that he could see exactly what had happened. The way the men had grabbed him, holding his arms while one of them punched him in the face and stomach. His strong, super-cool daddy had been helpless, while his mother screamed and shouted for someone to help him. His father had waited for the right moment and made his move, breaking free from his captors. He'd started swinging and punching. He was protecting himself, like a man should. Jared's father didn't mean to kill anybody, but when that man's head struck the floor, the police swooped in and took him away. They didn't know that Jared's daddy was a hero.

Chapter 18

Kimara dug through her purse for her ringing cell phone.

"Hello?" Kimara answered on the last ring, just before the caller would have been sent into voicemail.

"Hi, uh, Kimara?"

"Who's this?" Kimara asked, tucking the phone beneath her chin as she continued pushing a shopping cart down the grocery aisle. She had spent the entire weekend at Jared's apartment and they had completely cleaned the cupboards out, which wasn't hard considering that he lived like a true bachelor—keeping only the bare necessities such as milk and bread on hand. She'd promised Jared a gourmet dinner and aimed to tempt, tease and satisfy his pallet tonight with a meal prepared to perfection.

"Kimara, this is Harrell James. I got your number from the manager at the Roots and Culture Café."

"What can I do for you?" Kimara fingered a tomato, squeezing it to test its firmness.

"Well, I hadn't heard from you and I was just wondering if you'd had time to think about my offer?"

"Mr. James, I don't really recall you making any sort

of offer. You said that if I was interested in the recording business, I should call you."

"And since you haven't called, I guess I should take that to mean you aren't interested?"

"I'm sorry," Kimara responded.

"All right, well, no harm no foul. Do you mind if I ask why?" Harrell asked.

"Why?" Kimara repeated. Caught off guard by his question, she initially could think of no real response to Harrell, nothing that she could articulate. "Mr. James, I know that people look at the music business as glamorous and exciting, and I'm sure there are millions of people clamoring to get a record deal, especially young girls with pretty smiles and big dreams. But to be honest with you, I don't find it attractive. I took that stage purely as a fluke, and I didn't expect anything to come of it. I'm not an entertainer and have never held any notions of becoming one. None of this fits into my reality," Kimara answered, hoping that this got the message across.

Harrell's next statement gave pause to everything Kimara was thinking and had just said.

"I can respect what you're saying Ms. Hamilton, and you do make valid points. From what I've seen in this business, there are two types of people, entertainers are one, and artists who happen to entertain are another. Watching you on that stage, it was obvious to me that you are an artist. What you have is a gift, a natural talent that can't be learned or bought. Not many people possess that, in spite of what the record labels and video directors would have the public believe. So I ask you, Ms. Hamilton, what good is art if the world never gets to experience it? It's kinda like that tree that falls in a vacant forest."

Kimara laughed aloud. "You are a hard man to say no to, Mr. James."

"Then don't say it. Just come down to the label's

offices and let's sit down and talk. I'll tell you my ideas and you tell me what you think. After we're done, if you're still not interested, then cool. We part friends."

Kimara was definitely curious about what had this guy so convinced that she was what he was looking for. Finally, she agreed to meet with him later in the week.

By the time she returned to Jared's apartment, loaded down with packages of fresh vegetables, fish, baked bread and other provisions, she had all but forgotten her conversation with Harrell. At the forefront of her mind were her nagging concerns over Jared. She went about the task of preparing dinner, but remained preoccupied throughout the process. Two hours later, dinner was finished and Kimara, left with nothing to do, found herself overwhelmed by doubts surrounding her relationship.

Seated at Jared's kitchen table waiting for him to get in from work, Kimara drummed her fingers on the tabletop as her mind remained distracted by heavy contemplation. She couldn't get the things that Jared's mother had told her out of her mind. She hadn't mentioned anything to Jared, although she wondered why he hadn't told her the entire story. Maybe he had not reached a level of comfort with her yet that would allow him to share so much of himself. The real question which worried her was if he ever would. She had told him everything there was to tell about herself, yet there was this big piece of him that he'd kept hidden.

It was obvious that the pain caused by his father's incarceration had touched him profoundly. This need to help other people that he always talked about came from a place deeper than he'd ever alluded to and now that she knew what that place was, she wanted to help him deal with it. However, she knew that it would have to be his decision to let her in.

In spite of everything inside that wanted her to remain aloof and to not allow herself to become too deeply involved with Jared, she had done just that. She had fallen hard for the man before she'd had time to hit the brakes. He was a gentle, caring man who put time and effort into finding out what pleased her and did everything in his power to do just that. That was true in every aspect of their relationship, from the mental, the emotional, and the physical. While Kimara felt comfortable with him and didn't believe there was a single subject that she couldn't converse with him on, it appeared that Jared didn't quite feel the same way. The wounds he wore stemming from his father's tragic death might prove to be an impenetrable barrier.

"Mom, Dad, this is Jared Porter. Jared these are my folks," Kimara said.

"Nice to meet you sir . . . Mrs. Hamilton," Jared answered, shaking her father's hand.

"Please, call me Gena," Kimara's mother said.

"And it's William, son. How are you?"

William swooned over his daughter, telling her how beautiful she looked, which was actually an understatement. Kimara wore a mint-green Barami strapless dress. Her hair was swept upward, held in a gold barrette, soft tendrils of curls gracing the nape of her neck. With radiant skin flawless and delicately made up, she made him feel as awestruck as the day she was born. Jared had fallen all over himself when he picked her up at her apartment. He was still not used to the emotions which arose in him when he saw her, and today's effect was even more startling. Again, he found himself wondering how he had managed to land a striking, alluring woman such as Kimara. What's more, he worried how long he'd be able to keep her on his arm.

The group was standing in the rear of Mount Moriah church in Queens where Kimara's cousin, Terrance, was marrying his college sweetheart, Bridget. It was a huge wedding, with over 250 guests in attendance. It was also the first time Jared had met the members of Kimara's family and her friends, with the exception of Jasmine. The thought of introducing Jared to her parents had made Kimara nervous, considering the fact that the last time she'd brought a guy home had been three or four years ago, and they'd absolutely hated him. However, she expected her parents to receive Jared well as it appeared that the lousy first impression he'd made on her was an anomaly. Most people seemed to love Jared at first sight.

The signal was given that it was time for everyone to be seated, eliminating the opportunity for further discussion between Jared and the Hamiltons for the time being. The four of them took their appointed seats on the left-hand side of the church. Kimara looked around at the beautifully decorated sanctuary. Lavender and white organzas and lilies of the valley accentuated the ends of each pew, flowing satin ribbons adorning each bouquet.

After all of the guests had been seated, all attention was turned toward the altar. The minister entered, followed by Terrance and his best man. The organist began playing and the mother of the groom, Kimara's Aunt Tessie, was escorted down the aisle. The mother of the bride entered next, escorted by one of her sons. As the bridal party made its entrance, a hushed silence fell over the guests. When the bride entered on the arm of her father, tears sprang into the groom's eyes, which had a domino effect on the congregation. By the end of the fifteen-minute ceremony, there was not a dry eye in the house. It was a beautiful occasion made more special by the youth and sincerity of the couple who stood pledging their love with unfettered innocence.

The reception followed at a nearby banquet hall, where Jared and Kimara remained in each other's arms and on the dance floor for much of the night. Jared gave in to fantasizing that it was his and Kimara's wedding at which they were dancing. He knew that they had miles to travel before they would arrive at anyone's wedding chapel, and he wasn't even certain that that's where the relationship was headed. However, the feelings he held for Kimara were growing stronger every day, intensified when they were in romantic settings such as this and she was never as elegant and enticing as he found her to be right then. He didn't dare speak his mind to her, sure that she would tell him that he had gotten way ahead of himself. Little did he know that presently, Kimara's imagination was spinning its own fantastical yarn as she melted into the arms of the first man she'd ever fallen in love with.

At one point, William cut in for a dance with his daughter, for which Jared graciously stepped aside.

"Nice young man," William said as he took his daughter into his arms. He looked into her pretty eyes as they danced, and thought about how proud she had made him lately. When they'd asked her to move out, he was initially wrought with worry, unsure if she could make it on her own. However, in just a few short months, she'd managed to find a nice apartment, had possibly found a career in which she could flourish and show the whole world what he already knew about her. And, she had landed herself a young man who, from first impressions, William felt would make a nice son-in-law. His daughter had met their challenge head on, albeit reluctantly. Even her mother had remarked to him just that morning that Kimara finally seemed to be on the right track and that maybe their gentle shove had been just what she needed.

"Yeah, Daddy, he's one of the good guys," Kimara responded, smiling at her father. She knew that he would have something to say about Jared eventually, and she waited patiently for him to continue.

"You two seem pretty serious. How long have you known him?"

William hoped he didn't sound over protective, but

he couldn't help but notice that Kimara seemed to be quite taken with this young man. It was his duty to find out just how serious this thing was and what the young man's intentions were.

"It's not like that Daddy. We've only been dating for a few months and we're just enjoying each other's company right now. You know, kicking it."

"I see," William said skeptically. He knew his daughter well, despite the front she always tried to put on. "Well, I guess I'll tell your mother not to order those wedding invitations she was talking about earlier."

"Oh God, Daddy, please! I am so not on the wedding train and don't plan to be—not ever."

William laughed. "Never say never, sweetheart."

Later on, it was Jared who pulled William aside for a chat, although William had planned to do the same anyway. The two men walked to the parking lot. The night had turned muggy, black clouds hovering and threatening to rain on them.

"Mr. Hamilton—" Jared began earnestly.

"William," he corrected.

"Yes sir, uh . . . William. I just wanted to take a moment to let you know that I really care about your daughter. I mean, uh, I . . . she's a great girl and uh, I . . . well—"

William laughed. "Relax son, I get the point. Yes, my daughter is a wonderful person. She has a good heart and a bright mind. Pretty strong will, too, but I suspect you know that by now."

"Oh boy, do I," Jared agreed, joining William's laughter with his own chuckle.

"Well, just hang in there with her son, and I'm sure you'll be just fine."

"Yes sir, I plan to," Jared said.

"So, how long have you been on the force?"

"Almost five years."

"And I understand you're in law school too? That's a lot to juggle there son."

"Yeah, it's a load. But I figure if I work hard now, I'll be able to settle down in a few years and I'll have something to offer someone," Jared replied.

The more William talked to Jared, the more he liked him. He couldn't help but hope that some of Jared's work ethic had begun to rub off on Kimara. She certainly could do a whole lot worse for herself than a guy like Jared.

"I was wondering, William, has Kimara told you about the offers she's been getting for her poetry?"

"Yes she has. Kimara's been writing poems since she was a little bitty thing, but she never made a big fuss over them, so I guess that explains why this seems so out of the blue. She never entered any contests or anything . . . didn't even work on the school newspapers."

"Well, she was pretty upset with Jasmine when she entered her into that radio contest, but I think once she got over the initial shock, she enjoyed performing and receiving all that attention pumped her up."

When Kimara had told her parents about the contest and the performance, they had wanted to attend. However, it was Kimara who asked them not to come that night. She felt she'd be too nervous with them there, especially given the explicit nature of some of the lyrics of her poetry. Disappointed, but respectful of her wishes, they'd reluctantly agreed not to go.

"She hasn't made any decisions yet about these record companies has she?" William asked.

"I don't think so. In fact, I'm concerned that she might not say yes to any of them. These are once-in-a-lifetime opportunities she's being presented with. A chance to share her talents with the world, and she's acting like she could take it or leave it. Frankly, William, I don't get it," Jared admitted.

"The thing you have to understand about Kimara, son, is that she does everything in her own time and on her own terms. I love my daughter to death, but for the life of me, I don't understand why she limits herself the way she does. She's got some maturing to do and she's going to have to sit down and figure out what she wants to do with her life. But believe me, when she does, she's going to take this world by storm."

"No doubt," Jared agreed. "I just really hope she pursues this music thing though. You should have seen her up on stage. She was amazing."

William didn't miss the starry-eyed look that fell over Jared as he talked about Kimara's performance. No matter what his daughter said, these two definitely had it bad for each other.

"Listen Jared, here's what I'm going to do. I'm going to call a buddy of mine, Fred Townsend. He's got a brother who's a big-shot entertainment lawyer. I'll see if Fred can get his brother to talk to Kimara about the business. Maybe talk to these people who are trying to work with her. Make sure they're on the up-and-up."

"That's a great idea William. I just know that this will be good for Kimara."

"We'll see about that. Time will tell. In the meantime young man," William said, slapping Jared heartily on the back, "You take your time with my little girl. Be patient and be good to her. Anytime you want to talk, just give me a ring."

Jared thanked William for his encouragement. He almost felt as if he'd just had his first father and son chat. He'd grown up without the benefit of having a man to talk to, someone who would offer words of wisdom which he could soak up and use to guide him through life's minefields. His own father, try as he might, was not that person. Once he was incarcerated, it was as if the father and son relationship they'd shared got locked up too, sent to a place where neither of them could break free. Jared grew up on his own, with the nurturing hand of a mother, but minus the guidance of a father. He was a man-child who had to build his own bridge into manhood with limited resources and a broken spirit.

Jared rarely allowed himself to think about his father. It still hurt too much. He forced himself to focus on the here and now. From where he stood, with a job that he loved, a budding career which would hopefully allow him to make a big difference in the world and a strong, captivating woman like Kimara by his side, the present was not too shabby a place to be.

Chapter 19

"How do you come up with the stuff you write about," Jared asked as he stroked the fine hairs trailing down Kimara's stomach. His head rested in the palm of one hand as he propped himself up on an elbow. A cool breeze drifted in from the open window beside Kimara's bed and Jared pulled the sheet across her body.

It was early in the morning, just before sunrise and although he had worked a double shift the prior night, he could not find sleep. Kimara, curled on one side facing Jared, had been dozing, on the verge of sailing away on a magic carpet of slumber when his voice roused her.

"Mmm, I don't know," she answered slowly. "It just comes out. It's like . . . I don't really know what I'm going to write when my pen touches the paper but somehow, the words just come."

"Isn't that sort of a cop-out? I mean, it's like you're saying that you're not aware of what you're thinking until it's out in the universe," Jared wanted to know.

"No, no, I don't mean it as a cop-out. I think we are each the masters of our own thought. I guess subconsciously I do know, but maybe I don't want to know. You feel me?"

Jared nodded and a lazy silence enveloped them again.

"So being a poet stops you from hiding from yourself?"

"I've never thought of it like that but I guess, in a way it does. I mean, I didn't choose to write poetry. It's just there. It's not something that I can turn off. Even if I didn't write it down, the words would still be there . . . inside my head. It's like a mixture of rhythmic words, colors, emotions, and they are always swimming around in there and when they take shape and spill out of me, the world wants to call it poetry."

"What do you call it?"

"Breathing. Being."

"Being what?"

Kimara thought about Jared's question. She had never given structured thought to poetry or the motivation behind writing it—it was just something she did. She hadn't studied it, didn't follow other poets or writers in particular. She loved words, their sound. She appreciated different dialects and was intrigued by syntax, but not as an area of study or dissection. She didn't fancy herself a poet. Expressing emotions and telling stories in that fashion made up a small part of who she was.

"Being me, I guess," she answered finally. "Whatever that is."

Jared laid his head on Kimara's pillow and nuzzled next to her, his large arm draped across her tiny torso almost protectively. Her soothing aura and voice had unwound him and finally he felt sleep coming on. Just as he sank into that warm fuzzy place between being on and off, there was the sound of a loud crash and shattering glass coming from the living room. Kimara was jarred awake by the sudden noise and Jared jumped up and out of bed. He groped around the floor until he found his sweatpants. Deftly, he slid into them and turned to Kimara pressing a finger to his lips. He crept swiftly towards Kimara's dresser, slid the top drawer open and removed his service revolver and holster. He slid the gun from the case, disengaged the safety and crept toward the closed bedroom door.

The hallway was bathed in darkness and Jared slid quickly, yet quietly along the wall, his back grazing its cool exterior. When he reached the end of the corridor, his arm bent at the elbow and his gun poised in midair, he took a deep breath before bursting into the living room.

"Whoa buddy, don't shoot. Don't shoot," yelled a young Hispanic man wearing faded jeans and a tie-dyed shirt, throwing his hands into the air.

A sliver of light emanated from the kitchen, allowing Jared to read the man's terror-filled face. Behind him, Giselle was crouched, picking up shattered pieces of the large ceramic vase which used to sit on the sofa table. This was obviously the source of the crash.

Kimara came into the room and flipped a switch on the wall. Soft yellow lights from the half of a dozen tracks along the ceiling flooded the room. Jared lowered his gun and looked from Giselle to her friend and then to Kimara.

"Hey guys, I'm sorry about the noise. I've been living here forever . . . you'd think I'd know where stuff is by now," Giselle slurred. The sickening smell of too much alcohol consumption wafted across the room. Jared shook his head and retreated back down the hall without a word.

"That dude's a little uptight, huh?" the guy said.

"We thought somebody had broken in," Kimara answered. To Giselle she said, "I thought you were away with your dad this weekend at his beach house?"

"Yeah well, at the last minute he decided to bring the

wife and I'm telling you, five minutes with her is an eternity. Lucky for me, Miguel here showed up with a get-away vehicle and a stash of the good stuff. That bitch could ruin a wet dream."

Giselle ceased cleaning up the broken glass, plopped onto the sofa, placed her bare feet on the coffee table and pulled a sandwich bag of marijuana from her purse.

"You're welcome to join us," Miguel said.

"Kimara doesn't do pot. She's a good girl," Giselle giggled.

Kimara rolled her eyes and sighed. She hated being around Giselle when she got completely wasted, which seemed to be happening more and more frequently. She said and did the most asinine things. It was obvious that Giselle had some serious demons chasing her, her relationship, or lack thereof, with her father and stepmother being one of them. Of course Giselle would never admit that the situation bothered her in the least, and she was adamant that she was living her life the way she wanted to. In many respects, Kimara was loathe to tell her how she should conduct herself because hey, if partying, drugging and sleeping around was what made the girl happy, far be it from her to condemn. However, she also knew that there was a fine line between delight and destruction.

Kimara took another look at Giselle, shook her head and walked away, leaving the giggling Giselle on the sofa with her new companion, who had pulled out a pack of rolling papers and was picking the seeds out of his stash.

Jared was lying in the bed when Kimara entered the bedroom. She shut the door behind her and walked over to him. He was staring at the ceiling with his hands folded beneath his head. Kimara climbed onto the bed, straddling Jared's waist.

"Penny for your thoughts?" she said.

"Just wondering what makes some people tick."

"Hmm," Kimara answered. She began moving her

hips slowly in a grinding motion. Jared reached out and grabbed her waist as his body responded to her movements.

"I bet I know what makes you tick," Kimara said seductively.

The passion of their lovemaking drowned out all sound and memory of Giselle's giggling. Afterwards, they each lay silently staring into the darkness. Jared privately seethed over Kimara's living situation and worried that the trouble he predicted he'd find if he fell for Kimara was beginning to rear its head. Kimara too, lay with her own troubling thoughts, as she wondered if the divide she was beginning to feel between herself and Jared would eventually place in jeopardy the sweetest love she'd ever known.

The following morning found Jared pensive and brooding. Kimara knew that he was still pissed off about Giselle and the night before, but he wouldn't talk about it. In an effort to lighten the mood, Kimara retrieved an invitation she'd received to a new movie premiere. A guy who used to work at Club Silhouette had landed a small role in the movie and had invited her and a guest to attend the premiere and the after-party.

"I don't want to go," Jared said, barely looking at the invitation.

"Come on Jared, it'll be fun. We haven't been out in weeks," Kimara enticed.

"We just went to your cousin's wedding," Jared answered dryly.

"That's not like going out and you know it. I want to party."

"What else is new?" Jared asked.

"What's that supposed to mean?" Kimara paused, taken aback by the sarcasm dripping from Jared's tone.

"Kimara, in case you haven't figured it out by now, I

don't like clubs. I go out with you because that's what you like to do. Do you ever stop to consider, for one second, that that's not my scene? The clubs, the parties, the VIP lounges and the private after-parties. I've had enough of it."

"Whoa, somebody woke up on the wrong side of the bed," Kimara snapped, snatching the invitation from the rumpled sheets where Jared had left it. She glanced at Jared who sat frowning on the edge of the bed before sighing and getting up. She crossed the room, rummaged through her dresser drawers for her sweats.

"I'm going for a jog," she tossed at him over her shoulder before heading down the hall toward the bathroom.

"I'm going home to study," he yelled at her back.

He wanted to kick himself for his funky mood, but he couldn't help being angry with her. He felt like he had spoiled Kimara in these past months, giving in to anything and everything she wanted to do while all the time she paid no attention to how he felt about doing those things. She acted as though he should like whatever she liked and that his social calendar should be a mirrored reflection of hers. He wanted romantic dinners and quiet strolls, but she wasn't happy if she wasn't out shaking her ass somewhere. The words fed up didn't begin to express the way he was feeling lately.

He looked accusingly around Kimara's bedroom, believing that living in this apartment with Giselle had an increasingly detrimental effect on Kimara. He hated being in there. With Giselle and her raunchy lifestyle just doors away from them, he felt tainted.

Jared dressed slowly, his heart and mind heavy with conflicting thoughts and emotions. He didn't know how much longer he could go along if things remained the same. There were so many beautiful inspiring aspects to Kimara, things he'd fallen head over heels in love with. Yet there were other parts of her that he didn't understand and certainly could not accept. While his heart wanted her so badly that he felt it couldn't beat properly without her, his head told him that a future with her would not be one of growth and advancement. Kimara seemed to fight those two things with every inch of her being, and no matter how hard he tried, Jared couldn't understand why.

Chapter 20

"Jasmine, it's me. Where are you at this hour in the morning? All right, well, call me when you get in. It's important. Jared and I had another argument. Call me."

Kimara closed her cell phone, releasing the call and stuck it back into her jacket pocket. She had wanted to talk to Jasmine about the argument she and Jared had, just to take some of the edge off. Instead, she pulled the hood of her nylon jacket over her head to shield her from the light rain that fell and she began jogging.

Jasmine listened as Kimara left the message on her answering machine, and part of her wanted to snatch the receiver up. Kimara was rarely up that early on a Sunday morning, so she had to be very upset. However, Rick was at her feet, sending shock waves of tantalizing pleasure through her body as he dined on her toes. Each lick, each lap, each suck created a frenzy within her and she could not will herself away from him even if she'd tried.

With Rick working nights now, their days had become topsy-turvy. When he came in from his shift this morning, he immediately sat down to give her the pedicure he'd promised her the night before. First he'd placed her feet in the foot spa—a prior birthday present—to soak, adding to the water a concoction he'd found in the neighborhood beauty supply store which combined peppermint, lavender and tea tree oils. The result was invigorating. He dried her silky feet with a towel before rubbing peppermint foot gel on them, massaging from the tips of her toes to the tops of her calves. Her muscles melted under his touch, and her skin felt cool and refreshed from the gel. She laid her head back against the headboard of their bed and closed her eyes, relishing every moment. When Rick's mouth first made contact with her freshly bathed skin, the effect was riveting.

Rick traveled slowly up her body, molding flesh that felt even softer than he remembered. Touching parts of her body that had expanded and grown thicker excited him. The beauty of this woman who was carrying his first child was more erotic than he could have ever imagined. He had loved her when she was slim, but now with curves that were rounder, thickness in places that were previously thinner, she was even more beautiful to him.

Rick was a lucky man, to have found a woman like Jasmine at long last. He had been a confirmed bachelor for years, having given up on the idea of finding his soul mate. He had grown weary of all the game playing and the tap dancing that men and women do. His dreams of one day having children seemed to be becoming less of a possibility with each birthday, each new year. But then he met Jasmine and even though she was ten years his junior, he knew instantly that she was the type of woman with whom forever could be a reality. In the year and a half they'd been together, he had learned more from her about himself and about life than he could have hoped for. He was determined to spend the rest of his life treating her like the queen that she was.

Rick enjoyed making love to Jasmine due more to the pleasure it brought her than what he received himself. He knew that she was beginning to feel self-conscious about her weight and her body, and he did all he could to assure her that he had never found her more attractive. But it was at times like this, when he dined on her body as if he couldn't get enough, that served to reassure her more than his words ever could.

Their lovemaking had changed from the lust-filled, energetic race of newlyweds to a tender snails pace, in which they took their time exploring one another's bodies, all the time seeking new points of pleasure and new ways in which to satisfy each other. They found new positions which not only served to avoid putting any pressure whatsoever on Jasmine's growing belly, but also brought them to new heights of pleasure as their bodies made contact with one another.

The undulating motion of Jasmine's widened hips drove Rick wild as he pleasured her from behind, his arms wrapped around her, his hands cupping her breasts. He lifted her hair, reminding himself to tell her later how much he loved her hair in braids. His lips teased the back of her neck, her shoulders and the tips of her ears. His climax was complete and, for him, earth shattering, yet he remained buried inside of her, not willing to rest until she, too, had reached orgasm. When she did, she shivered as she moaned his name over and over again. They fell asleep still connected, feeling utterly fulfilled.

Just before she drifted off, Jasmine thought of Kimara's phone call. She felt guilty for not picking up, but not enough so that she could tear herself away from her husband. Kimara was in love, and despite the fact that she and Jared were having problems, Jasmine knew that if Kimara was feeling half of what she was feeling, she'd understand.

Chapter 21

Kimara awakened to the sound of raised voices. She sat up, confused. She glanced sideways to the empty space next to her where Jared had lain. He was gone. She looked at the digital clock on the nightstand and learned that it was close to two o'clock in the morning. She kicked the cotton sheet from her legs and walked around the bed to the other side of the room. The voices grew louder as she retrieved her bathrobe from the hook behind the bedroom door and stepped into the hallway.

"What's going on?" she asked as she made her way into the living room.

Jared, Giselle and her new boyfriend, Kyle, were standing in the center of the room facing off. There was another guy whom Kimara did not know seated on the sofa. Giselle was topless, holding her arms across her body in a useless attempt to cover her nakedness. She looked from Jared to Giselle and back, and then her eyes landed on the coffee table. On its surface was a cornucopia of illegal narcotics, starting with a pile of about twenty or so pills, different colors and sizes. Next to that was a pack of rolling paper, several plastic sandwich bags full of marijuana and a smoking bong. A small glass mirror also lay on the table with a razor blade on top of it and a white powdery substance.

Kimara looked back to Jared. His face was contorted in anger. His solid chest rose and fell heavily as he breathed, the veins in his thick neck visibly taut. Giselle looked pale and tense. She blinked her glassy eyes rapidly, as if in an attempt to sober up. She looked briefly at Kimara and then down at the floor.

"Jared?" Kimara looked pointedly at Jared, who remained in quiet contemplation.

The others were also quiet as they waited for Jared to make a move. The guy seated on the couch looked as if he were about to try to make a run for it. He seemed to be sizing up Jared and measuring the distance to the front door.

Finally it was Kyle who spoke. "Aren't you cops ever off duty or something?" Kyle stupidly remarked.

"Shut your mouth punk before I haul your ass to jail," Jared spat.

Kyle closed his mouth and took a seat. His beady eyes remained defiantly fixed on Jared. In the few weeks that Giselle had been seeing Kyle, Kimara had already figured out that he was a spoiled rich kid who thought he owned the world. The son of a famous plastic surgeon, he was used to doing whatever he wanted to do without reprimand or censorship. He thought a lowly city cop beneath him and wore that contempt on his smug face with its thousand dollar nose and sculpted chin.

"Jared, you don't have to talk to him like that," Giselle said, seeming to have found her voice again.

Jared whipped around to face her. "You don't tell me how to talk 'cause there's plenty of room downtown for you too."

"All right, everybody just calm down. Jared, let's go in the bedroom and talk. Please?"

Jared glared at Giselle for another moment before turning to Kimara. His expression changed to one of defeat as his eyes searched hers. "You know what Kimara, I don't need this crap. I've got enough to deal with."

"Jared—" Kimara placed a hand on his shoulder.

"I don't need this," Jared repeated, shoving her hand away. He walked back to her bedroom and angrily snapped the light switch on. Hastily, he searched for the jeans he'd worn earlier. Upon finding them, he slid quickly into them and then his sneakers.

"What are you doing, Jared?" Kimara asked.

When he didn't respond, she approached him. Standing in front of him, blocking his path, she posed the question again.

"I'm getting out of here. I'm not going to let you and your friends ruin my career . . . my life. Do you know what could happen to me if I get caught in this apartment with that kind of stuff going on out there? Every week there's something else. Some different guy, some wilder partying. I don't know what I'm going to walk in to from one day to the next."

"Jared please, let's just talk about this."

"Move Kimara," he said, spotting his T-shirt on the dresser behind her.

She would not budge. He attempted to step to the left to go around her. Kimara moved in front of him. Jared's nostrils flared and his eyes lowered into tiny slits. The anger rose off of his body like tiny volts of electricity, but Kimara was relentless. She could not let him leave like this. She knew instinctively that if he walked out now, there would be no coming back. This had to be fixable. If he would just calm down, she could find the words to fix this.

"Jared please. Don't do this. We can work it out," Kimara pleaded.

"The only way we can work this out is if you pack your things and walk out that door with me," he answered suddenly.

"What?"

"You heard me Kimara. I've had enough of this. The clubbing, the parties. It's like you're not happy if you're not living *la vida loca* every damned night. Then you come home and there's different guys every night running in and out of here. I'm fed up with the drugs and your coked-out friends."

"Jared, those are Giselle's friends, not mine. I don't have anything to do with what goes on out there, and you know it."

"Do I?" Jared asked purposely.

"Yes, you do," Kimara snapped back.

"Kimara, I can't take this anymore. I love you and I want to build a future with you. But not like this. You don't want the same things as I do, and I just don't see how we can work it out."

"You said it didn't matter that we were different. You said it was all good. What happened to all that? Was that just game you were kicking to get at me?"

"No, it wasn't. But this . . . this is crazy. You don't know what you want and I'm not going to wait around and get caught up in some of Giselle's bullshit while you try to figure it out. Either you move out of here or—"

"Or what?"

Jared stepped to the right of Kimara, snatched his T-shirt from the dresser and slipped it over his head.

"Or what Jared? Don't you dare give me an ultimatum," Kimara yelled.

"Call it what you want. Are you coming?" he asked.

Kimara looked away from him, her own anger spilling out in blinding tears. She felt sick to her stomach and her heart throbbed with a brutal aching. The sensation of having been bullied and beaten rose in her and she felt as cornered and powerless as a caged animal. Here it was—the inevitable.

She didn't know why she thought it would be different this time when she knew that people always ended up placing demands on her, no matter how different she thought they were or how special she thought her relationship was. People tell someone they love him or her just as they are and then always end up trying to make the person into something else. That's just the way it was, she was convinced.

Defiance gripped her and with a set jaw and unwavering eyes, she looked at Jared. "You know the way out," she said, her voice too loud for her own ears.

Jared turned his back and took a step forward before hesitating. He stood in the doorway and for a moment, Kimara thought that he would turn around. He didn't. He started walking, down the hallway, through the living room and into the foyer. She heard the apartment door open and slam shut. Then there was nothing but silence, save for the sound of her heart breaking like a delicate piece of fine china.

Chapter 22

Kimara refused to talk about Jared. She had given Jasmine a brief synopsis of what had transpired between them, remaining indignant about the demands he'd placed on her. She told Jasmine that it was the for the best and that their reaching the end was an inevitability for which she had prepared herself. Then she implored Jasmine to move on and let it go. She swore that she was fine, even though inside she felt like she was drowning.

After awhile, Jasmine stopped trying to get Kimara to talk. Besides, Jasmine had her own problems to deal with. Rick was insisting that they move to Virginia before the baby was born. He had applied for a position with the Virginia Department of Rail and Public Transportation and had just gotten word that there would be an opening in a few weeks. He had also engaged the services of a realtor to help them find their dream home, despite the fact that they had only managed to save just over ten thousand dollars. He informed Jasmine that the market was much different there than in New York and that they could do quite nicely with what they had saved.

Rick was bullheaded in their discussions. He cited the fact that he desperately wanted the baby to be born in

Virginia, near his parents and siblings. He felt that there
was no better time than the present and promised to
work double shifts if he had to in order to make sure
they had enough money to begin their new life together. Rick didn't see any reason for them to delay
their plans any longer.

But Jasmine saw many. For one, it was early in a new
school year. She had already formed bonds with her students and didn't want to walk out on them now. With
budget cuts and limited resources, the public school
where she worked would have a hard time finding a
qualified replacement with such short notice. Also, she
had wanted to have the baby in New York, and be near
her own mother at first. Add to that the fact that no
school district would hire her at this stage in her pregnancy, which meant that she would be out of work
longer than she would like to be.

Finally, there was Kimara. No matter what she said,
Jasmine knew that Kimara was grieving over breaking
up with Jared. She tried to put on a tough front and act
like it didn't bother her, but Jasmine was no fool. How
could she, in good conscience, leave her best friend
right now? On top of that, there were people coming
out of the woodwork wanting to work with Kimara on
her poetry and Jasmine knew that if she wasn't around
to push her, Kimara would not pursue it.

No, she kept telling Rick, now was not a good time
to pack up and move. He didn't understand her reasons
and felt that she was putting too many things and
people before him and their baby. As a result, they
argued daily. Jasmine hated the tension between them
but stood fast to her beliefs. She began spending more
time at her mother's house, not wanting to be home
with Rick and the stress began to show on her.

"You look like crap today," Kimara told her one day as
they sat in Jasmine's mother's kitchen reading over a

contract which had come via overnight mail from Smithtown Records.

"Gee, thanks. You sure know how to make a girl feel good about herself," Jasmine replied.

"Sparing your feelings is equivalent to telling you a lie. You don't look good. How have you been feeling?"

Jasmine sighed. "Tired."

"Are you taking your vitamins?"

"Yes, I take those nasty horse pills and the iron pills too. I drink six glasses of milk every day, ten glasses of water, no soda, no caffeine and no alcohol. I eat my veggies, I rest . . . basically, I'm a model prisoner."

Kimara looked at her friend, considering her state of being. Her face was puffy and her eyes were red. Gone was that blissful glow of the early part of her pregnancy, replaced by the haggard look of a much older and very weary woman. Worry colored her voice when she spoke again. "You and Rick still fighting?" Kimara asked.

"Yeah. He's like a dog with a bone over this Virginia thing."

"He just wants to get you away from me. He probably thinks I'm going to corrupt you or something," Kimara joked.

"Kimara, not everything's about you. Rick just wants what's best for us, and I love him for that. I just wish he could see my side," Jasmine said. "Enough about my problems. I'll work them out. What's up with these Smithtown people? Do you think you want to do something with them?"

"It's a tough call. Penchant wanted to sign me as a solo artist, but talking to them was scary, what with their big fancy offices, and team of lawyers. They were asking me to practically sign with them for life, you know? I'd be making records for them when I'm ninety-nine with cataracts and a crooked back, bent over from osteoporosis."

"Not a cute thought. How'd you leave it with them?" Jasmine asked.

"I told them I needed some time to think. I know that they've got a solid reputation and they're talking about a lot of money, but I don't know."

Jasmine read a few more paragraphs of the Smith-town contract. "These guys seem like they're just trying to get on the map," she said, tapping the contract. "They're a major record label, but they don't have as many years in the business as Penchant does. Basically, it looks like they're the baby of the business whereas Penchant is already full grown and all over the place."

"I know," Kimara agreed.

"But on the other hand, the fact that Smithtown is trying to make a name for themselves in the business means they're thirsty. They're going to work hard for you because they have to in order to grow. Penchant doesn't have to prove anything. If your records don't sell, I don't think it'd be that big of a loss to them."

"Listen to you. *My records.* You say that like this is everyday business. A few months ago, I was a closet poet who worked at a nightclub and now people want me to make music. It's crazy."

"It is crazy but that's how these things work Kimara. Quick, fast and in a hurry. You've got to either get on board or watch the train pull out of the station without you. There's no time for hesitation."

"Okay, Miss Berry Gordy. Check you out. You act like you've been down this road before," Kimara joked.

"I read *Rolling Stone, Vibe* and I watch *E! True Hollywood Stories.* That's a crash course in the business, so trust me when I say I know what I'm talking about," Jasmine said seriously, truly believing herself to be an authority on the subject.

"Well look, I'm really leaning toward Smithtown, if I even bother with any of this," Kimara said.

"What do you mean, if you even bother with any of this?" Jasmine snapped.

Kimara got up from the table and walked into the pantry area at the rear of Mrs. Mitchell's kitchen. Silently, she scoured the shelves. "Does your mother have any Bisquick in here?" she asked, peering at Jasmine.

"I know you're not about to pass up the opportunity of a lifetime," Jasmine continued.

Possessed with a one-track mind, Jasmine had no intentions of letting Kimara's offhanded comment slide.

"I feel like baking. Oh, here's the Bisquick," Kimara stated, ignoring Jasmine.

She busied herself gathering various ingredients from Mrs. Mitchell's pantry. From the cabinet next to the stove, she retrieved muffin pans. She sauntered past a perturbed Jasmine, opened the refrigerator and removed three green apples from the vegetable bin. Kimara peeled the skin off of the apples and diced them into fine pieces. She returned to the **refrigerator,** fishing out eggs and butter. She felt Jasmine's eyes **on** her but refused to acknowledge them.

After twenty minutes of silent preparation, Kimara filled the muffin pan with the batter and placed it in the oven. She proceeded to clean up after herself. Finally, when there was nothing left to do, she returned to her seat at the table.

"Kimara if you don't want to go through with this, then you shouldn't," Jasmine said finally.

Kimara chewed her bottom lip thoughtfully. "I just don't know if I can do it," she admitted quietly. More than anything else Kimara hated to appear vulnerable. This entire situation, while not one of her choosing, filled her with an expectant excitement. However, she was also afraid of so many aspects. Would she be received well? Or, once her album dropped, would no one be feeling her besides Jasmine, her parents and the people she worked with? She was being asked to put herself out there for the whole world to see and judge. That type of exposure terrified her and she felt like she would be relinquishing control over her own life. She wasn't quite sure that she was brave enough to do that.

"Kimara, you can do anything you set your mind to. I've watched you since we were little kids and never once did you fail at anything that you wanted to attain. Your failures were all by choice. When we were thirteen, you wanted to learn how to ride dirt bikes like the boys—you did it. When we were fifteen, you wanted to make captain of the cheerleading squad, a position usually reserved for seniors, but you did that too. If there was a cute boy who you wanted to date, you pulled him. You made average grades in school simply because you chose to. Whatever you set your sights on, it's yours and this won't be any different. So I guess the real question is not whether you can do it, but whether or not you want to."

Jasmine stood up from the table and walked to the oven. Opening it, she peered inside at Kimara's muffins, the tantalizing aroma already causing her to salivate in anticipation.

"Maybe you shouldn't get involved in this music thing," Jasmine said. "Your baked goods are a heck of a lot better than your poems anyway," she said with a smirk.

Chapter 23

"Kimara, meet Delphina and Simone. Ladies, this is Kimara."

"Hi, nice to meet you both." Kimara smiled, shaking hands with each singer in turn. She had met Harrell James in the lobby of an office building on the West side of Manhattan and they rode in an enclosed glass elevator to the 29th floor. When they stepped off the elevator it was as if they'd stepped into a whole new world. There was a swarm of activity—people running in and out of offices, telephones ringing, music playing. They walked down a long corridor, the walls covered with framed color photographs of singers, bands and other well-known people in the industry. They passed conference rooms and lounge areas and finally entered a room whose door was marked Studio A in gold lettering.

"You too. I heard a tape of you at the Roots and Culture Café. Miss Thing, you rocked the house," Delphina said.

"Thanks," Kimara answered shyly. She had still not become accustomed to the way people had responded to that night's performance.

Kimara had agonized for weeks over the offers from both Penchant and Smithtown. She was wined and dined by both labels and conferred endlessly with both Jasmine and her parents. Finally, she decided to sign with Smithtown. While she'd read all about the horrific experiences some artists had gone through with managers, producers and record labels, there was something about Harrell James that Kimara felt she could trust. He seemed genuinely interested in making music. He took her in to meet the big wigs at the label and even met with the entertainment lawyer her father had found through his trumpet-playing friend, Fred Townsend, and answered all of his questions.

Everything seemed to move at the speed of light after that. Now, on this, her first day in the studio, she felt as if she had been racing on a treadmill, her mind panting behind her trying to catch up.

"And Kimara, over here is Big Mike, the best engineer in the city," Harrell said, pointing to a large, buff man seated before a Macintosh computer. His high cheekbones and round face gave him a Native American appearance, but his complexion and thick bushy ponytail indicated that his heritage was definitely mixed with those of African descent.

"Mike, how're you doing?" Kimara greeted Big Mike, who rose from his chair and languidly kissed the back of her hand.

"Okay Romeo," Harrell joked. "Over there is Jonathan, affectionately known in these parts as the Wizard 'cause he's magic on the beats. He'll be producing ninety-nine percent of the tracks on this project."

"Welcome aboard, Ma," Jonathan said. He was seated on a long leather sofa sifting through reams of paper spread across the oak coffee table in front of him. He had a head full of neatly braided, intricately designed cornrows. He was a slim guy, not very tall with soft effeminate features. He had a tattoo of a panther on his neck.

"Okay, time is money people so let's get it popping. Here's what I think we should do. Delphina, Mo', you two go into the booth and just lay down some of the harmonies. Big Mike will run some of the tracks and you ladies just free style it or do some of the hooks. I want Kimara to get a feel for the sound we've been working on. Let's get a nice vibe flowing up in here and take it from there. Cool?"

"Works for me," Delphina said, heading toward the vocal booth.

"Let's do it," Simone followed.

"Pretty lady, you can sit here next to me," Big Mike said.

"All right." Kimara took a seat in front of a large box-type piece of equipment covered with dozens of switches and buttons. "What's all this?" she asked.

"This right here is the track board. I use this to switch back and forth between the tracks. And this here is where I run all the music from. We use a software called Protol."

He flipped a few switches and the lights inside of the vocal booth came on. Through the glass partition, Kimara watched as Delphina and Simone placed head-sets on their heads and adjusted the microphones. Simone took a sip from a bottle of Evian she carried and then Delphina nodded at Mike. He typed a few strokes on the computer's keypad and suddenly the room was filled with a mellow beat.

Delphina took the lead and began singing in a slow moan. Her voice was deep, a low alto. She reminded Kimara of Lauryn Hill. Delphina, the shorter of the two, was slim with cocoa-brown skin and deep-set dimples. She looked a lot younger than she actually was, which made the soulful voice which sprang from her body all the more of a surprise to the listener. At the moment that Delphina began singing actual words, Simone came in picking up on the harmony, her soprano voice light and airy.

Simone was a tawny complexioned woman with wide

eyes and a full round face. She was what the fellas called thick, with shapely legs, a small waist and a fair amount of junk in the trunk. Together, their sound was amazing, as if they'd been singing with one another for years.

"How long have they been together?" Kimara whispered to Harrell who was standing behind her chair.

"About six months. They were a part of a threesome but it just wasn't working. We scrapped that project and spent the last few weeks trying to find another singer. But then we found you."

"Oh," Kimara said. She couldn't believe they sounded that good after only six months. Suddenly, she grew nervous as she contemplated how she would fit in with this pair. She had yet to hear a recording of herself and wasn't certain that she'd sound good. Once again she began to get that feeling in the pit of her stomach like she'd set herself up for a big-time fall. She bit on her lower lip, listening to the singers and becoming increasingly disillusioned. As if sensing her discomfort, Harrell placed his hands on her shoulders from behind and squeezed gently.

Kimara closed her eyes and just listened. She allowed all of her other senses to take a backseat to her ears. She followed the melody, the cadence of their voices infecting her in a soothing manner. And then she was with them, imagined herself right there in the booth with them. She began flowing. Words from a poem written years ago slipped from her lips.

Jonathan looked up from his paperwork and stared at Kimara, just as Harrell and Big Mike were doing. She paused after spitting a few verses, her body rocking to and fro to the beat.

Big Mike switched tracks again, an up-tempo rhythm seeping through the speakers. Kimara quieted, listening for a while until she found the new rhythm. Then her voice, like fine silk, found a place in the melody, tucked itself in between Delphina's alto and Simone's soprano and on the night went. It was a persistent give and take between the music and the artists. By the time Mike had played the last track, the room was on fire.

"Damn girl, you can flow. You've got mad skills," Jonathan said.

"What'd I tell you guys? This girl is the real deal," Harrell beamed.

Kimara was surprised herself at how freely the words escaped from her mouth. The feeling which came over her was magical and intense. Maybe she could do this after all. While she had no idea how the trio would be received by consumers, she decided they had about as fair a shot as anybody else.

Harrell immediately drafted a rehearsal schedule and the group tossed around ideas for an outline of the pattern of the album. They agreed that they wanted an original sound, something that combined hip-hop, jazz and soul but didn't sound concocted.

As the new addition to the group, Kimara quickly learned that she had a lot of catching up to do. Harrell signed her up with a vocal coach and registered her for courses in musical theory, note reading and piano. She objected vigorously to the piano lessons, having been forced by her parents to suffer through a year of private lessons when she was ten years old with an old battle-ax named Mrs. Murphy. Kimara still had nightmares about that woman, visions of the hair mole on her neck and her crooked finger still haunting her. Despite her protests, Harrell was insistent. Her schedule was rapidly taken over by her new career and she jokingly wondered when she'd be able to fit sleep into the mix.

Kimara was surprised to learn that Delphina was a year younger than she, but was a wife and mother of a five-year-old son. Simone, who was the youngest at age twenty-one, was single and childless like Kimara, but was working a full and a part-time job to help raise her three younger siblings. Feeling guilty about her own laziness,

Kimara stepped up and accepted the demands Harrell placed on her. How could she complain when these two women were working twice as hard as she was to achieve their dreams?

The up side of it all was that she should be left with very little time to think about Jared, whose image still ran rampant through her memory.

Chapter 24

"That's a nice color on you," Gena Hamilton said as she leaned against the doorframe of the bathroom.

"Thanks," Kimara answered as she applied Mac's Desire Lipglass to supple, parted lips.

It was a little strange for Kimara to be back at her parents' apartment in Queens. She hadn't visited in over two months. Her father had changed the wallpaper in the bathroom and all of the bath accessories were new. Kimara didn't really like the new look, the color her mother called dusty rose looked more like bubble gum pink, but she didn't say anything for fear of hurting her mother's feelings.

When she'd stopped by the night before, she hadn't planned on staying over. Her mom had prepared baked porkchops and potato salad for dinner, two of Kimara's favorite dishes. They sat at the dinner table for hours. Gena and William were as excited as kids on Christmas Eve as they listened to the details of Kimara's foray into the music world. They wanted to know everything about the people she was working with, the type of music they were making and when they'd get to hear their daughter on the radio for the first time. She promised to take them into the studio one evening real soon so that they could get to meet the rest of the crew and get a first-hand look at what she was doing. While she was too proud to admit it, it pleased Kimara to see her parents so impressed by something she had done. For the first time in a very long time, she felt like they were proud of her and she relished every minute they spent oohing and aahing.

Later on, alone in her old bedroom, Kimara recalled the evening and realized that not once had her mother been critical or disapproving. She was, to the contrary, extremely complimentary and seemed genuinely impressed. It was quite a change from their normal conversation and it made Kimara feel happier than she'd felt in weeks, especially since her breakup with Jared.

Kimara awoke late the next day and had a big breakfast with her parents. Shortly before noon she prepared herself to meet the girls at the studio. Kimara grew uncomfortable under her mother's watchful eyes.

"What?" she asked.

"Nothing. I'm just watching. You think you want to put a little something around your eyes? The skin looks a little dark."

"Yeah."

"Haven't you been sleeping well?"

"I'm fine. Just been working hard and stuff."

"Oh. Are you still working at that phone store?"

"No, just four nights at the club. But I'm also in the studio all the time."

"I see. How's Jasmine?"

"Big as a horse."

"Kimara that's not nice. It's hard enough being pregnant without people telling you how big you are all the time," Gena reprimanded.

Kimara laughed. "I don't say it to her face, but trust

me, if she gets any bigger she's gonna need her own zip code."

"You're bad. Well tell her I said hello. And tell her to try soaking her feet in tepid water with sliced cucumbers in it. It'll help."

"Yuck," Kimara answered as she smoothed a little warm bronze cover-up beneath each of her eyes.

"You haven't mentioned Jared since you got here. You two had a fight or something?" Gena asked.

"Or something. He walked out on me a couple of months ago."

"And?"

"And what? It's over." Kimara hoped her voice sounded as nonchalant as she was working to make it sound. She didn't want her mother to know the sad truth that she was actually breaking down inside.

"Just like that?"

"Just like that," Kimara snapped.

"Hmm, well, if you're sure it's over . . ."

"I'm sure," Kimara answered with a finality that she didn't feel.

The last thing she wanted to do was to talk about Jared with her mother. The fact was he was on her mind every minute and the past nine weeks had seemed like an eternity. With each passing day she grew more uncertain of the righteousness of her part in their breakup. Now she realized that she shouldn't have let him walk out the way she had. A lot of what he'd said was true.

Giselle's apartment was, at times, like a three-ring circus. She never knew who or what she was walking into when she came home at night. Last week, Kimara had installed a lock on her bedroom door after she'd been lying awake watching television late one night and one of Giselle's male friends had opened the door and walked into Kimara's bedroom. He claimed he'd merely taken a wrong turn on the way from the bathroom, but Kimara was spooked nonetheless.

While Kimara realized that having Jared spend time with her in Giselle's apartment had been inappropriate and potentially problematic for him, she still didn't like the fact that he'd issued an ultimatum to her. He didn't even want to try to work it out. It had seemed to her that he wanted to break up with her for some reason other than what he was saying and that that was just a convenient excuse.

Kimara really didn't know what to think now, other than the fact that she missed Jared terribly. She had hoped that with time, the dull ache in her heart would ease, but it hadn't. She loved him, plain and simple and no amount of time or space would change that fact. All the changes that had begun taking place in her life seemed to lose some of their shine since Jared wasn't there to share them. He and Jasmine were there at the very beginning. If it weren't for him, she probably wouldn't even have gone through with the show after Jasmine had entered her into the poetry contest.

"I'm not trying to tell you how to live your life Kimara. I just wanted to say that . . . well, I know sometimes it's difficult for you to follow through with things. You have a tendency to quit when the going gets a little tough," her mother said, pulling her from her own train of thought.

"Yeah, I do have a habit of not finishing what I've started. But this is different. I feel like the group, the music is where I was meant to be all along. Putting my poetry to beats, giving them life, it's like nothing I've ever felt before," Kimara answered.

"That's wonderful Kimara, and I'm so happy for you. But I wasn't talking about the music," Gena said. "I was talking about Jared."

With that, her mother walked away, leaving a speechless Kimara to marinate in her words.

Chapter 25

Remorse for my losses
Embarrassed by my accomplishments
Stressed when I underachieve
Pointless if I try?
Miserable when I quit
      Life—is this it?

Considered the sacrifices
Embodied by selfishness
Persuaded by routine
Negate my fortune
Humbled by poverty
      Love—is this it?

Scarred by misunderstanding
Understand what to be grateful for
I war for peace
But before war
Is that peace discomfiting?
      This is my apology

Chapter 26

Kimara ran her sweaty palms down the sides of her hip-hugging jeans. She glanced at her watch again, noting that Jared's shift had been over for about twenty minutes. It was just after midnight and she had been standing outside of the station house for half an hour. When she'd called the station that afternoon to find out if Jared was on duty, she had learned from the desk sergeant that Jared was no longer working the graveyard shift but had moved to the four to midnight.

Several other police officers entered and exited the building and each time the doors opened, a herd of butterflies tickled her chest cavity. She couldn't believe how nervous she was. After she had made up her mind to pay Jared a visit, it seemed as if it would be the easiest thing in the world. Now, standing outside of his job only minutes away from seeing him, she realized exactly how much was riding on this surprise meeting.

Finally, the doors opened once again and Jared appeared, talking to a coworker. The sight of him caused her heart as well as her loins to stir. He looked as sexy as she remembered, possibly even more so. He wore an Atlanta Hawks fitted cap pulled down low over his brow, a black leather jacket, jeans and black Gortex boots. His face was clean shaven, but when he smiled Kimara noticed that his eyes didn't join in on the act. They seemed to be thinking of other things and other times.

He shared a brotherly handshake and hug with the guy before heading down the steps. He was looking out into the street and didn't notice Kimara approaching him. She took a deep breath before calling out his name.

"Jared," she said softly.

He turned in her direction, his gaze falling squarely on her face. He stopped abruptly on the last step, his expression a mixture of shock and something else which she could not read.

"You look like you've seen a ghost or something," Kimara joked.

"Or something," Jared said, a slow smile spreading across his mouth. This time his eyes smiled too. He descended the final step and stood in front of Kimara.

"You look good," he noticed.

The pretty honey-brown face was as breathtaking as he remembered. The bright chestnut eyes still sparkled and the full pouty lips still seemed to be waiting to be kissed. He was afraid to look at the length of her, memories of her sexy frame and how she felt in his arms had been too hard to forget.

"You, too."

A moment of pained silence followed as Jared waited to find out why Kimara was there and she worked up the nerve to tell him. A gentle breeze blew, lifting Kimara's hair and leaving a few strands in her face. Jared resisted the urge to reach out and sweep the silky hair back into place. Instead, he stuffed his hands into his jacket pocket.

"I uh, I'm sorry to just pop by like this, but uh, I had something to tell you," Kimara began. She took a deep breath and was immediately intoxicated by the heady masculine scent of Izzi Miaki cologne. "I have to tell you that . . ." Kimara paused.

Jared waited patiently, hanging on every word that poured from the pretty, supple lip-glossed mouth.

"I'm sorry," she blew out. "I'm sorry for the way things ended and sorry for the way I acted. I know we both said some things that we may not necessarily have meant but . . . uh . . . wow, this is harder than I thought it would be." Kimara paused.

She looked up and down the empty sidewalk, the stillness of the air around her uncharacteristic for October in New York. She looked at her shoes then up at the sky and finally continued.

"Look Jared, you didn't deserve to be treated that way and well . . . I'm sorry."

There, she'd said it. She looked up at Jared, trying to gauge his reaction. There was a look in his eyes that was unmistakable because it was the same longing look she'd seen reflected in her own every day since they had parted. She became emboldened by the realization that he had missed her as much as she had missed him.

"I've missed you terribly, more than I'm capable of saying right now, and I was hoping that maybe—" Kimara's words were cut short by the approach of bright headlights. A shiny black Mercedes SLK 230 Roadster screeched to a halt at the curb inches from where they stood with its top down. The driver's door swung open and out stepped a long-legged woman, with skin the color of butter pecans and curly, auburn hair which seemed to have a life of its own. In an instant she had danced onto the curb and proceeded to languidly kiss Jared's lips. She turned to Kimara and introduced herself.

"Hi. I'm Millicent, Jared's fiancée. And you are?"

The territorial glare in Millicent's eyes was a direct contrast to the buttermilk sweetness of her voice. Kimara stared in disbelief at the glittering marquise diamond Millicent so graciously flashed in front of her. Rendered speechless she looked at Jared who looked like the cat who ate the whole bird sanctuary. The silence screamed into the air as the three of them stood waiting—Millicent waiting for the opposition's next move, Jared waiting for Kimara to free him from her spell and Kimara waiting to wake up from what had to be a nightmare.

Another look at Millicent's startling diamond made it all a reality. Feeling as though she had been mortally wounded, Kimara turned to flee into the night, hot tears of shame burning her cheeks with each departing step. Jared called after her, but his words fell on deaf ears.

"Who was she?" Millicent asked.

She had tried to talk to Jared after the woman ran off, but he refused to talk. She was incensed at his calling after her and then standing there for several additional moments, looking as if he were about to run behind her.

They rode in silence back to his apartment in Clinton Hills, Brooklyn. She parked her car on the quiet tree-lined street in front of his brownstone and waited for some sign from him that things were okay. It never came.

Jared got out of the car and climbed the building's stairs. Millicent followed, anxiety building with each passing silent moment. Inside the apartment, Jared went directly to the kitchen, barely holding the front door for Millicent who trailed behind him. He opened the refrigerator and withdrew a Heineken. Roughly, he popped the top off with a bottle opener and took a long swallow. Millicent stood in the doorway, watching his Adam's apple bob up and down as he drank heartily.

Jared's striking appearance still caught her off guard sometimes. His smooth skin, the color of coffee beans, was as alluring to her now as it had been the first time she'd laid eyes on him. For some inexplicable reason she remained surprised that she had attracted a man as handsome as Jared. While she considered herself fairly attractive, men as ruggedly sexy as Jared never seemed to gravitate toward her. She recognized that the difference between Jared and most other handsome men was that Jared was not conceited. It was as if he wasn't even aware of how attractive he actually was. For her, his humility made him all the more alluring.

When he'd drained the bottle, Jared sat it on the counter beside him, removed another from the fridge and was halfway through that one when Millicent found the courage to pose her question again.

"Nobody," Jared answered gruffly. His head felt as tight as a rubberband being stretched to its full length. He didn't want to talk to Millicent right now, but despite his wants, he could not think of anything short of the world coming to an end that would help him avoid it.

"Didn't seem like nobody to me."

Millicent was timid yet determined in her manner. She didn't want to upset Jared. Certainly didn't want to threaten the already fragile ground on which their relationship stood. She had loved Jared since the day she met him, six years ago. They were both students at John Jay and had met on the first day of classes in Economics 1000. Jared was quiet and relaxed, taking a seat at the back of the class and keeping to himself. Millicent stumbled into the class midway through the hour, disheveled and tense after a rough day of late registration and battles over tuition with the bursar's office. The only available seat was at the back of the class, next to Jared. She took the seat as inconspicuously as possible, disturbed by the annoyed look she received from the professor. Jared calmly explained what she'd missed, let her copy from his notes and by the end of that first class, she had fallen head over heels in love with him.

Millicent had been convinced that she'd met the man she wanted to marry. Their breakup, three years later had thrown her for a loop. She had tried to be supportive of Jared and his problems within the police department. She knew of his troubled past, but was a firm believer in the *just get over it* adage. She was happy, in love and at the beginning of a fabulous career in forensic science. She wanted to plan for the future with the man she loved and quickly grew tired of his morose moods.

She stopped trying to get him to talk and ceased thinking up creative ways to try to ease his tension, because nothing she did seemed to help anyway. Eventually, she began to complain fearsomely about his behavior and his self-imposed depression. When Jared broke it off with her, she had been surprised but not completely caught off guard.

Millicent had spent the next few years wondering what could have been. After much introspection, she realized that she should have been more supportive of Jared during his crises. The time she spent in the dating pool made her realize that she had found a true gem in Jared and was foolish to let him go. Her unsolicited phone call to him this Fall appeared whimsical to him, but was, in fact, the result of her long-planned designs to rekindle their love. She was pleasantly surprised when Jared said that he was still single, and she jumped at an opportunity to see him again. At the time she felt no cause for concern when he mentioned that he had just come out of a relationship. Now, it seemed, she should have been wary.

Jared sighed, pulled out a chair at his table and motioned for Millicent to do the same.

"Look, when you and I got back together, I told you I'd recently broken up with someone."

"So that was her?" Millicent asked.

"Yes, it was. Kimara and I were only together for a few months and . . . well . . . we just didn't see eye to eye on a lot of things."

"And?"

"And nothing. We parted ways and that's that. You're back in my life now and that's all I'm concerned with."

"What did she want?" Millicent pressed.

"Just wanted to say hello I guess," Jared lied, looking away from Millicent's face.

He couldn't stand to see the scared look in her eyes. That was one of the things he disliked most about her. She always needed reassurance about his feelings for her. Any attention he received from another woman sent her into this worry mode where she grew increasingly fearful that he was going to leave her. On the surface Millicent appeared to be a confident, self-assured woman but in actuality, she was a scared rabbit. She rarely disagreed with him and it was beginning to feel like he was marrying a puppet instead of a woman.

Kimara was the exact opposite, her assertive demeanor a direct contrast to Millicent's compliant personality. She had an opinion about everything and loved to express it. But she was far from being opinionated or pushy. She loved to debate and to hear what others had to say. However, when she believed in something, Kimara stood her ground, no matter what. And Miss America could walk into the room and she wouldn't bat an eye. She was the least insecure person he'd ever met. Kimara did what Kimara wanted to do. She was considerate of other people's feelings, but not at the expense of her own. That's the thing he loved the most about her. But he also realized that was precisely the thing he'd let come between them.

But, he'd put a ring on Millicent's finger. He'd felt like it was the right thing to do for himself, for his life. He could not keep running around, just dating. He felt like he was getting too old for that. Besides, he and Millicent had some good times together and she was smart, pretty and ambitious; a good catch by any standard. What's more, she led a lifestyle that was complementary to his. She didn't party much and was a homebody like he was. Settling down with her would not be the worst move he could make. While it may not set his soul on fire either, he told himself that it wouldn't be a bad thing.

"Jared, are you even listening to me?" Millicent asked, her voice rising slightly.

"Huh? Yeah, I . . . look Millie, let's not make a big deal out of this. What Kimara and I had is in the past, dead and buried. It's over, and you don't have to worry about her," Jared said absently.

Jared rose from the table and went over to Millicent's side. He bent down and kissed the top of her head. He didn't believe entirely what he'd just said, but the words were a comfort to his anguished soul. He hoped that they would comfort Millicent as well.

"I'm going to take a shower and hit the sheets. I'm exhausted."

Jared rinsed the two empty bottles and placed them on the counter next to the sink. He left the kitchen, unaware of the tears that had begun to form at the rims of Millicent's woeful eyes. She sat for a long time at the table, twisting her engagement ring around her finger as the salt water escaped her lids.

Chapter 27

"Ssh, sweetie, it's okay," Jasmine purred as she stroked the back of Kimara's wild head of hair.

Kimara's long tresses were a matted, tangled mess. She was laying on Giselle's sofa, her head in Jasmine's lap. Snot and spittle pooled beneath her face and onto Jasmine's maternity jeans. Jasmine snatched several tissues from the box next to them, handing them to Kimara and taking the soiled ones from her.

"It hurts so much, Jazz. I thought I was over him, but seeing them . . . seeing her . . . that ring, was like being punched in the gut."

"I know honey, I know. But you're going to be okay. You'll get through it. Just cry it out and it'll feel better."

Kimara cried for a while longer and soon, there were no more tears left to cry. She continued to lay on Jasmine's lap, playing with the round beach ball that had become her friend's belly. The baby began kicking and stirring about and Kimara lay feeling its movements and talking baby talk. Feeling no better, but exhausted from feeling so bad for so long, she got up. She dialed the number of an Italian restaurant nearby and ordered chicken marsala for herself and eggplant parmigiana for Jasmine.

Having lain around in the same clothes since seeing Jared the night before, Kimara was disgusted with herself. She decided to take a shower while they waited for their food to arrive. She allowed the water to run over her completely, from head to toe, the temperature as hot as she could stand it. She washed her hair with the same scented soap that she used on her body and exited the bathroom covered by a full-length, fluffy bathrobe with her hair wrapped in a thick towel. By the time the food arrived, she felt refreshed, but found she didn't have much of an appetite. Jasmine and baby happily ate enough for all of them.

Once again, Jasmine was her rock in her time of need. She stayed with her all afternoon and slept over until the next morning. They talked, Kimara cried some more and Jasmine even managed to make her laugh a little in between. Disbelief that Jared had become involved, no less engaged, so quickly, eventually dissolved and gave way to feelings of betrayal and disappointment. Finally, emptiness settled in and Kimara felt as though the past few months of her life had all been in vain.

After Jasmine left, Kimara closed herself in her bedroom and watched *Love Jones*, her all-time favorite love story, on DVD. By the time the love-struck couple broke up and Nia Long had left town for good by train while Larenz Tate ran, unseen, alongside of it, she was in tears again. She clicked the television off before they reunited, unwilling to watch them attain on screen something that was lost to her in real life.

The afternoon passed slowly and finally, as she teetered on the brink of depression and unconquerable despair, she threw on a pair of leggings and a hooded sweatshirt and went for a jog. Her goal was to run until she felt something close to normalcy, if that was possible.

The sun had set and the night air was crisp and inviting. Kimara stayed on the outskirts of the park, knowing that a darkened park was no place for a lone jogger. She jogged down 5th Avenue, past closed stores with pretty window displays that failed to catch her eye. She hadn't gone running since she and Jared broke up and she was amazed at how quickly the body regressed when left dormant for too long. She ran until the muscles in her neck hurt as much as those in her calves. However, no place ached as much as her heart did, so she continued jogging until even that spot was numb.

She was sweaty and exhausted when she returned to her apartment. After a quick shower she tossed herself across her bed and fell asleep with the ease of a newborn baby. She slept hard, mentally and physically exhausted by the preceding events and was grateful for the opportunity to lay her burdens down, at least for a little while.

Chapter 28

"Stop. Stop. Everybody take five," Harrell shouted over the loudspeaker.

Kimara slid the headphones from her ears and tossed them onto the table. Delphina and Simone glanced quizzically at her, then at one another before leaving the booth.

Harrell entered the vocal booth where Kimara sat alone. She was staring at the sheet music in front of her, unable to make sense of anything.

"Kimara, what's up? You're all over the place today," Harrell asked.

"I know. I'm sorry. Look maybe we should try this another time," Kimara agreed. She hated wasting everybody's time but she just couldn't get into the right frame of mind. She kept forgetting her words, words that she had written herself and she was missing the cues. Her voice sounded false even to her own ears.

"Kimara, there is no other time. You've missed the last two sessions. We've got to get this album finished yesterday. What's up with you? Talk to me. Please?"

Harrell took Kimara by the arm and led her out of the studio. They walked a short way down the corridor and then he turned the doorknob to an empty lounge.

He sat her d( )m on the sofa and held both of her hands in his.

"I know it's not nerves Kimara 'cause you've got nerves of steel. So what's going on with you?"

"I feel like such an idiot," Kimara sighed, feeling a fresh pool of tears forming behind her eyes. She closed them and swallowed in an effort to push them back down to where they'd come from.

"I loved Jared so much, and I don't think I ever told him. And now . . . now it's too late."

Harrell put his arm around Kimara's shoulder and pulled her body until she was leaning into his. He rubbed her back as she began to shudder with the falling tears.

"Kimara, I don't know if this Jared guy was worth all this or not, but there is one lesson I have learned in my lifetime. That is, anything that is meant to be, will be. No matter what."

Kimara cried for a moment more and then sighed heavily. She wiped her face with the back of her hands and looked gratefully at Harrell. He had been so patient and helpful to her and was becoming a real friend. She knew, however, that he had a job to do. It was his job to make her do hers, and she hated inconveniencing him the way she had over the past couple of weeks.

Before she'd realized what had happened, this new-found career had become really important to her. She wanted to do a good job and she wanted to make all of the people proud who had invested so much time and money into her. At that moment, she made up her mind to be a professional and not let her broken heart ruin things for everyone around her. She stuck out a defiant chin and pulled herself from Harrell's embrace.

"Well, brother man, I guess this wasn't one of those things. But don't worry about it, I'm cool." She stood up and headed for the door. "Let's go lay down some tracks."

The rest of the session went much better, as Kimara

remained steadfast in her determination to block everything else out and concentrate on giving her all.

With seven completed songs, Speak Easy was only slightly behind schedule. The label was shooting for a December release for the album and had already begun promotions. Everything seemed to be happening so quickly that the group scarcely had time to process it all. For Delphina and Simone, who had been singing all of their lives separately and had come together earlier in the year, this journey was a long time in the making and they looked forward to all that lay ahead. Kimara, however, who up until a few months ago never dreamed she'd be signed to a record label and reciting her poetry for all the world to hear, looked toward the future with an equal dose of trepidation and excitement.

As everyone prepared to leave the studio, Kimara lagged behind. She didn't want to go to the apartment, but didn't want to go anywhere else either. For one fleeting moment, she thought about popping up on Jasmine's doorstep, but then nixed that idea. Jasmine had enough of her own problems. Just yesterday when Kimara spoke to her, she was complaining that her back was hurting and that she was beginning to doubt that she'd be able to work up until her thirty-sixth week of her pregnancy as she'd planned. Of course, the added stress of Rick pushing for them to move sooner rather than later had Jasmine feeling like she was being pulled in too many directions.

Kimara didn't want to bring her funky mood to Jasmine tonight, feeling certain that she would be pretty poor company. The last thing Jasmine needed was the added chore of trying to cheer Kimara up.

She sighed heavily as she stared at the music sheets for the group's next song. At a time when she should be experiencing nothing but happiness, it seemed as though the forces were conspiring against her. Ever since her breakup with Jared, she had been re-examining, among other things, her living arrangements. While Kimara did not blame Giselle for her having lost Jared, things were definitely strained between them. Giselle's partying had reached an all-time high and she had begun entertaining in the apartment on a nightly basis. Sometimes she and her friends got so loud that the neighbors complained. Giselle had received a letter from the co-op board, reminding her of the rules and regulations governing her tenancy, at which she just laughed. Kimara expressed to her that she should take their warning seriously, but Giselle simply tore the letter up without giving it another thought.

It was definitely time for Kimara to consider other living arrangements, but the task of searching for an apartment and moving seemed more than she could handle just then. It was everything she could do to concentrate on her poetry. Her days were divided between the studio and the vocal lessons that Harrell had her taking three days a week, in addition to her job at the club, where she still worked four nights a week.

She knew that it was just a matter of time before she'd have to leave Club Silhouette and she would definitely miss working there. Gino had been good to her, giving her the job even though she didn't know the first thing about mixing drinks. Lately, he had taken to questioning her about Giselle, who no longer worked at the club at all. He was worried about her and it showed all over his face. Kimara tried to assure him as best as she could that Giselle would be just fine, but she wasn't so sure she believed that herself. She tried talking to Giselle, but Giselle had a habit of making everything into a joke.

Kimara had so many things to work out right now, but lacked the motivation to do so. The loneliness which had invaded her soul recently was foreign to her. She was used to good times and carefree living. Now it seemed that when she wasn't paying attention, everything had changed. The real question was whether or not she was ready for the changes.

"Hey you. What are you still doing here?" Harrell said, entering the room and breaking Kimara's train of thought. He sat down on the sofa next to Kimara and placed his hand over hers.

"Just hanging around. What about you?" Kimara asked.

"Had a meeting with the boys upstairs. They're really excited about this project you know. They're sure you ladies will be the next TLC."

"That's good," Kimara said somberly.

Harrell didn't like the lack of enthusiasm which underscored Kimara's tone.

"You're really down in the dumps, aren't you? This guy Jared must have been the real deal," Harrell suggested.

"It's not just that. I don't know, Harrell . . . I feel like my life is somehow spinning out of control. Don't get me wrong, I'm happy to be here and to be giving this music thing a try. Never in my wildest dreams did I picture anything like this happening to me. And believe me, I know it's a once-in-a-lifetime opportunity. I don't want you to think I don't appreciate everything you've done for me," Kimara said.

"I don't think that. I'm just worried about you," Harrell said. He had begun to regard Kimara as a little sister of sorts. There was no doubt that she was a beautiful woman and he knew that under different circumstances, he might very well have tried to hook up with her. But right now, he couldn't afford to have any sort of entanglements. It was vital to his career that Speak Easy blew up. In essence, their success would be a win for him, one that his career needed desperately. He was thirty-two years old and had spent the last ten years running around this business, doing whatever he had to do to get down.

He had been at Smithtown for the past four years, toiling away. There had been no task too menial, no responsibility too trite. The way you made it in the recording business was to make contacts, put yourself in the right places at the right times and build a reputation as a "can do" sort of person. The project with Speak Easy was his first real opportunity to fly solo, and he didn't have any intentions of letting it flop.

Seeing the light having dimmed in Kimara's eyes now, underscored another reason why he would not allow himself to view her in anything but a platonic fashion. Her heart belonged to another man and probably would for a long time to come. While he prided himself on being somewhat of a good catch, he knew from experience that it didn't matter how much you had it going on, once a woman had given her heart to someone, nobody else stood a chance. He just hoped for Kimara's sake that she either got over this guy or worked things out with him. He hated to see a wonderful woman like Kimara suffering so, and he also didn't want to see her sabotage what could be a great career for herself.

"I know you're worried Harrell, but don't be. I promise you, I'm not the type of person who hangs around down in dumpsville for long. I've just got to get focused and straighten a few things out."

"Anything I can help out with?" Harrell asked with genuine interest. If he could help Kimara find balance in her life, he'd do so gladly.

"First thing I need to do is find an apartment. Second, I think it's time I quit working at the club."

"I thought you liked that place."

"Yeah, I did. But right now, I think I need to devote all of my time to this. Besides, I'm supposed to be getting paid lovely now, as Smithtown's brand-new recording star," Kimara joked.

They label allotted Speak Easy an album budget of six hundred thousand dollars, which, while it sounded like a great sum of money, would easily be stretched to the max. From that figure, each member of the group was given a fifty thousand dollar advance. In addition, that budget was designed to cover the video costs, production costs, costumes, vocal and speech coaches, and more. While Kimara had also received a bonus of fifty thousand dollars upon signing the contract, she was extremely far from making Janet Jackson-type money. She had no intentions of blowing through that money until she knew for sure that more would follow.

"You ladies do your thing in the studio and then on the road, and you'll be writing your own ticket before you know it," Harrell promised. "Hey, I've got an idea. Come with me," he said, pulling Kimara up from the sofa.

They took the elevator down to the garage level and retrieved Harrell's black Camry from its reserved space. Harrell drove downtown as Kimara sat in the passenger seat, quietly watching the busy city streets zip by. When Harrell finally pulled over they were in the heart of Tribeca—downtown Manhattan's premiere residential district. He parked in front of a warehouse-looking structure on Reade Street.

"Who lives down here?" Kimara asked.

"Possibly you—in your new apartment," he answered, shutting the engine off.

"What are you talking about Harrell?" Kimara asked.

"Just come on," Harrell said getting out of the car.

Kimara followed him into the building. He rang the bell marked superintendent and waited. After a couple of minutes, they heard the muffled sound of slippered feet making their way to the door.

"Who is it?"

"Uncle James, it's Harrell. Open up man."

"Hey, boy," James said as he opened the door and hugged Harrell. "Whatcha doing downtown?" he asked. Looking over Harrell's shoulder, he spotted Kimara.

"Hi," she said waving.

"Hello young lady," James said, stepping aside to allow the pair to enter his apartment.

"Uncle James, this is Kimara Hamilton. Kimara, this is my Uncle James. He's the super of this building. Uncle James, Kimara is part of that new group I told you I was working with."

"Nice to meet you," Kimara said, shaking James extended hand.

"Oh, so you're a singer?" James asked.

"No, not really. I do poetry, spoken word stuff," Kimara answered. It was the first time she had referred to herself that way, falling short of actually using the word poet. In spite of herself, she realized that she liked the fact that what she was doing had a definition to it. Something that people could understand and appreciate.

"Listen, Uncle James. Is that apartment upstairs still vacant?"

"The studio? Why, yes it is," James said, scratching the stubble on his chin. "Had somebody in this morning, but she never called back so I'll be showing it again tomorrow. Why do you ask?"

"Kimara is looking for a new apartment. You think she could take a look at it?"

"Well, I don't see why not. The landlord is using a realty company, but it's been vacant for a couple of weeks now. They definitely don't like losing money. Hold on a minute, let me get my keys."

A few minutes later, after climbing a flight of stairs to the second floor, Kimara was standing in the middle of a huge studio apartment.

"There are six apartments in this building, beside mine and they're all lofts but they differ in size and design. This one is one of the smallest and it's only got one main room, a kitchen and a bathroom," Uncle James explained.

The floors were covered with terra-cotta tiles. The apartment's two windows were huge, almost floor to ceiling, and they faced Church Street, a busy main street filled with numerous art galleries, photography studios and other businesses. The kitchen nook contained brand-new sparkling white Kenmore appliances, earth-toned granite countertops and retracted ceiling lights.

"I like this," Kimara said, as she peered into the apartment's solitary closet, a huge walk-in one. The bathroom was small and square, with the toilet cramped between the sink and the bathtub. However, the bathtub was almost as spacious as the one in Giselle's apartment.

"How much are they asking?" Kimara inquired when she returned to the main room.

"A thousand a month, utilities included," James said.

Kimara did the math in her head. She had yet to spend any of the money she'd received from the label and had also managed to save a few pennies from the club over the past few weeks. Ironically, her breakup with Jared had left her in such a funk, she hadn't felt much like partying or shopping, two of her favorite pastimes. Staying home night after night had proved seriously beneficial to her bank account.

Kimara beamed. "Well, Uncle James, I want it! How soon can I move in?"

"If is was up to me sweetheart, I'd say right now. But you're going to have to fill out an application and leave fifty dollars for a credit check. You got good credit darling?" Uncle James said, raising his eyebrows.

"Yes, Uncle James. My credit is good." Kimara smiled, crossing her fingers. With the exception of her cell phone, which she had occasionally paid a little late, she was sure that she didn't have any outstanding or delinquent debt.

Over the past twenty years Tribeca had gone through a rebirth of sorts. Bordered on the north by Canal Street, the east by Broadway, the west by the Hudson River and the south by Vesey Street, it was previously an industrial area, once considered the dry goods capital of the country. Now, Tribeca was home to artists and small business entrepreneurs, as well as families. The spacious apartments were attractive to New Yorkers, as much as the artistic atmosphere and trendy venues. Kimara knew that she would fit in well downtown, away from the elitism of her current Central Park address and the stuffiness of midtown Manhattan.

"Okay then. You know how some of us are—credit bad as I don't know what but we're running around applying for stuff everywhere!" James laughed.

"So how soon do you think she could get the place?" Harrell asked.

"The apartment's all ready. If everything checks out, I'd say the first of the month. How's that?"

"That's perfect. Thank you so much," Kimara said.

They went back downstairs to James' apartment, where Kimara filled out the application, giving her parents' and Jasmine's contact information as references and wrote a check. Back in Harrell's car, Kimara could hardly contain her excitement.

"This is so cool. I like it down here. And you know that rent is dirt cheap for Manhattan right? Look, over there on Duane Street is that gallery/café, A Taste of Art. I used to hang out down here with this guy I was dating a couple of years ago. There is so much to do. There's the Hudson Lounge, which is hot and the Elixir Juice Bar. Ooh, and you can get to almost any subway line from down here. And—"

"I take it you're pleased?" Harrell said, amused by Kimara's enthusiasm. It was good to see a smile back on her pretty face, and he was proud that he had played a part in putting it there.

"Oh Harrell, this is perfect. Thank you so much for looking out for me. I can't believe my luck," Kimara said.

She thought briefly about Giselle. She knew that she

would be disappointed when Kimara told her she was moving out, but it was definitely for the best. She hoped that they could remain friends but part of her knew that Giselle was in a place in her life where Kimara just didn't fit in and vice versa.

Kimara's next concern was the fact that for the first time, she would be living alone. The thought gave her pause as she thought about her safety.

"Relax. Uncle James is right downstairs and believe me, he's a pretty tough old dude," Harrell said when Kimara expressed her concern. "Besides, I'm right over the bridge in Brooklyn. Any problems, you just call me and I'll be there in ten minutes flat."

A brief moment of silence passed before Harrell broke into the Jackson 5's 1970 hit, "I'll Be There." Kimara begged him to keep his day job because singing was not one of his strong points. The comment prompted laughter from both of them.

"Harrell, you can't spend all your time taking care of me. I'm sure you've got enough to do without having to babysit me," Kimara remarked seriously.

Harrell smiled. "Nah, I really don't have anything else to do. Besides, I can't have my star falling to pieces on me. We need you."

"You are great guy, you know that? I'm sure your girl-friend is not going to be too pleased about you running around New York rescuing me from myself."

"There you go. For your information, I'm not seeing anybody right now. I've got, correction, *we've* got too much work to do to be losing our heads chasing after love. So, Ms. Hamilton, now that we've all but got your living arrangements taken care of, what else can we do to make it all better?" Harrell asked.

The earnestness with which Harrell asked that ques-tion made Kimara look at him more intently than she had ever done in the past. He was a very attractive man, a fact that hadn't gone unnoticed by her previously.

However, she had met Harrell at a time when she only had eyes for one man. Now that the place that once held Jared's image was vacant, she was able to appreciate Harrell's handsome profile.

Briefly, she let her mind wander to the possibility of a romance with Harrell. People swore all the time that the best way to get over a broken heart was to move on. Almost as quickly as the thought entered her mind, she dismissed it. The last thing she needed was to complicate her life by getting involved with someone she had to work so closely with. She did, however, definitely intend to move on. It was apparent that Jared had, so why shouldn't she. She'd find someone new too, and erase all memories of old what's his name.

"Nothing at all, I promise. I'm going to get my head on straight and trust me, I won't be dragging ass anymore," Kimara said with conviction.

Chapter 29

The feeble waves lapped lazily against the rocky shore. Kimara watched their foamy advance and subsequent retreat back into the ocean. Behind her, in the house, the music played loudly and conversation flowed as effortlessly as the Cristal. She had escaped the festivities by stepping through the sliding glass doors and out onto the verandah, shutting the door behind her.

The South Beach house belonged to Bronson Chandler, a senior A&R at Smithtown. He was Harrell's boss, as well as superior to the other A&Rs at the label. A&Rs were charged with the responsibility of identifying new talent for the label. As a senior A&R, Bronson served as the liaison between the A&Rs, the producers and the artists on one side and the vice presidents, and the label president and CEO on the other. Bronson had invited a bunch of Smithtown artists to his house for a celebration. They'd flown into Miami early that morning and were scheduled to spend the next couple of days meeting with, among other people, a famous production team who worked out of Miami. Bronson took Speak Easy on a personal tour of the city when they'd arrived that morning. Tonight, as they partied at his private beachfront house, the young artists got their first real taste of the good life. The champagne flowed in rooms dotted with celebrities and label executives. Caviar and other exotic delicacies were carried around on trays by a large waitstaff as people elbowed their way into exclusive circles vying for attention.

For Kimara, it was all a bit overwhelming. She despised the pomposity which clung to many of the party's inhabitants and couldn't stand the wide-eyed adoration which seemed to follow them around the room. This was one part of celebrity life that she knew she would never be able to get used to—once she became a celebrity. People were too caught up in the fantasy of what famous people were supposed to be like to acknowledge the fact that famous people were just like them. No better, no worse.

"Planning a quick getaway?" Bronson asked as he joined Kimara on the verandah.

"Huh? Oh no, just getting some air," she responded.

"Let me freshen that up for you," he said, motioning to the almost empty glass in her hand. He filled her glass from the bottle of Cristal he carried, then added more to his own glass.

"These type of parties can be a bit much to take in, I know, but you'll have to get used to them because it's part of the game. This is where you'll do a lot of business, make contacts, you know what I'm saying? More work gets done at a party than in the office all day long," Bronson instructed.

"I guess I do have a lot to get used to," Kimara agreed.

"You should stick around after the party. I can give you a crash course in the business—you know, what to expect, what to watch out for."

"Thanks Bronson, that's sweet of you. But I'm going to head back to the hotel soon. It's late, and we've got a long day ahead of us tomorrow. In addition to the meeting with the guys at Brainstorm, Harrell wants to meet with some beat makers while we're down here."

"Nonsense. You won't turn into a pumpkin. Besides, I have plenty of room. If it gets too late, you can crash here," Bronson all but ordered.

"Again, Bronson, it's nice of you to offer, but I'm going to have to take a raincheck. Harrell expects us to get an early start in the morning," Kimara answered, uncomfortable with the tone of insistence apparent in Bronson's voice.

Bronson Chandler was a tall, light-skinned black man who wore his hair in a low Caesar. His wire-framed, tinted Gucci glasses hid eyes that were small and set far back into his head, giving him a sinister look. His pearly white smile seemed to have been snatched right from the pages of a toothpaste advertisement, but it seemed fake, as if thoughts quite the opposite of those that rested on his lips lurked in his mind. He was the type of man who was used to getting what he wanted. He was new-money rich and flaunted it shamelessly. Bronson thought that Versace suits and alligator shoes were his ticket through life. He was pretentious, conceited and arrogant—three traits which were at the top of Kimara's hate list.

Kimara fought to remain cool as Bronson eyed her with a self-assured stance. Despite her dislike of the man, he was the boss, and she knew that he had his finger over the controls when it came to her project. She didn't want to piss him off, but deal or no deal, she wasn't about to be used. She smiled as she gathered her shawl around her shoulders and prepared to leave.

Bronson, however, did not return the gesture. No was not a word that was said to him often and he honestly didn't seem to know what to do on the rare occasions, like now, when it was directed at him. He stared intently at Kimara before letting out a loud, shallow laugh.

"Look, I know right now you think Harrell is the man because he got you into Smithtown and he's got you in the studio laying down songs and what not. But let me tell you something you may not know. Harrell is nothing but a street urchin. One word from me and he'd be back out on the block with his boom box harmonizing and spitting rhymes with the other bums. He doesn't call any shots. I, on the other hand, I'm on the fast track to the president's office. One day real soon, I'll be running everything at Smithtown. And—" He paused as he threw back the remains of his drink. "I can either make things real good for young, sexy artists like yourself, or . . ."

A nasty leer hung from Bronson's filthy mouth. He reached forward to stroke her hair and Kimara quickly ducked her head, moving out of his reach. Her eyes shot daggers at him as she quickly stepped around him and moved across the verandah, re-entering the house through the glass doors.

"Hey girl, where are you go—" Simone began as Kimara breezed past her. Kimara neither saw nor heard her, as blind fury brewed within.

Kimara continued walking, pushing her way through the crowd as she made a beeline to the door. From across the room, Harrell spotted her. He then turned to see Bronson trailing her, the color drained from his face, making him appear even lighter than his natural complexion. Harrell jumped up and followed Kimara. As she reached the door, Bronson put his hand on her shoulder. She shrugged it off forcefully just as Harrell approached.

"Hold up Kimara," Harrell said, looking Bronson squarely in the face. "I'll drive you back to the hotel."

"Thanks," Kimara said. She continued through the door. Bronson took another step in her direction before Harrell cut him off.

"Back off man," he spat, squaring off with Bronson. Bronson, the taller of the two was also the frailer man. He didn't stand a chance against Harrell, whose eyes warned Bronson of this fact.

"Whatever," Bronson said as he turned his back on Harrell and headed back into the party.

Kimara was waiting beside Harrell's rental car, parked at the beginning of the circular driveway, when he approached. He clicked the locks and Kimara hastily snatched open the door and jumped inside. She cursed as she broke a nail slamming the door shut behind her. Harrell got in and started the engine without saying a word. He backed out of the driveway and turned onto the secluded road which would lead them back onto the highway. He sped away, driving for several minutes, eager to put some distance between them and the party. Finally, he pulled over to the shoulder of the road, the tires spinning as they hit the dirt and gravel, and placed the car in park.

"What happened?" he asked. He had noticed the special attention Bronson had been paying to Kimara since she'd come on board. It was subtle at first and didn't raise suspicion in Harrell initially. Bronson didn't spend much time in the studio with the artists, although he did drop by on occasion to see how the projects were progressing. From what Harrell observed, he'd always been cordial and encouraging in his exchanges with Speak Easy. But Harrell knew a snake in the grass when he saw one and he knew that Bronson was as slimy as they come. The man chased skirts like it was open duck-hunting season and his penis was his rifle. He flashed his cash and credentials, and boasted and bragged his way into many a bed.

When Harrell spied him chatting Kimara up a couple of times in New York and more intently since they'd arrived in Florida, he was inclined to warn her. After thinking on the matter more, he realized that his concerns were unwarranted. Kimara was far from being some starstruck, ignorant little groupie and Bronson's charms would be wasted on her. The more he thought about it, the more he thought that maybe it was Bronson who

should be warned. Kimara was round-the-way tough and
he was certain she could cut a brother down to his knees
if she needed to.

"That tacky, wanna-be down, son of a bitch had the
nerve to try to push up on me—hard too. Like I would
be interested in his sorry behind. He's so full of himself,
so arrogant. I hate brothers like that. He gave me this
look like who am I to turn him down. Oooh, Harrell,
you don't know. It was all I could do not to punch him
dead in his face," Kimara shouted. Her hands were
shaking as if itching to make physical contact with Bronson and her heart pounded furiously in her chest.

Kimara had never been one to fight. Although her
self-assured, militant demeanor would lead people to
think otherwise, she actually hated confrontation and
avoided it wherever possible. In school and around the
neighborhood as children, it had been Jasmine who
balled up her fists and lashed out more often than
Kimara. Jasmine, who seemed like the more mild-
mannered of the two, would pounce the second that
she felt that her own honor or safety or that of Kimara's
were in jeopardy. Kimara had grudgingly learned from
Jasmine and from her own mother that sometimes
people will back you into a corner and at that point, you
had to be just as ferocious as they were to avoid being
swallowed whole. Bronson had barked up the wrong
tree that day, thinking she was one of these easily in-
timidated young girls who were so starved for fame and
fortune that they would willingly barter flesh to get it.
Kimara had never wanted anything that badly in her life
and no matter how much flash was dangled before her,
she couldn't see herself ever becoming that desperate.
For Kimara, flesh and soul were intricately woven together and could not be cut up into little pieces and
sold at a swap meet.

"All right, all right, calm down Kimara," Harrell said,
attempting to soothe her, while his own anger had him

seeing red. "That bastard," he snapped suddenly, slamming his fist against the steering wheel. "I should drive back up there and beat him down".

"No, Harrell, don't do that. Hey, weren't you just telling me to calm down?" Kimara asked. They looked at one another for a few seconds, before smiles and then outright laughter took over. The outburst served to relieve the stress that had both of their bodies tense and wound so tightly that they threatened to pop like a string on an overworked guitar.

"We're a mess," Kimara said finally. Once again she was amazed to see how much Harrell cared about her. He had taken her side and had her back without the slightest hint of hesitation. "Listen, I don't want to drag you into this. He's still your boss, you know?"

"So what? That doesn't give him the right to treat you like that. That punk thinks he's above the rules, but I've got another trick for his ass," Harrell said.

He was sick of guys like Bronson, who ran around thinking they had the game on lock. The music business was full of Bronsons, guys with no talent and no real love for the music, but who were guided by the almighty dollar and snaked and sniveled around in order to get it. Guys like Bronson Chandler thought they were more important than they ever would be in reality. They expected respect but were ill-equipped at doling it out.

Harrell had never had any affection for Bronson, but he had treated the man with the professional courtesy which his position as senior A&R deserved. As long as Bronson had stayed out of Harrell's way and left his artists, producers and crew alone, they had no beef. Obviously, that unspoken understanding had been broken and things had changed. There would be some repercussions behind Bronson's disrespectful treatment of Kimara today. Harrell would make sure of that, no matter what it cost him.

"Listen Kimara, I don't want you to worry about

Bronson. Just concentrate on this project and let me take care of that punk. Now, let's go have some fun," Harrell said suddenly, a smile softening his angered expression.

They drove along the coast, lush scenery bringing a serenity to both of them and serving to push to the background the unpleasantness of the episode with Bronson. They found parking near Washington Avenue just as the sun set and the bright lights of downtown Miami lit their way.

Harrell took her hand as they strolled down the numerous blocks, crowded with people from all walks of life. To the average onlooker they appeared to be just another handsome couple. To them, they were two people who had met under the guise of business but had become the kind of friends for whom sex and sexuality were not an issue. They were comfortable with one another and had formed a camaraderie in the fickle business of making music. Kimara felt as if she had known Harrell for years and knew instinctively that she could trust him to have her back with no strings attached. Dealing with men like Bronson Chandler would be made all the more easy just because she knew she had someone like Harrell on her side. For his part, he enjoyed Kimara's company, enjoyed her humor and her vivaciousness and none of that had anything to do with wanting to be anything more than friends. Thus, the easy nature of their relationship made sharing the experience of South Beach nightlife all the more special.

Ocean Drive was a virtual party in itself. They stopped at one of the many restaurants on the strip and Kimara bought an order of fried calamari. She tried with all her might to get Harrell to take a bite, but he turned up his nose, refusing to eat something that had once had that many arms. A steel band played outside of another restaurant, while listeners danced along the sidewalk like they were in a club. It wasn't long before the beat caught hold of Kimara and she dragged Harrell into the middle of the mix to dance.

"You're wild," he laughed in spite of himself.

By midnight they were at Wet Willie's, a popular watering hole, sipping on daiquiris and sharing more of their life stories. A karaoke machine was set up at the back of the bar and patrons took turns singing popular tunes in predominately awful voices.

"I bet you won't get up there," Harrell said, pointing to the microphone.

The two daiquiris Kimara had consumed caused her to lose all inhibition. With a wicked smile, Kimara downed the rest of her drink and made her way to the back of the bar. She flipped through the selections offered, made a pick and when the microphone was free, she stepped up. Whistles came from the crowd as two burly men lifted Kimara onto a table, the makeshift stage, and handed her the mike.

The music began and Kimara blew a kiss toward Harrell who laughed. The words appeared on the screen and she began performing Angie Stone's "Brotha". It wasn't long before she had the crowd jumping, singing and clapping along with her. Once again, she felt that high that came from being able to move people with the sound of her voice and she loved every minute of it. Two songs later Harrell good-naturedly dragged her from the stage and out of the bar, cheers sailing after them.

They ended the evening strolling on the beach behind the Fontainbleau Hilton, the resort at which they were staying. The temperature still hovered in the low seventies, a warm breeze blowing across the sands.

"I'm so excited about this project, it's all I can think about these days," Harrell said.

"I still feel like none of this is really happening. Like I'm dreaming or something. I don't know what to make of it all," Kimara responded.

"All you have to concentrate on is the fact that you're about to blow up. You're gonna be a star, girl. Soon, people are going to be screaming your name and running you down for an autograph. Watch, you'll see."

"I don't know about all that. I just know that being in the studio feels so good. It's like making magic when the girls and I get in there and a vibe gets going. We're in the zone and it's all good. I never knew I could enjoy something so much," Kimara revealed.

Harrell laughed. "And just think . . . you were playing all hard to get at first. I practically had to wrestle you down to get you to give it a try."

"Okay funny man, you don't have to go there," Kimara said, punching Harrell softly in his arm.

They walked the length of the beach, enjoying the night air and each other's company. It was very late when they entered the hotel and went to their respective rooms. Before they parted, Harrell repeated his earlier promise to Kimara that he would take care of Bronson. He vowed not to let Bronson upset or harm her in any way. Kimara knew that she could take him at his word, and knowing that made her rest easy that night. Besides, she had come too far to let a man as insignificant as Bronson throw her off track.

Chapter 30

"What's up girl," Kimara asked Jasmine.

"Kimara, I can't talk to you right now. I'll call you back later," Jasmine said before hanging up without waiting for an answer.

Kimara was surprised by Jasmine's abruptness and started to dial her back immediately, but decided against it. She had not spoken to her since she and Rick had left for a long weekend in Virginia two days ago. He had convinced her to drive down with him to look at a few properties and while she had not committed to a firm move date yet, she was willing to at least allow him to put things in motion.

Kimara was saddened by the thought that Jasmine would be moving so far away from home, but she realized that she could not selfishly expect her not to go. Jasmine was a married woman with a child on the way and those had to be her first priorities. As much as she would miss having her nearby, she kept reminding herself that their friendship was a lot stronger than a five-hour car ride. Besides, who knew what avenues this new career would take her down. She would definitely have to travel away from New York herself, and it was unfair to expect Jasmine to stay put while she did not.

Things had gone well in Miami. The producers they met with were feeling Speak Easy's style and were eager to work with them. The team's services were pricey, but would be well worth it. Harrell hammered out the details for a two song production deal and received immediate approval from the label heads. The remainder of their time in Miami was spent meeting with stylists and video directors as they worked to create the group's visual image.

Upon their return to New York, Harrell had them back in the studio immediately. The time was approaching when the label heads would want to hear the project in its entirety. From past experience, Harrell knew that there would be a few songs that would not get approved because someone would either feel they weren't right for the group or didn't fit with the rest of the album. Therefore, he wanted to have a minimum of eighteen completed tracks for the boys upstairs to select from.

Kimara continued practicing the new song the group would be working on in the studio the following day. She glanced at the clock and noted that a couple of hours remained before she'd have to head downtown to meet with her speech coach. That in itself was a trip. Here she had been talking all of her life, believing herself to be fairly articulate and now she had some guy reteaching her everything from diction, to pronunciation, to tone. It was his job to prepare her to appear before an audience and to give interviews in which she was engaging and well spoken. She needed to be able to lob questions like a tennis pro and at the same time to make whomever she was dealing with feel connected. Unlike many people, this came very easy to Kimara since she was an extrovert who loved dialogue and loved people. However, Professor Poissant still felt like she had a ways to go. He was working her harder than her high school English teacher had. A middle-aged speech therapist by trade, he took himself so seriously that it was difficult for Kimara not to crack up in his face every time they met. She couldn't believe the behind-the-scenes work which she was now discovering went in to creating the artists who ended up on television and on stage.

Just as her thoughts drifted back to Jasmine and her weird behavior, the phone rang.

"Hello?"

"Hey girl, it's me. Sorry I had to cut you off earlier."

"Yeah, that was extremely rude. What's going on down there?"

"You would not believe the drama if I told you," Jasmine said, her voice sounding tired.

"What happened now?" Kimara asked.

"You will never in a million years believe who I ran into yesterday."

"Who?" Kimara asked, intrigued. She closed the binder of sheet music and lyrics from which she had been reading and sat up on her bed.

"Rick had been dealing with these two guys who own their own land development business. Basically what they do is buy vacant lots and build new homes on them which they sell for a substantial profit. Anyway, we had an appointment with them yesterday morning to see a home that they'd just finished and had recently placed on the market."

"Okay."

"Rick never mentioned the company name and I never asked, but when we pulled up to the house, I saw their sign on the lawn."

"Uh-huh."

"It read Mitchell & Bigelow Developers, Inc."

Kimara repeated the name, not understanding the importance of it.

"So?"

"*Mitchell*," Jasmine said again.

Kimara sat silent for a moment, trying to figure out

what Jasmine was getting at. All of a sudden, a light
came on in her head. "No!" she gasped, surprise knock-
ing the wind out of her lungs.

"Yes," Jasmine said. "He came out of the house when
we pulled into the driveway. It was him. Sixteen years
older, but otherwise looking exactly the same as the last
time I'd seen him."

"Jasmine, please tell me that you're not saying the
man Rick is trying to buy a house from is your father?"

"It was him Kimara. I couldn't believe it. I couldn't
move. Rick got out of the car and came around to my
side, but I couldn't move. He kept asking me what was
wrong, but I couldn't speak either. I just sat there."

"Oh my God! This is surreal." Kimara could scarcely
catch her breath as she listened to Jasmine. "What happened?"

"Well, finally Rick was able to pull me from the car,
but I could not walk, even if my life depended on it. I
just leaned against the hood. Rick called him over and
was about to introduce us when I told him there was
no need. That man looked me in the face and I could
tell he had no idea who I was."

"Stop."

"No Kimara, I'm serious. He was all smiles, right up
until I said, 'Hello, Daddy.' Then he looked like he was
gonna pee in his pants."

Kimara remembered the day that Jasmine's father
moved out of the family home. The girls were ten years
old and it was the middle of a very hot and humid
summer. Early one Saturday morning Jasmine had
come over to Kimara's house to watch Saturday morning cartoons as was their usual routine. They had just
finished watching an episode of the Power Rangers
when the telephone rang. It was Mrs. Mitchell calling.

"Jasmine, your mom wants you to come home now,
sweetheart," Kimara's mother yelled from the kitchen.

"Come with me," Jasmine had asked nervously.

"You in trouble?" Kimara wanted to know. She picked up their empty cereal bowls and headed toward the kitchen. She placed the bowls in the sink and followed Jasmine to the front door, where she slid into her sneakers.

"I don't think so," Jasmine said. "My mom and dad were arguing when I left though."

Kimara could tell that Jasmine was worried about something, so she followed her home without a word of protest.

Mr. Mitchell had always been a pretty quiet man. Likeable and lenient would be how Kimara would have described him. Nothing could have prepared her for what they saw and heard when they walked the two blocks to Jasmine's house and found Mr. Mitchell shoving bags of clothing into the back of his Toyota.

"Here she is, here she is," Mrs. Mitchell yelled. "Tell your daughter what you're doing Howard. Tell her to her face. Don't be a coward and try to just slip away."

Mr. Mitchell looked his wife squarely in the face and the look of rage he wore was undeniable. Jasmine and Kimara stood side by side on the front lawn, dumbfounded. Finally, after several long moments in which Kimara, feeling like she was witnessing something she shouldn't and wishing she could disappear, Mr. Mitchell slammed the trunk of his car shut and walked over to Jasmine.

"Princess," he said grimly, "Daddy's gotta go away. I'm gonna call you . . . real soon and we'll talk about everything. I promise." He kissed Jasmine on the forehead and turned away quickly. He jumped into his car and sped off without looking back.

Mrs. Mitchell began wailing and ran inside the house. Kimara and Jasmine continued standing on the lawn, numb and unsure of what to do.

"You wanna go back to my house?" Kimara asked.

Jasmine shook her head and proceeded to walk toward her house. She stood in front of the open door for a minute before going inside and shutting the door behind her.

Kimara turned and walked the two blocks back to her house alone. When she arrived and told her parents what had happened, her mother advised her to give Jasmine some time alone and not to go back over there that day. Kimara didn't really understand what had happened, but she knew that it was something that Jasmine wouldn't get over any time soon. Later that evening Kimara's mother baked a pan of lasagna and took it over to Jasmine's house. She stayed over there for almost two hours and when she returned home she explained to Kimara that Jasmine's parents were getting a divorce and that, naturally, Jasmine was pretty torn up about it.

Indeed, Jasmine spent the next few weeks falling into crying spells and she hardly came out of the house at all. Kimara visited her faithfully, bringing her pop rocks and Now & Laters from the candy store, ice cream when the Good Humor trucked rolled down the block, and trying to make her laugh with tales of fights and folly from the neighborhood. Jasmine's father never called and after a few months, she stopped sitting by the telephone. Eventually, she stopped talking about him as much, rarely mentioning him. It was as if he'd died or something, only this was worse because knowing he was out there somewhere and just chose not to be in touch with her cut like a knife. Jasmine never got over it, but she did move on. Kimara could only imagine what a shock it must have been to stumble upon him the way she had.

"Wow. Talk about it being a small world. So what happened next?" Kimara asked now.

"Well, Rick was standing there with his mouth wide open and all of a sudden I had to go to the bathroom—badly. We went into the house, and I used the bathroom and when I came out, they were sitting on the front porch and Rick's mouth was still wide open. I was like, 'Babe, close your mouth before you swallow a fly.'"

"You're crazy," Kimara laughed. "What was your father doing?"

"He was staring at me, like I was an apparition or something. Then he started crying, talking about how much he'd missed me and how beautiful I was and how sorry he was. I'm looking at him, thinking to myself, 'Look at this clown.' Finally, I couldn't stand anymore. I told Rick to get me out of there. We got in the car and drove away, back to Rick's mother's house, and left his silly behind standing there blubbering."

"That's cold. Well deserved, but cold just the same."

"He's lucky I didn't spit in his face," Jasmine said.

"I know, I know. How are you feeling now?" Kimara asked, concerned because Jasmine sounded like she was out of breath.

"I haven't slept a wink and my back is killing me. It feels like my diaphragm is being pushed up into my throat. On top of that the baby's been resting on one side of my body and it feels like pins are being stuck in my thigh. I'm a mess and so is Rick. He's falling all over himself trying to make up for it all, like it's his fault that my father is a reject."

"Well, he probably feels bad because he's the one that was pushing for this move and hooked up with your father's company and all. I mean, Jazz, this is the wackiest coincidence I've ever heard of in my entire life."

"I know," Jasmine agreed wearily.

"So what are you going to do?"

"I don't know. He's been calling here nonstop and begging to talk to me. Rick is about two seconds from going out and whipping his butt. But I don't know. Yesterday I was sure that I didn't want to talk to him, but today . . ."

"Today you realize that you need to talk to him, huh?" Kimara sympathized.

"Yeah."

"Look, Jazz, just call the man up and listen to what he has to say. After that, if you still feel like telling him where to go, then by all means do it. But you need to just get it over with, one way or the other and move on."

"You're right. Man, this is about the last thing I needed to deal with right now."

"I know baby girl, but you'll be all right. If you want, I can catch a train down there. That way I can hold him down while you pimp-slap him," Kimara offered. This prompted a much needed laugh from Jasmine.

"No, I got this one, but thanks girl. I'll call you later on."

"All right. Try and get some rest. I don't want my god-baby coming out all stressed and old looking, just 'cause her mama's bugging out. Okay?"

"Later, crazy."

Jasmine hung up, while Kimara sat holding the telephone in her hands, still too dazed to act. She hoped for Mr. Mitchell's sake whatever excuses he offered for abandoning Jasmine the way he had had better be good.

Later that night, after her speech session, Kimara was back at Giselle's apartment packing her belongings. She had gotten the studio just as Harrell's Uncle James had promised and was all set to move in the following week. She hadn't seen Giselle since she'd received the news and the note she'd left on her bedroom door telling her that they needed to talk was still taped there, untouched. All Gino could tell her was that Giselle had left him a voice mail message stating that she was going to Cancun for a few days with some friends, but expected to be back by Sunday. Today was Tuesday and nothing. Kimara had every intention of telling Giselle face to face that she was moving out and she was also going to pay her share of next month's rent since it was such short notice. However, if Giselle didn't return by the week's end, Kimara intended to turn the keys and the money over to Gino and be done with the whole situation.

Cleaning out her dresser drawers, she came across a police academy sweatshirt which belonged to Jared. In a moment of nostalgic regress, Kimara pulled the sweatshirt over her head and slid her arms into the sleeves. She wrapped her arms around herself and sniffed the sweatshirt. All she could smell was Downy fabric softener; no Jared. She pulled the sweatshirt over her head, balled it up and tossed it in the wastebasket. If she was going to go full speed into the fabulous future, there was no sense in hanging on to remnants of the painful past.

By eleven o'clock Kimara had the three suitcases and the garment bag she'd first come to Giselle's place with all packed up. Additionally, she had five boxes of books, photographs, linen and other personal items taped shut and stacked against a wall. Two more boxes remained open to receive the items she would continue to use over the next few days. The only furnishings belonging to her were the television set, the stereo and a beanbag chair. She had reserved a U-haul van which Harrell had graciously agreed to drive for her on moving day.

Kimara lay in bed eating a bowl of strawberry ice cream when her telephone rang. Jasmine's cell number flashed in the caller identification.

"How'd it go?" she asked, skipping the preliminaries as she pressed the mute button on her television's remote control.

"Let's just say that you could knock me over with a feather right now," Jasmine answered.

"What happened?"

"Okay, okay, I'm going to tell you, but it ain't pretty. I had Rick call him and invite him over. He came and brought his partner with him, a Robert Bigelow. Mr. Bigelow is European, born and raised in London. He's in his mid-fifties, nice looking man. But the thing that struck me the moment I met him were his mannerisms. Now, while I'm not one to judge a book by its cover, the moment we shook hands I could tell that he was gay."

"Okay, so your father's partner is gay. So what about it?"

"No, Kimara, you're not hearing me. When I said his partner, I didn't just mean his business partner. I meant his partner partner."

"Get the hell out of here!" Kimara screamed into the phone. She dropped the bowl containing the remaining ice cream onto her lap. As melted ice cream spread across the comforter and down its side, the bomb Jasmine had just dropped commanded all of her attention.

"Kimara, I swear I'm not lying. You can't possibly imagine how I tripped out over that one. Here I was expecting my father to come in there telling me about how hard it was living with my mother, or how oppressed he felt by society, or I don't know, anything but that he was gay and that's why he left my mother and me," Jasmine said.

Jasmine was laying on a queen-sized bed in the guest room of her mother-in-law's home, rubbing her belly. Rick had just gone out to get her some frozen yogurt and she was anxiously awaiting his return. She had been unable to eat all day long, feeling nauseated at the sight or smell of food. A few moments ago she had gotten a craving for something cold and sweet and Rick, eager to get something in her stomach, had made a mad dash in search of an open grocery store or ice cream parlor.

"This is some straight up Montell Williams, Sally Jesse Raphael crap. Please tell me you're pulling my leg Jasmine. Please?"

"Sorry my friend, but it's the God's honest truth. He explained that all of his life he had been in turmoil regarding his sexuality. He said that while he'd truly loved my mother as a person, he was not happy. When he finally admitted the truth to her, that he was attracted to men, she wouldn't accept it. She wanted him to see their pastor, to go to church and pray his way through it. Needless to say, they began to argue a lot and things got really strained. When he finally worked up the courage to leave, she took it really hard."

"Well duh, why shouldn't she have taken it hard? The man she married and had a child with tells her after, what, ten, eleven years that he's gay. I would have taken it a whole lot worse than *hard*. I probably would have drop-kicked him into next week," Kimara snapped.

"Yeah well, suffice it to say, she was all torn up and so was he. He was also ashamed and embarrassed and so he broke out. He says he was depressed for a long time and his family turned their backs on him, so he had no one to go to. Eventually, he ended up down here and he went through therapy, started his real estate business and rebuilt his life."

"Just like that?"

"Yep. He met Robert about five years ago and they're a couple and run the business together and are as happy as two pigs in mud."

"Uh, Jazz, that's all sweet and everything, but that doesn't explain why he never contacted you," Kimara replied sarcastically.

"Well apparently, after he got his head together he felt like so much time had passed that I probably wouldn't want to see him. Plus, he claims he didn't know how to explain things to me. Basically, he was a coward."

"Have you told your mother about all of this?" Kimara wanted to know. Mrs. Mitchell was a devout Christian woman full of old-school beliefs. She attended a Baptist church, which meant Bible school, choir practice, usher board meetings and all-day service on Sunday. The news about her ex-husband would surely send her reeling.

"No, I just didn't feel up to talking to her yet. You

know how dramatic she is. I'll be home tomorrow and maybe I'll go see her then or the next day. That'll be soon enough."

"You're right. How'd the meeting end?"

"I told him that I was happy that he'd made a life for himself and that I wished him well. I also told him not to ever contact me again."

"Really?"

Kimara couldn't imagine saying something like that to her own father, but then again, she couldn't imagine her father breaking out on her like that.

"You know something Kimara, it's like all my life I've been wondering and worrying over that man. I prayed every night before I closed my eyes and every morning when I opened them that he was okay, alive and healthy and that one day he'd come back to me. I convinced myself that no matter what, I'd always love him and I'd welcome him with open arms when he came back. But looking at him today, listening to what he had to say made me realize that for as much as I loved him and was willing to put him before my own hurt and pain, he didn't do the same for me. I don't care that the man is gay. I wouldn't have cared if he was a cross-dressing drag queen. But he let his issues, his depression, his whatever, come before me for sixteen years. He didn't love me enough to risk being embarrassed to come and see me or to pick up the phone and call me. What do I need somebody like that in my life for?"

Kimara quietly considered what Jasmine had said and realized that she was right. Things were not always going to go the way people planned in life, but if they really loved someone, they should be willing to tough it out for his or her sake.

"I'm about to bring a child in this world, and I want him or her surrounded by people who will be there for her. People who will have her back no matter what life brings. As far as I'm concerned, Robert Mitchell is not one of those people."

"I hear you girl. I hear you. But Jazz, it's gotta hurt like hell, doesn't it?"

"Yeah, it does. Thank God I've got a good man like Rick on my side. He's proof positive that unconditional love does exist." Jasmine sighed, briskly wiping the tears that rimmed her eyes away. Although she felt like she was losing her father all over again, she refused to cry about it. She did not want to transfer any sadness or negativity to her unborn baby.

"I'm glad he's there for you. And call me as soon as you get back. You know I'm here for you too, don't you?"

"I know, Kimara. Goodnight, sweetie."

Kimara cleaned up the mess she'd made with the ice cream and went to bed with raw emotions that night. Before she drifted off to sleep, she asked God to help her understand why love had to hurt so much and why people could never do what they promised you they'd do.

Chapter 31

"It's so hard sometimes, knowing what the right thing to do is," Kimara answered in response to her mother's question about how she was doing.

"Sweetheart, it doesn't have to be hard. If you follow your heart, you can't fail."

"It's funny hearing you say that," Kimara challenged. She was surprised to be having this conversation with her mother of all people. She was the most pessimistic, critical person she knew.

Kimara was surprised when her mother offered to come by her new apartment to help her decorate and settle in. Kimara had moved a few days before, but had scarcely had time to unpack. Unbeknownst to Kimara, her mother had purposely asked her father not to join them. She had long felt a need to right things between herself and Kimara. She had always imagined that she would share a close relationship with her daughter and they would have a tight bond, spending afternoons lunching together while sharing girl talk, going on shopping sprees, maybe even vacationing. She also knew that she had been to blame for the fact that she and Kimara were not close. She awoke one day to realize that she didn't even really know her own daughter. Hopefully, it was not too late for them to forge a relationship.

"I was young once too Kimara. Just as full of life as you are. I was wild and crazy and believed that I could outrun time. You have no idea," Gena said as she retrieved a sponge from a bucket of sudsy water. Her rubber-glove covered hand worked rhythmically, scrubbing the shower tiles in Kimara's new bathroom.

"What happened?" Kimara asked skeptically. She lay down her own sponge and leaned against the bathroom sink, watching her mother intently. It was difficult to imagine her mother being any way but the way she'd always known her.

"What do you mean, what happened?" Gena asked.

She ceased scrubbing and looked away, staring into space momentarily. It was obvious that she was becoming uncomfortable as the conversation turned from Kimara to herself, but Kimara didn't care. She felt like this was her one opportunity to really talk to her mother, woman to woman. There were so many things that she wanted to know and had never felt right asking. Maybe now was the time for that wall between them to come down.

"What went wrong for you . . . in your life?"

"Kimara, life does not have a road map. You can't plan every second, every journey, every day. Sometimes you start out on a certain path and things happen to turn you around and send you in an entirely different direction."

"So what direction did you want to go in?"

"I don't know," Gena said wistfully. It was hard to look back and examine the ups and downs in life objectively. "I guess I grew up believing in fairytales. I thought that I'd grow up, marry a man who loved me to death and whom I loved equally and everything else would just fall into place. But fairytales are just that and you have to work real hard at everything else," she finished.

"Do you regret marrying daddy?" Kimara asked fearfully. She didn't want to hear her mother answer in the affirmative, but she also felt like she needed to know.

"No, I wouldn't use the word regret at all. You're too young to remember this, but your father and I went through a real rough patch and I don't know that we've ever fully recovered."

"What happened?" Kimara asked.

"You father and I were unhappy with each other and we just didn't know how to express it. We both said hurtful things to each other, and I think the only thing that kept either of us from walking out was you. But, your father met someone and for a while, I guess she made him forget all the problems at home."

"Daddy cheated on you?" Kimara gasped. She was horrified at the thought and couldn't believe what she was hearing. The father she knew was a kind, honest, compassionate man. He couldn't do something like that. Could he?

"Yes, Kimara. Your father had a relationship with another woman for several months. When I found out about it, I walked. I left you and our home, and I walked. I was gone for half a year and in that time, I realized that it was my fault just as much as it was his."

Kimara felt like she had been cheated, wronged somehow, although she couldn't quite figure out how. Maybe in time she could look at this objectively and realize that her parents were just people, her dad just a man and not the superhero she always believed him to be. But not now. Right now it seemed as if everything she had ever believed was a lie. "Listening to you . . . to this, just makes me feel even more hopeless. It's like, there's no point in trying, no point in caring . . . in loving. It always gets jacked up anyway," Kimara said. She walked out of the bathroom, wanting to get away from her mother and her truths.

Right on her heels, Gena followed her into the

kitchen. "Hold on a minute Kimara. I'm not telling you all this so that you can judge your father, or me for that matter. Marriage is hard work and even though we stumbled, we didn't fail at it. We also made sure you had the best life possible."

"But wasn't it all pretense?"

"No it wasn't. Your father and I loved each other very much and still do. And you . . . you were the best thing that could have happened to us."

The women stood face to face, a short distance of space between them. Gena looked at her daughter, now grown, for the first time in what seemed like a hundred years. On the surface, she saw a beautiful young woman. But looking deeper, into eyes that were so much like her own, she saw the delicate spirit of a baby bird learning how to take flight. She looked scared and at the same time determined. Gena had never felt more proud of Kimara than she did at that moment. She reached out to stroke the side of Kimara's face. Kimara grabbed her mother's hand and held it, that simple gesture serving to close the divide that had existed between them for so long. Gena moved closer, taking the other side of Kimara's face into her free hand.

"All I'm trying to get you to understand Kimara is that we don't always know what life has in store for us. All we can do is prepare ourselves, store up all our strengths and hold on for the ride. Sometimes that ride is going to be bumpy and sometimes it'll be smooth sailing. But if we have faith and love in our hearts, it'll turn out okay."

"Will it?" Kimara asked in a small voice. She wanted to believe her mother, but part of her, the unsure scared little girl in her didn't know if she could.

"Oh sweetheart, yes it will. Maybe Jared wasn't the one. Maybe he was but it was just not the right time for you two. That doesn't mean that you should give up on love. Don't harden your heart because you're too afraid of the possibility of being hurt. Don't ever feel like you can't love or be loved."

"I still miss him so much," Kimara admitted, to her mother and to herself.

"I know, I know." Gena put her arms around her daughter and hugged her. She wished she could take some of the pain away but knew that she could do nothing to ease the grown-woman, broken heart type of pain Kimara was feeling. All she could do was be there for her and hope for the best, which she intended to do.

The sound of the doorbell ringing intruded upon their moment. Kimara opened the door and was greeted by a large bouquet of yellow balloons.

"What in the world?" she exclaimed as hands behind the balloons pushed them into the door. She shoved the balloons aside, reaching out to find the hands, which she grabbed.

"You nut," Kimara shouted once she cleared the doorway and found Jasmine standing there grinning. Beside her stood Rick, holding a pastry box and a gift-wrapped liquor bottle. "What are you doing here? I didn't know you were coming today," Kimara asked.

"It wouldn't be a surprise if I told you I was coming. Now move out of my way and let me see this little chic chateau of yours," Jasmine said, waddling through the doorway. "Mom," she exclaimed, hugging Kimara's mother as closely as her belly would allow.

"Lord girl, what are you carrying in there—a whole football team?" Gena beamed, rubbing Jasmine's protruding stomach. "Hi Rick, how are you honey?"

"Can't complain, Mrs. Hamilton," Rick said as he kissed Gena's cheek. He turned to Kimara. "These are for you."

"Thanks, Rick," Kimara answered, taking the box and the bottle from Rick's hands. "Come on in and make yourselves at home. Everything's still a mess in here so be careful where you walk."

"Ooh, this is too cute. Look at the bathtub Rick. I want a tub just like that when we move," Jasmine squealed. "Right now I can barely fit in our tub."

She finished the tour of the loft apartment in a matter of minutes and then plopped down on the sofa.

"Tired?" Kimara asked, clearing a space next to Jasmine so that Rick could sit too.

"Yeah, it's getting harder by the minute. My doctor says I've gained too much weight, but I can't help it. I'm always hungry, even right after I've eaten," Jasmine complained.

Noticing Jasmine's swollen ankles, Kimara slid a hefty bag filled with clothes nearer to the sofa for her to prop her feet up on.

Gena looked suspiciously at Jasmine's feet and ankles. "Jasmine, how's your pressure? You're carrying a lot of water in your feet." Gena's concern was apparent as she pressed lightly against the puffy flesh around Jasmine's ankles.

"It's a little high," Jasmine admitted. She hated that everyone was so worried about her condition, but she did enjoy them fussing over her. "I'm okay though. I'm getting down to the home stretch now and everything is looking good."

While Kimara didn't know much about pregnancy, it was clear to her that Jasmine was beginning to have a difficult time. She had just entered her twenty-ninth week and she looked like she was overdue.

"Could the doctor have calculated your due date wrong, Jazz?" Kimara wondered.

"No, the sonogram confirmed it. I don't know why I'm so big because the baby is actually pretty small still," Jasmine replied.

"Well just take care of yourself, honey. Stay off your feet as much as possible. Rick, are you making sure she's getting enough rest?" Gena asked.

"Yes ma'am. And I've got a woman coming in twice a

week to clean the apartment. Jasmine's hard-headed though, so I have to watch her carefully."

"Ya'll knock it off. I'm fine. And if it makes you feel better, I'm leaving work in two weeks. So I'll spend a couple of months laying around getting even fatter," Jasmine joked.

The group spent the remainder of the afternoon talking and munching on the pastries Jasmine and Rick had brought. Kimara and Gena hung drapes over the windows and unpacked boxes of dishware and utensils in the kitchen. Rick assembled the small entertainment center Kimara had purchased from Pier 1 and when he was finished, he placed her twenty-seven-inch television on it, connecting the cable wires for her. The ten o'clock news had just begun when he turned the set on. The lead story that night was of a cop shot from the ninth precinct. Jasmine gasped and Kimara froze as the reporter spoke.

"Tonight, cops from all over the city hunt for a brazen suspect who allegedly shot a police officer two blocks away from the station house on fourteenth street. The ninth precinct, regarded as one of the top precincts in Manhattan, is mourning the loss of one of their own," the reporter said solemnly.

"Oh God," Kimara whispered as she turned the volume of the television up.

"What?" Rick asked.

"Ssh!" Jasmine ordered sharply.

"The incident unfolded around four o'clock this afternoon when the officer and his partner pulled the suspect's car over for a traffic violation. The officer approached the vehicle, ordering the suspect to place his hands outside of the window. While details are still sketchy, it appears the suspect leaned out of the open window and opened fire, without warning. He then sped off in a 1990 Honda Accord."

"What about the license plates? They didn't get the-license plate number?" Gena shouted through trembling hands which covered her mouth.

"The identity of the officer is still being withheld at this hour pending notification of his family. However, sources say that the officer, a five-year veteran of the force was an African-American male in his mid-twenties. Police are asking for anyone with any information regarding this crime not to hesitate to call their local precinct. Back to you in the studio," the reporter concluded.

Jasmine struggled to get up from her seat, huffing and puffing until she was on her feet. She came to Kimara's side and grabbed her by the shoulders.

"I'm sure he's okay. Don't get upset. I'm sure it's not him," Jasmine said.

"What if it is, Jazz?" Kimara whispered. All the blood had drawn from her face and her eyes were wild with fear.

"Are you sure that's Jared's precinct?" Gena asked, as she too came to stand near Kimara, reaching out to touch her shoulder.

"Yes," Jasmine answered.

"Can't we call the station and ask?" Rick said, finally putting the pieces together. Concern had filled his eyes as well.

"They won't tell us anything over the phone and none of us are family," Kimara answered. She had begun trembling, as she replayed the reporter's words in her mind. A twenty-something year old African-American officer who was a five-year veteran of the force pretty much narrowed down the possibilities. She could not pretend that the probability that it was, in fact, Jared was not extremely high. Even though it was over between them and she had willed herself to get over him, the mere thought of him being hurt, or worse, killed, made her whole body seize with pain. She thought about his mother.

How could that woman make it through the pain of losing again. Hadn't she suffered enough?

Jared had hurt her pretty badly, there was no denying that fact. Be that as it may, Kimara still loved him. At that moment she realized that no matter how much time had passed, no matter how many other people came in and out of her life, she would love Jared until the day she closed her eyes for good. And who knew, maybe there was a possibility that, in time, they could find their way back to each other. Anything was possible, until this. Now, there was no hope at all and that simple fact was devastating to her.

"What's his home number?" Jasmine asked, reaching into her purse and retrieving her cell phone.

Kimara looked at her blankly for a moment. At Jasmine's urging she recited his telephone number. As Jasmine dialed the digits and waited while the phone rang, Kimara went into the kitchen and leaned on the counter. She couldn't bear to hear what Jasmine said into that phone to whomever answered it. She also didn't want to see her face if the worse case scenario became reality.

Jasmine shook her head as the line just rang. Finally the answering machine clicked on, but she hung up without leaving a message. The next hour passed painfully by, Kimara quiet and withdrawn while Gena and Rick filled the dominant silence with nervous chatter and Jasmine discreetly redialed Jared's number a half a dozen times. Finally, her call was answered.

"Hello? Jared?" Jasmine cried.

Rick turned the television to mute as all ears tuned in to Jasmine.

"Yeah, who is this?" Jared answered.

"Oh thank you, Jesus. Jared, this is Jasmine, Kimara's friend."

Kimara looked up and Jasmine mouthed the words *he's okay* to her. Kimara let out an audible sigh and returned to the living room. Tears slid down her cheeks as she released the breath she hadn't realized she was holding. Gena rubbed her daughter's back, as she said a quick prayer thanking God for Jared's safety.

"Oh hey, Jasmine. What's up?"

"Jared, we just heard the news . . . on the news they said someone from your precinct was killed this afternoon."

"Yeah, uh, they haven't released his identity yet. What . . . you thought it was me?" Jared asked.

Jasmine sighed. "Yes. They were so cryptic in their description it could very well have been . . . oh well, I'm so glad to hear you're okay."

"I'm fine. The media had no business giving any sort of description whatsoever. I guess I'd better call my family and let them know before they hear that report."

"Yeah, you should do that. I'm sure they'll be worried. I'm so sorry . . . this was an unspeakable act of cowardice . . . shooting that man like that," Jasmine said as she prepared to hang up.

"Don't worry, we'll get that piece of garbage," Jared said through clenched teeth. "Listen Jasmine, is Kimara . . . did she hear it too?"

"Yeah. I'll let her know, okay Jared?"

"Yeah . . . all right then. Thanks for being concerned Jasmine. You take care."

"You too. Bye Jared." Jasmine hung up the phone.

Jasmine and Kimara locked eyes for a moment, before Jasmine pulled Kimara to her, wrapping her arms around her. Kimara cried silently and Jasmine patted her head.

"It's okay. He's all right."

But it wasn't okay after all, Kimara knew. It still hurt just as much as it had before, and Jared was still just as far from her reach.

Chapter 32

"Well now, looks like it's my turn to ask you what you're doing here?" Inez said, greeting her son at her door.

Jared stood on the porch of his mother's two bedroom ranch house, located on a rural stretch of road in Deerwood, Maryland. He bent down to kiss his mother's soft cheek as she opened the door wide enough for him to enter.

"Hey Mama, I just came down to see you . . . to check up on you and that big-headed little brother of mine," Jared answered.

At five-feet-three inches, Inez Porter barely reached her son's chest. She tilted her head back in order to get a clear view of his face and narrowed her eyes with one hand on her hip. Jared rubbed the top of her head as he passed her. He walked straight toward the kitchen where the aroma of something delicious called out to him.

"You drove three hours, without calling, just to see me?" Inez said as she followed her son into the kitchen. "You never was a very good liar," she said as she smacked his hands away from her simmering pots.

Inez had been laying on the sofa wearing a pair of

jungle-print lounging pants with a matching top, and reading a book when she heard Jared's truck pull into the driveway. She'd peered through the curtain, surprised to see her son walking up the front path, and snatched open the door before he could get his spare key out of his jacket pocket.

Now, Inez reached into the cabinet and removed a plate for Jared. Just as she had had to do every day when he was a little boy, coming in straight from the yard covered in dirt from head to toe, she sent him into the bathroom at the end of the hallway to wash his hands and proceeded to pile his dish high with collard greens, turkey wings and baked macaroni and cheese. Jared returned to the kitchen and immediately dug in, having missed his mother's down-home cooking more than he'd realized.

"Where's Javon?" he asked through a mouthful of food.

"He went down to the university for that big game. You know Mrs. Thomas' grandson plays football there now."

"Oh yeah, I remember seeing him around the neighborhood. That kid's got a powerful arm," Jared said, pausing to take a huge swallow from the tall glass of freshly-squeezed lemonade his mother had placed before him.

"Mrs. Thomas sure is proud of that boy. She goes to every home game and even some of the away ones too. Javon drove down there with her other grandson and some boys from 'round here. I don't know all their names," Inez reported.

Jared steamrolled through a second helping of his mother's cooking before sitting back in his chair, stuffed.

"That was good Mama. Thanks."

"You're welcome, baby. Now, are you going to tell me what brings you down here?"

"I had a couple of days off, and on the spur of the moment I just decided to jump in my truck and come down. That ain't a crime is it?" Jared asked, feigning innocence.

He didn't want to tell his mother how unsettled his life had begun to feel. That would worry her unnecessarily. Besides, he was too old to be crying on his mother's shoulder. Truth was, Jared didn't even know how to cry anymore. It was as if the tears had packed up and ran into hiding the very day that his father went away.

He was only seven years old, but he remembered that night as clearly as if it were the night before. It was his mother's birthday and she and his father were all dressed up and headed out for a night of partying. They were planning to meet some friends at a club on the west side of town. Some place that they had never gone to before, but had heard nothing but good things about. It was supposed to be an upscale joint, with chandeliers, top-shelf liquor and a live band. For a tiny town in the South, that was a treat. He had never seen Inez so excited. It was the first time she and her husband had gone out to a party in over a year. Money had been a little tight and Sean had been working two jobs to make ends meet.

Jared remembered looking up at his father and thinking that he was the coolest dude in all of North Carolina, possibly the world. The burnt-orange polyester bell-bottomed slacks he wore with the butterfly-collared patchwork shirt made him look sharper than any Mack Daddy Jared had seen on television. Sean's afro was perfectly rounded, his mustache trimmed and his shoes polished until they gleamed. He was tight. His Old Spice cologne made him smell even more manly and strong than he looked. This thought ran through Jared's mind as his father picked him up, lifted him in the air and swung him around, before setting him down, patting his butt and reminding him to behave and listen to Mrs. Jenkins, the downstairs neighbor who would be watching the two boys that night. Jared promised to be good as he sniffed his pajama shirt, feeling heady from the potent scent of his father's cologne, which had rubbed off on him, while Javon got his turn at being tossed into the air.

And then they were gone and hours later, only one of them returned. For weeks after that night, Jared kept that particular pajama shirt stuffed beneath his pillow, inhaling the scent his daddy had left behind. Even then, he couldn't cry. By the time the smell had faded and his father had been sentenced to prison, Jared's smile had gone the way of his tears and the scent of Old Spice.

He couldn't bring himself to sit at his mother's table now and tell her how badly he had been feeling since he lost Kimara, nor could he tell her that he had realized that he was once again making a mistake with Millicent. He had tried so hard to be a man after his father left—to be the man his mother needed. He wouldn't falter now. The compulsion that sent him racing down to Maryland that afternoon was not strong enough to allow him to break down. He'd have to figure this thing out on his own. Just being at home, in the company of his family would be enough to ease his mind, or at least allow him to rest peacefully for a while, he believed.

Jared took his mother's hand in his and smiled what he hoped was a reassuring smile, but said nothing.

"No, that ain't a crime," his mother answered, knowing that there was, indeed, a reason for his visit and that with time, he'd tell her what it was.

Jared followed her into the living room and settled on the sofa next to her. Absently, he picked up the remote and flipped the television from station to station. He finally settled on CBS when his mother mentioned that the show playing was her favorite Friday night series. They watched television for a while, Jared dozing comfortably. The serenity that being back home in his mother's house brought him was priceless.

"I'm going to bed," Inez said finally. "Javon'll be home after a while."

"All right Mama. I'll listen out for him. Good night."

"There's some peach cobbler in the fridge," she tossed over her shoulder, knowing that her son would be hungry again real soon.

Jared stretched out on the sofa to watch television, but fell asleep five minutes into an episode of *Real Sports*. He slept hard and didn't even hear his brother come in later. He awoke when the sun began shining through the curtains and into his face the next morning. He found a blanket had been laid across his body and his brother was sitting opposite him on the matching loveseat, watching television as he ate cereal from a huge plastic bowl.

"What's up?" Javon said when he realized that his big brother had awakened.

"Nothing man," Jared answered, scratching his head as he sat up. "What time is it?"

"About eight."

"Where's Mama?" Jared asked, noticing how quiet the house was. By eight o'clock in the morning, his mother would have already cooked breakfast and been either cleaning or working in her garden. The local gospel station would be playing on the radio if it was a Sunday or soft jazz would be piping through the house. Jared could neither hear nor smell the telltale signs.

"At the cemetery," Javon answered, watching his brother's expression as the words registered with him.

"Oh," Jared said, rubbing his forehead. He'd forgotten the date. Today would have been his father's forty-eighth birthday, had he lived. He knew that his mother had gone to place flowers on his grave, just as she still did for every birthday, their wedding anniversary, the anniversary of his death and all major holidays.

"You didn't go with her?" Jared queried.

"Nah, I kinda sensed that she wanted to go alone today. She gets that way sometimes."

Jared looked at his little brother, noticing that he really wasn't so little anymore. In fact, Javon was bigger than Jared now. Two to three inches taller, with legs as thick as tree trunks and a massive upper body, Javon was a full-grown man. Somehow Jared had forgotten that just as time had passed for him, so it had for his brother and his mother. Javon was twenty-two years old now. He had a degree in engineering, had landed a very good job with a top firm and had been with his current girl-friend for close to two years. Javon had a full, adult life, complete with all the things that should be there. Jared was grateful that his brother had grown up to be a re-sponsible young man—no drugs, no gangs—despite the fact that he'd had no father. Jared had tried to be the best big brother and male role model that he could be for Javon, and he felt proud that in some way it had counted.

"Javon man, have you been spending any time with her? I mean, you know she's been a little lonely—"

"Lonely? Mama? Man, please. I'm here more than she is," Javon scoffed.

"Say what?" Jared asked surprised.

"You heard me. Mrs. Inez Porter be out ripping and running more than I do. She's doing her thing, believe that. Between work and church, she's always got some-thing going on. Then she's got her card playing pals and Mr. Edwards, and—"

"Who's Mr. Edwards?"

"Frank Edwards, the guy who owns the meat market over there near the high school. He and Mama been kickin' it for the past few months."

"What? Mama's dating?"

"Duh! Where've you been?" Javon laughed, getting

up from his seat. He went into the kitchen to refill his cereal bowl, Jared following.

"Ain't this something. How you down here letting Mama date some dude?"

"What is she supposed to be doing man? She's a grown woman. Besides, even if I did have a problem with it, which I don't, ain't a damn thing I could do about it. You know how Mama is."

Jared opened his mouth to protest but immediately closed it. Javon was right—if one of them even thought about questioning something their mother did, she'd be all over them like a bad rash. But the news of her dating was more than he had bargained on hearing during this impromptu trip.

Jared freshened up and dressed quickly. He wanted to see for himself if his mother had truly moved on into this great, full life that Javon had described.

After a short drive to the other side of town, Jared parked his car at the end of the long line of parked cars in the lot and began walking. It was a cold morning and the sky looked like it was ready to open up and rain. Charcoal-gray clouds hung low and thick, menacing and threatening. He pulled the collar of his peacoat up around his neck and stuck his gloveless hands in his pockets. The tiny winding path between the numerous headstones had not changed since the last time he'd been there, half a decade ago. Somehow, he still re-membered the way, as if that walk had been engraved on his memory. He stopped a few yards from where his mother stood, her hand resting lightly on the top of the stone, her back to him. She wore her long beige wool coat with the beaver collar, a gift from Jared, purchased with his first paycheck as a police officer. The belt was cinched tightly around her tiny waist and tied in front. Jared noticed how slim his mother was, still carrying the shapely, thin figure of a woman half her age. He'd never thought of her as a woman, with needs and desires, only as Mama. Obviously she was still turning the heads of men she encountered, at the meat market no less. Just because Jared had never envisioned it, didn't mean it was not right and natural. Still, it was a shock to his system.

"Mama," he called lightly, not wanting to startle her.

"Yes, Jared," she answered, without turning around. It was as if for some reason she had been expecting him to come.

Jared approached his mother and placed an arm around her shoulder.

"You okay?" he asked.

"Of course. I love coming here from time to time to talk to your daddy. Seems like I feel closer to him in this place. Maybe it's 'cause it's so quiet here."

"You still miss him?"

"Sure, I miss him a lot. We were supposed to grow old together. But the memories of the precious time we did have together makes it okay."

Inez regarded her son for a moment, proud at how handsome he was and how well he'd turned out. Looking more and more like his father as the days turned, she thanked God that at least she and Sean had had enough time to bring two such fine boys into the world.

"What about you?" she asked, "you still miss him?"

Jared was quiet, having returned to a place inside that still felt like an open wound, even after all these years. He nodded his head.

"I loved your daddy with all my heart and when they took him away, I thought for sure God had to be playing the cruelest joke on me ever heard of. It took me a long time to realize that my God is not a mean God, and he does not do anything just to spite us," Inez said.

Jared chewed on his bottom lip as he soaked in what his mother was saying to him. "It feels like part of me has been in limbo since he left. Like no matter how right things are, how good things seem to be going for me, there's something that's off. A piece of the puzzle that just doesn't fit exactly where it's supposed to fit. Does that make any sense?" Jared asked.

"All that means is that you haven't learned to let it go. Just let it go baby and give it to God. Your daddy would want you to be happy and free. He would want you to smile and to love and to live life, not just exist in it. Believe me, if you just let go, it won't hurt so much anymore."

"I don't know how," Jared admitted, hanging his head in shame.

He felt like a big kid and was embarrassed by what he felt were his inadequacies as a man. Inez patted her son's back, patted and rubbed like when he was a restless baby who was terribly exhausted but could not fall asleep. Flashes of childhood crept through Jared's mind, happy days with both of his parents, visits to Grandma's house, Javon as a baby. It all zipped through his head, one memory after the other and soon tears were sliding down his manly cheeks as he remembered how sweet things had been. Then the days and months after his father was jailed, the strength his mother showed, the way she took care of them and tried to make their lives as normal as possible. He remembered the tortured visits to the prison, the weekly letters and phone calls from his father. How he had looked forward to his father finally coming home, how he'd counted down the years, then the months, then the weeks. He had just begun believing that they were going to have a normal life again, that they would all be together, and it would be as if the past ten years had never happened. Then the phone call came and this time Daddy was gone forever.

Jared cried openly now, cried a river as deep and as long as the Nile River. Against his will, he let it out, let it go as his mother had advised. Seventeen years of anguish poured out of him, emptied from his heart in sweet salt water. Inez stood by her son, a man now, as he cried the little boy tears that he had never shed. Surprisingly, when he finished, he didn't feel less of a man; he felt like a lighter man, as if he'd lost a hundred pounds. Jared hugged his mother, whose own tears of joy streaked her cheeks.

Later, Jared lay on his brother's bed and stared at an article in *VIBE* magazine. He was unable to take his eyes away from the quarter page picture of Kimara posing with the other two members of her group. She looked radiant, more beautiful than he remembered. She was wearing a floral sarong skirt and matching bikini top, which strategically, but barely covered her glistening body. The article talked about the group's upcoming debut, the buzz being that Speak Easy would turn the music industry on its ear. Their star was already on the rise. Jared couldn't have been more proud of Kimara. She had taken a chance on something, and it was going to pay off for her. He had never doubted that she was a star, one too bright to be contained as he had tried to do. He regretted that aspect of their relationship more than anything else.

He knew what he had to do and prayed for the courage to do it. He also knew that Millicent would be hurt by it, but there was no way that he could marry her. While he had love for her and cared about her, he was not *in* love with her. Had he been honest with himself and with her from the start, he had never truly been in love with her.

The next step would be to win Kimara's heart back. He didn't know if that were possible, but he would try. She meant more to him than anything else on this Earth and like his mother said, love was the only thing that he could really count on; the only thing worth preserving. He had to recognize that he could not control everything around him and that sometimes things were

not going to go the way he'd like them to. Kimara had
been so right for him even when he had behaved so
wrongly. He had been selfish and uncompromising, a
fact he recognized now that he had dared to examine
himself more closely. Jared had no way of knowing
whether he stood a chance, but he also knew that life
was too short for him not to go for broke.

Chapter 33

"Kimara, my pretty girl, how have you been?" Gino greeted. He kissed her cheek warmly and hugged her tightly.

"Not bad, boss man. How're you?" Kimara returned.

"I'm doing my thing, as you kids would say," Gino laughed, in his deep, scratchy voice.

Kimara laughed with him. "I should say so. Look at this place—it's packed tonight. Business is definitely treating you well, huh?"

"Oh, but that's only because they all heard you would be here tonight. You and these pretty ladies you sing with," Gino said, motioning to Delphina and Simone.

At this stage in the development of their music project it was decided that it was time to begin making promotional appearances. The more hype the group was able to drum up before the album dropped, the better sales could be expected. When searching for clubs in the area for the group to perform, Kimara suggested Club Silhouette. The fact that she was like a second daughter to the owner made it a done deal that they would be welcome there.

Kimara showed the ladies to the employee lounge where Gino said they could sit and relax until show

time. Kimara returned to Gino's office so that the two
of them could have a private moment.

"So Gino, what's up with Giselle?" Kimara asked.

Gino sighed heavily as he leaned back in his chair. He
smoothed his thinning hair and shook his head. "Kimara,
that girl is going to drive me stark-raving mad one of
these days. I don't know what went wrong. I thought I was
doing everything right by her. I gave her everything and
I let her be. Didn't want to crowd her and be overbearing
like my parents had been. When her mother died, she
was just a little girl, and I wanted to make up for it. I
wanted to just take all the pain away. But I guess I
couldn't do that."

"You're a good father Gino, and Giselle loves you. I
know she acts like she doesn't give a damn about anybody or anything, but I think it's just a front," Kimara
consoled.

"Yeah well," Gino said, sighing again, "time will tell.
Right now she's in a clinic in Maine. It's supposed to be
one of those new age rehab places where you connect
with your spiritual self while you kick whatever monkey
is on your back. My Giselle . . . I don't know if she's
strong enough to do this."

Kimara sat quietly with Gino, holding his hand across
the desk. She felt bad for the man because all he'd ever
done was try to love his daughter. Giselle had a lot of
issues, her biggest one being that she didn't realize how
much her father loved her.

"I don't know what it's going to take for Giselle to get
her act together, Gino. For a long time, I was a lot like
her. I was so busy trying to ride this life 'til the wheels
fell off that I didn't realize how my actions where affecting those who love me. Just keep being there for her
though. Eventually, she'll get it together. I know she will."

"Here," Gino said, reaching into his desk drawer and
pulling out a slip of paper. "This is the address to the

place she's at. You write to her, let her know that she's got people pulling for her."

"I will," Kimara promised, taking the slip from his hands.

"That's if you're not too busy being a big star to remember us little people," Gino mocked.

"Never Gino, never," Kimara promised.

Speak Easy took the stage at Club Silhouette that night and they rocked the packed house. Gino gave them an open invitation to come back any time they wanted.

Kimara smiled as she thought back on that now, seeing Gino laughing and dancing in front of the stage was unforgettable. She'd written to Giselle, but had yet to receive a response. That was okay, however, because Kimara knew that Giselle had a lot on her plate at the moment and maybe she wasn't quite ready to communicate with the outside world.

Staring in the mirror, Kimara studied her reflection. She ran her hands through her new short hairdo, the naturally curly pattern of her hair giving her face an exotic look. She had also had it dyed a light honey-brown color, which brought out the striking color of her eyes even more. She loved the new look, feeling more soft and feminine than she had with longer hair.

So much had changed in her life over the past few months. Spring had brought a love so breathtaking and so surprising to her that she scarcely had time to prepare for it. With summer came the exposition of her life's work, her poetry. The opportunity to share her gift of expression presented itself, and with the understandable fear of the unknown, she moved haltingly forward and accepted the challenges that opportunity presented. Fall stole in unexpectedly and crept out just as suddenly, taking her love with it and leaving her heart naked and unprepared for the cold winter. Yet somehow, she'd managed to survive and weather the storms and now, here she was, close to facing a new year and feeling so completely changed. She wanted to see if those changes were reflected in her skin, her eyes, her soul. They were.

She thought about the photo shoot a few days before and how exhilarated she'd felt standing in front of the camera. The group had been nervous going in, aware that the pictures they were taking were for the album. This was their one shot to make a good first impression. Jean-Michel Dervais, a man whose stellar reputation proceeded him, was the photographer for the shoot. He spoke halting English and issued directions mostly in his native language, French, which sounded like music. Kimara loved the way he said her name, the way it rolled off of his tongue like melted butter. He had a knack for making women feel comfortable, making them more aware of their sexuality, grace and beauty. He encouraged them to lose themselves in front of the camera and to tease and flirt with the lens as much as they wanted to. He worked them and they, in turn, worked the camera. Kimara couldn't wait to see how the pictures turned out.

Right on cue, the doorbell rang. Harrell had promised to come by with the photos before the end of the afternoon.

"Hey," she said to Harrell as she opened the door for him, Delphina and Simone.

"What's up?" he asked.

"Girl, would you believe he would not let us look at the pictures until we were all together? He's so uptight," Delphina complained, waving her hand in Harrell's general direction.

They all took turns teasing Harrell as they took seats in Kimara's living room. Harrell reached into his oversized tote bag and retrieved a manila envelope. From this envelope he delivered the two dozen 8 x 10 glossy photographs of Kimara, Delphina and Simone. "Feast your eyes on these, ladies."

They lined the photos up across the floor and took turns surveying them, one at a time. Most of them were pretty good and a handful of them were downright fantastic. Kimara almost didn't recognize herself and doubted seriously anyone who knew her would.

"I look like a different person," she commented.

"No, you don't. Beneath the clothes and the makeup, that's definitely you," Harrell said.

"Wow, Jean-Michel is the man. I can't believe how good these are," Simone commented.

What Jean-Michel had given each woman was an almost fantastical image of themselves and with that came a feeling of sensuality and feminine power on a whole new level.

"This calls for a toast," Kimara announced.

She popped the bottle of champagne that Jasmine and Rick had brought her as a house warming gift. After she poured four glasses of bubbly, she raised hers in the air.

"Success, fame and fortune are all perks with which we will undoubtedly be blessed. However, the true gift from all of this is the newfound friendship we've built. To my new family—my sisters in song, Delphina and Simone, and to my big brother, Mr. pit bull himself, Harrell. You guys embraced me, right from the start and made me feel welcome. So here's to you and to us," Kimara said from the heart.

"Cheers," Harrell responded. Glasses clicked against one another and hugs and kisses were shared amongst the group.

"Let's go out and have dinner or something," Simone chirped.

"Sounds like a plan," Kimara agreed.

Reluctantly, Delphina begged off because her son was suffering from the chicken pox and she didn't want to be away from him for too long. As the group headed out, Kimara marveled at how close they had become in such a short period of time. The long hours they had been putting in could easily have brought tension into their relationships, but instead, it had made the challenges they faced easier to deal with. Each respected what the others brought to the situation and the support and concern shared between them made everything run smoothly. Kimara hoped that unlike many groups, past and present, they would be able to hold on to the bonds they'd secured, thereby avoiding some of the traps of their predecessors. Making music and performing was definitely not something she would want to do alone, and although she had a hard time compromising in relationships, she vowed to do better than her best this time.

Chapter 34

Harrell's signature rap on the door had become a familiar sound to Kimara. Clad in a long T-shirt and boxer shorts, she opened the door for him without hesitation. He had come by the building to review some contracts for his uncle. Uncle James was looking to make some real estate investments and Harrell wanted to make sure everything was on the up and up. James later sent Harrell upstairs to Kimara's apartment toting breakfast of pink salmon and grits.

"I'm going downstairs to give Uncle James a big kiss after I finish this," Kimara squealed, as she wiped the buttermilk biscuits he'd also sent across her plate.

"Don't be getting my uncle all excited, now. He ain't a young man you know!" Harrell joked.

They spent the morning going over the dates lined up for them to do promotional shows at more local venues like Club Silhouette, which had been like going home. Performing at her old haunt had been a great ice breaker for her, although she was still trying to get used to the idea of taking the stage anywhere.

The group also had their first video shoot set for the following week and Harrell had managed to get one of the most sought after directors in the business to agree to direct it. Everything seemed to be on track and to her own surprise, Kimara was blossoming under the pressure. An unexpected bump in the road, however, threatened to derail the train before it really left the station.

"That's not possible. There's got to be some sort of mistake," Harrell said into his cell phone.

Kimara glanced at Harrell from where she stood at the tiny counter space in her kitchen. She held the knife with which she had been slicing a honeydew melon, poised in midair, the uncharacteristic agitation in Harrell's voice commanding her attention.

"Mr. Vogel, trust me, this is news to me. I don't know what happened sir, but I'm certainly going to find out."

Harrell paused, listening respectfully as George Vogel, CEO of Smithtown Records bellowed at him through the phone. In the four years that Harrell had been at Smithtown, he had always had pleasant dealings with Vogel, up until this point.

George Vogel was a well-traveled, highly respected man in his mid-fifties. He was a veteran in the business, having worked with a lot of the jazz bands of the sixties and seventies. Vogel was known for being fair-minded and even-tempered. He treated his artists with respect and was even known to go out on a limb on more than one occasion. For instance, a couple of years ago, one of Smithtown's premier artists was involved in a hit-and-run accident and faced serious criminal charges and other legal penalties. Vogel personally remained at that artist's side, and provided legal counsel, financial support and damage control by way of public relations. It turned out that the artist was not under the influence of alcohol as the police had charged, but was suffering from an undiagnosed neurological disorder which caused him to fall asleep at the wheel. Vogel helped find medical care for the artist and when he had recovered and was able to work again, Vogel made sure his project picked up right where it had left off.

Harrell knew that if Vogel was this upset, it was with good reason. He listened intently, allowing the older man to blow off as much steam as he needed to, despite the fact that it was directed at him. They ended the conversation with Harrell promising to take care of the problem and Vogel, almost back to his calm, collect demeanor, advising Harrell that he had less than twenty-four hours to do so.

"That snake. That fake, wanna be Damon Dash . . . brown-nosing little punk!" Harrell shouted as Kimara entered the living room.

The juice from the melon she'd just bitten into slid down her wrist. She sat the tray of sliced fruit on a snack table next to Harrell, placed a hand on her hip and waited expectantly.

"You won't believe what Bronson did," Harrell spat.

"Oh, Lord," Kimara sighed.

She was so tired of Bronson Chandler and his antics. One would think that she was the crown jewels the way he'd gone after her. It was truly pathetic for a man to be so pressed over one woman. Whatever miniscule amount of respect that may have remained for him after he so rudely came on to her at his beach house had completely vanished in the ensuing weeks. She did not know what Harrell had said to Bronson, but whatever it was seemed to have made him back off of Kimara. However, he succeeded at getting to her in other ways. His attitude toward Harrell was childish. He'd also taken to barging into the studio and demanding changes in everything from the group's hair, makeup and clothing choices, to the vocal arrangements and the position of the tracks on the album. He was doing everything in his power to make both Kimara and Harrell uncomfortable. Unfortunately, his actions were also affecting the rest of the group and the entire production staff. While Kimara was truly apologetic for being the unwilling cause of the discomfort, she refused to do anything to soothe Bronson's wounded ego. She spoke to him in monosyllabic terms only when necessary and didn't attempt to hide her disdain.

Delphina, the self-designated caretaker of the trio, had made an attempt to smooth things over with Bronson. Without knowing much about the disagreement between Bronson, Harrell and Kimara, she decided to try to ease some of the tension which entered the room anytime Bronson did. She'd approached him one evening after rehearsal and asked him what was bothering him.

"What's up with you Bronson, man? You've been running around biting everybody's head off like a hungry lion lately," Delphina joked.

"Oh really? Is that what everyone is saying?" Bronson asked.

"No, that's what *I'm* saying. Don't tell me, Mr. Player himself is having girl troubles?"

Bronson smirked. "Come on now Delphina, you should know better than that. I don't have any problems in that department."

"So what is it? You know what Bronson, on second thought, I don't even want to know what it is. Just do me a favor and lighten up a little. Life's too short for you to be stressing out like this." Delphina smiled her dimpled smile, lightly patting Bronson's arm.

"Your man Harrell needs to get his act together," Bronson said hotly. "Then, maybe I wouldn't have to keep running behind him and fixing his screwups. Keep messing around with him and you ladies may do more fizzling than sizzling, if you catch my drift," Bronson said.

Delphina shook her head and began walking away. It was obvious that Bronson was still and always would be a jackass and no amount of reasoning on her part would change that.

"Listen, Del," Bronson called after her, "What do you

say you and I go out for a drink. Maybe we could talk about you doing a solo project or something?"

Delphina rolled her eyes and sucked her teeth, her jaw set tight with anger, showing off her dimples again, but this time in not so friendly a manner. Her definitive answer was loud and clear as she let the studio door bang shut behind her.

When she told Kimara what had happened, they both laughed at his arrogance. Secretly, Kimara worried that things would get a lot stickier with Bronson before it was all over with.

"What did he do now?" she asked, almost not wanting to hear Harrell's response.

"That backstabbing bastard told me that he had gotten the track releases for the two remakes we did. He said it was all taken care of and filed with the legal department. It turns out that he only got one. He never spoke to anyone in Bobby Wallace's camp and never got a release for us to use his song, *Tuesday's Lover.*

"What?" Kimara exploded. "How could he overlook something so important as the releases?"

"He didn't overlook it, although I'm sure that's what he'd swear if confronted. He did this crap on purpose, knowing full well that we can't release the album without permission from Bob Wallace to use the song. Everything's been printed, there are three hundred thousand copies of the album packed up and ready to be distributed, and Wallace's people told Vogel that if the album drops, they're going to sue the group, the label . . . every damned body."

Harrell was pacing the floor, his hands flailing about as the anger within him railed against his body.

"How'd they even know about the remake of the song if they never heard from anyone at Smithtown?"

"Oh, are you ready for this one? Some little birdie delivered a promotional copy to them. I don't have to tell you who the dirty, stinking pigeon who did that is, do I?"

"To hell with this," Kimara snapped. "To hell with all of this. I don't need anymore of this drama. I'm not going to spend my life dealing with shady turncoats like Bronson Chandler. This cutthroat business just isn't for me. I can't take it." Kimara collapsed onto the sofa and held her head in trembling hands.

"Stop it Kimara. Just stop right there." Harrell pointed a shaking finger at her. "I'm not quitting on you, so you damned well better not quit on me. We've put too much into this project to do that."

"But what can we do Harrell? It's too late to change the song and from what you've said, it doesn't appear that Mr. Wallace is going to give us the okay now. What can we do?"

"You go and get dressed and let's bounce," Harrell said as he began packing his calendar and notes back into his bag.

Without a word, Kimara grabbed a pair of slacks and a sweater from her closet and went into the bathroom to change out of the bed clothes she'd been wearing. Minutes later they were in Harrell's truck, racing across Manhattan. Neither of them spoke, each lost in his and her own thoughts of how totally messed up the situation was that Bronson had created. If he was standing in front of her right now, Kimara wouldn't hesitate to backslap him twice.

Harrell drove through the Queens Midtown Tunnel and then jumped onto the Long Island Expressway. Ninety minutes later they were pulling into a long circular driveway in Sag Harbor, Long Island. Harrell parked in front of a stone-faced colonial house. She followed him to the front door where he rang a bell that chimed like a gong. Several minutes later, the door opened and an older black woman wearing a domestic uniform answered.

"May I help you, sir?" she asked.

"Yes, ma'am. I'm here to see Mr. Wallace."

"Whom shall I say is calling?"

"Uh . . . tell him it's Harrell James from Smithtown Records. I'm here to discuss an urgent matter with him."

"Come in," she replied as she stepped aside. "Wait here." She closed the massive door behind them and walked away, down the center hall, disappearing through a doorway at the end of the corridor.

"I can't believe we're actually inside of his house," Kimara whispered. She glanced around the foyer, too nervous to move from the spot where she was standing. She thought briefly about the fact that her daddy would be tickled pink to be standing there, waiting to see a legend. She herself, in fact, was excited and amazed, but, on the other hand, the reason that had brought them there caused much of that excitement to lose its shine.

The woman returned to the foyer. "You two can follow me. This way," she said.

Harrell and Kimara followed her down the same path she had taken moments before. She ushered them into a spacious living room, once again pulling the massive brass-handled doors shut behind them. The room was stunning, styled in various hues of burgundy and wine, with a large vaulted ceiling, fireplace and a custom hardwood pool table designed with sparkling mother of pearl accents.

If the room itself was intimidating, seated on a leather sofa smoking a cigar was Mr. Bobby Wallace himself, looking every bit the legendary award winning soul singer that he was. Kimara nervously followed Harrell farther into the room.

"Mr. Wallace, thank you for agreeing to see us. We're uh . . . sorry to just barge in like this . . . without an appointment, but it's critical that we talk to you," Harrell said, extending his hand to Mr. Wallace.

"Sit down son," Mr. Wallace said in a gruff voice.

Kimara and Harrell took seats in the high-back arm-chairs directly across from Wallace.

"Uh, sir, this is Kimara Hamilton from Smithtown's new R & B group, Speak Easy. Perhaps you've heard of them?"

"Oh yeah, I've heard of them. Got a whole earful from my lawyers about them. How do you do, young lady?"

"I'm fine sir, and yourself," Kimara answered self-consciously.

"Living darling, I'm living. Now, what it is that I can do for you two?" Wallace replied.

"Well sir—"

"Call me Bobby, young lady. Everybody just calls me Bobby."

"All right, Bobby. We're here about *Tuesday's Lover*. We remade the song and—"

"Without my permission, right?"

"Well sir, Bobby, that's the problem," Harrell inter-jected. "We thought we had your permission. We would never have touched the song without it. But it seems someone dropped the ball and the paperwork was never sent to your people. I assure you, I take full re-sponsibility for this mess."

"I see."

"Look, Bobby, you've got to know that you're a legend. My parents and their generation love you and your music is as respected now as it was back in the day," Kimara added.

"She's right. We wanted to remake *Tuesday's Lover* be-cause it's good music, everything from the tracks to the vocals on that joint is hot. In doing that song over, we were trying to give you your props too, for having made so many good songs during your career."

Bobby Wallace took a short drag on his cigar, rolled the smoke around on his tongue and then blew it up into the air. He regarded Harrell and Kimara, tickled by their enthusiastic appeal. They reminded him of himself and the other young musicians he came on board with in the fifties, eager and determined to leave their marks on the world. He didn't have a real problem with them using his song, but he realized that he couldn't let them off too easily. These kids today needed to understand how to take care of business first.

"You know, a lot of times people call themselves re-making somebody else's music like they can do it better. As if there was something wrong with the original and it needed to be done over. I don't dig that," Bobby growled.

"We certainly don't feel that way and we weren't trying to imply anything by redoing the song," Kimara explained.

"I'd like to hear this song for myself, this *remake*," he said.

"No problem, I've got it right here," Harrell said, pulling one of the promotional disks from his bag.

Bobby directed Harrell to the stereo system which was built into the room's south wall. Harrell inserted the disk, pressed a few buttons and soon the room was filled with song. Speak Easy's cover of *Tuesday's Lover* was on point, of this both Kimara and Harrell were certain. The question remained, however, would Bobby Wallace agree. Three and a half minutes passed, Bobby's face re-maining expressionless the entire time. When the song ended, Harrell pressed the stop button and looked ex-pectantly at the legend as he took another pull from his cigar.

"You ladies sound divine," Bobby said finally.

Kimara and Harrell beamed.

"Thank you. That's high praise coming from you," Kimara said.

Bobby reached over to the coffee table in front of him and picked up his telephone. He quickly dialed a number.

"Yeah, this is Bobby Wallace. Let me speak to Tom."

Kimara and Harrell stole hopeful glances at one another, but sat quietly.

"Hey, Tommy, it's Bobby . . . nothing much, can't complain. Listen, I need you to take care of something for me. That new girl group, Speak Easy . . . yeah . . . *Tuesday's Lover* . . . uh-huh." Bobby stopped speaking momentarily as his lawyer explained the situation further to him.

"I see," he said finally. "Who is this Bronson Chandler?"

Anger flashed in Harrell's eyes as his suspicions were confirmed.

"Well I've got part of the group sitting in front of me right now, along with Mr. James. I think it's a good effort and these kids, they're on the right track. I say we give them the green light . . . uh-huh, okay. Make sure when you call down there, you let them know what's what. All right Tommy, take care and kiss Angela for me."

Bobby hung up and for the first time since they'd entered his home, he smiled at Kimara and Harrell.

"Thank you so much Bobby. We really appreciate this," Harrell beamed.

"No problem, young blood," Bobby said, shaking hands again with Harrell.

They prepared to leave, Bobby walking them to the door personally. "Listen here," he said, placing a hand on Harrell's shoulder. "You've got somebody in your camp who ain't particularly on your side, but I suspect you know that already."

"Yes sir, I do."

"All right then. Watch your back. And you young lady," Bobby said, turning to face Kimara, "you my dear are breathtaking, talented and humble—a triple threat. You take care of yourself 'cause this business is not for the meek or mild at heart. Mind my words and stay true. You'll be a star for sure."

"Thank you, Bobby," Kimara said as she leaned forward and hugged him.

Outside, Kimara and Harrell danced all the way to his car. Lady Luck had definitely shone on them that day, but surely Bronson Chandler wouldn't be able to say the same.

Bronson leaned back in the leather armchair in Mr. Vogel's office, puffing a cigar as he waited for him to enter. Vogel had called from his car as he headed into Smithtown's offices and asked his secretary to track Bronson down and tell him to meet him in his office right away. There was an urgent matter to discuss. Bronson smiled to himself now, certain that this urgent business was something to his own benefit. Maybe it was the raise and promotion he had been angling for. Everyone knew that Vogel was hoping to be able to take a backseat role in the company soon. In order to do this, he needed to have someone he could trust to fill in for him, take care of some of his duties and Bronson was planning to be that person. He had been working for Vogel for years now, and it was time he got his due.

George Vogel entered his office a short time later, a somber expression on his face.

"George, my main man, what do you know?" Bronson greeted, oblivious to the serious look his boss wore.

"Bronson."

"Listen George, I was already thinking ahead, about making moves. I just want you to know that I'm your man . . . whatever you need me to do, I'll get it done. You can count on that."

George Vogel studied the young man in front of him, disgusted by his brown-nosing as much as he was by Bronson's recent transgressions.

"Bronson, before you set yourself up for making

those moves you speak of, there's something you should know. I received an interesting phone call last night."

"Really? An interesting phone call . . . from who?" Bronson replied, the ingratiating smile he wore slowly dimming.

"Thomas Brickshaw, the attorney for Bobby Wallace. Ever heard of him?"

"Uh . . . no, well, I mean of course I've heard of Mr. Wallace. He's a legend . . . but uh, his attorney?"

"Yes, his attorney, Thomas Brickshaw. It seems Mr. Brickshaw got a call from his client instructing him to get in touch with me."

Bronson began sweating, realizing that this conversation was far removed from the conversation he thought he'd be having with Vogel. A sickening sensation arose in the pit of his stomach as his mind flip-flopped, trying to decipher what Vogel was not saying.

"Bronson, I recognize that you're an ambitious young man. In fact, that was one of the things I liked about you when I first hired you. Smithtown needs thirsty, go-getters who will overcome any obstacle to do what needs to be done to move the company forward."

"Well, yes, George, th . . . that's what I try to do . . . always," Bronson stammered.

"That drive to move forward, however, cannot be one born solely of personal ambition. I want people working for me who see their personal futures tightly interwoven with that of Smithtown."

"Yes, of course. And I assure you—"

"Let me finish Bronson. I have watched you over the years, watched you in your dealings with artists, with staff, and with individuals outside of this company. I had hoped you would have learned by now how things are done. I had also hoped that you would always take an ethical approach in everything you do, especially as it relates to this company. Unfortunately, that is not the case."

"George—"

"Quiet," Vogel demanded. "Please don't sit in my face and try to deny the facts Bronson. The fact is, you have a personal grudge against Harrell James. The fact is, you purposely set out to sabotage Speak Easy's project. The fact is, you withheld the paperwork for the track release from Wallace's people, and then turned around and sent them a promo copy of the album, knowing full well that they would go ballistic over that song. This company could have been slapped with a multi-million-dollar lawsuit because of your actions."

Bronson sunk further into his seat as bile rose in his throat and a pasty look cloaked his face. "Mr. Vogel . . . I don't kn . . . know what Harrell t . . . t . . . told you, but I didn't—"

"You *did* Bronson. And what's more, Harrell never told me anything. Harrell dealt with the situation and took the heat off of Smithtown without ever implicating you. It's funny, you've been so busy trying to be the *man*, you've failed to do the *job*. Son, I hope you learn something from this situation . . . something that will aide you in your future endeavors."

"Future endeavors?"

"Yes, Bronson. As of today, you're no longer an employee of Smithtown. Clean out your office within the hour."

Bronson protested, begged and pleaded and finally, with his tail tucked between his legs, slunk out of Vogel's office. Ironically, as he headed down the corridor leading to his office, past the studios, one of Speak Easy's tracks traveled with him, piping through Studio A's open door. He kept his head down as he passed.

Chapter 35

Kimara sprang from the hard plastic chair in which she had been sitting, gazing out of the window, when Jasmine stirred. She moved closer to the bed.

"Hey girl. How long have you been here?" Jasmine asked yawning, shifting in the bed, and trying with great difficulty to sit up.

"Here, let me help you," Kimara said. She propped the pillows behind Jasmine's back and held her arms as she shifted her body into a sitting position.

"A little while. I didn't want to wake you," Kimara answered when Jasmine was settled against the pillows.

"Have you seen her?" Jasmine asked referring to her brand new daughter who was less than three hours old.

"Yeah. Rick told them I was your sister and they let me into the neonatal ward. She's a dollbaby."

"Yeah and she's tough. She's going to be just fine," Jasmine smiled.

Kimara glanced away, afraid to look Jasmine in the eye. She didn't want her doubt to show. When Rick had called her that morning to say that Jasmine had gone into labor early, Kimara's heart just about stopped. She called her mother and together they'd prayed for the safety of both mother and child. By the time they'd finished, she'd felt sure that everything would, in fact, be all right. She'd gone to the hospital and waited downstairs until Rick came down to get her.

Looking at the baby had been the most heart-wrenching thing she had ever done. At three pounds, eight ounces, with tubes running every which way through her tiny body, it was hard for Kimara to be optimistic. The doctors had given a laundry list of the things that could go wrong with the baby and while they also explained all the strides which had been made in caring for premature infants, they were cautious in their predictions.

"She's going to be fine, Kimara. I just know it," Jasmine said again, her voice rising in demand that Kimara share her belief.

"Yes, she is. She's strong like her mama." Kimara surmised that if she allowed herself to say the words often enough, eventually she would believe them. "How are you feeling?" she asked the weary looking new mother.

"I'm okay. Tired as hell though. Who knew pushing a little baby out could drain you like this?" Jasmine asked with a laugh. "And girl, that mess hurt like hell. It felt like somebody was kicking me in the gut with steel-toed Timberland boots."

"Uh-uh," Kimara gasped, holding her hands to her mouth. "See, that's why I'm not having kids. You know I can't get a paper cut without passing out."

Jasmine laughed softly. "Oh, don't make me laugh. It still hurts downstairs."

"Sorry," Kimara comforted, stroking Jasmine's bare arm. "By the way, thanks to you and your impatient little bundle of joy, I had to cancel your baby shower."

"We're sorry about that. But once we come home you can go ahead with your plans for us. Since you're making those big bucks now, you'd better be doing something big and extravagant for us!"

"I'll just have to check my schedule now and get back to you guys when I'm free," Kimara mocked.

Jasmine rolled her eyes, laughing as softly as she could manage. "Where's Rick?" she asked.

"He's with the baby."

"He's been by my side for hours, ever since I went into labor. And I don't think he's slept at all, much less had anything to eat," Jasmine worried.

"How 'bout I go relieve him. I'll sit with the baby, and he can go home for awhile. Maybe get a little rest."

"Would you Kimara? You don't have to work in the studio or anything do you?"

"Girl please, I'm going to sit with my pretty little goddaughter and that's that. Harrell and the girls will get along just fine without me."

"Don't blow off business on account of us Kimara. You know—"

"Mother hen would you please knock it off already! I don't have to be anywhere. Now, get some rest and I'll see you later."

Kimara kissed Jasmine quickly on the forehead and headed toward the door.

"Thanks Kimara," Jasmine sighed. "And make sure Rick goes home to get some rest. Don't take no for an answer," she commanded.

A few minutes, a short elevator ride and several twists and turns down the long hospital corridors later, Kimara was back in the neonatal ward. She washed her hands and put on a paper gown with the aide of a young nurse. When she took a seat beside Rick, she watched in amazement as the heart monitor ticked, other gadgets whirred, and oxygen was ushered into the baby's tiny lungs. All of these contraptions were connected to the baby—who lay tucked inside an incubator—monitoring every aspect of her new life.

The baby's skinny limbs were covered with a fine layer of hair over thick, pale pink skin. Her rounded belly and puffy face were the biggest things on her little body. Her eyes were taped shut, but Kimara could tell that she was not asleep from the wild intermittent thrashing of her legs and arms. Each time the baby moved Kimara gained more confidence that she was going to be just fine. There was definitely no denying that this baby had her mother's fighting spirit.

"You're going to have to beat the guys off with a stick you know," Kimara whispered to Rick.

"Yeah, she's gonna be as pretty as her Mama," Rick agreed.

"Let's just hope she doesn't have that mouth," Kimara laughed. "Listen," she added, "your wife wants you to go home, have a bite to eat and get some shut-eye. She gave me permission to knock you over the head and drag you out of here if you resist."

Rick smiled, unable to take his eyes off of his baby just yet. He reached his hand through the pocket in the incubator and rubbed the baby's tiny leg.

"Did Jasmine tell you her name?"

"No," Kimara said, realizing for the first time that not only had Jasmine failed to mention it, in all the excitement Kimara hadn't even thought to ask. All of her focus was concentrated on willing the baby to live and be healthy it seemed, sending naming her to a distant second place.

"Her name is Faith." To the baby he grinned, "Right little girl . . . baby Faith," Rick repeated. "Jasmine named her," he added.

"Hey little Faith. A pretty name for a pretty girl," Kimara said.

They sat together for a half an hour before the fatigue really began to wear on Rick. His eyes drooped heavily and his head nodded a couple of times before Kimara nudged him and reminded him of Jasmine's orders.

"I'm glad you're here, Kimara. When Jasmine went

into labor, she kept telling me, 'Call Kimara, call Kimara.' You mean a lot to her . . . to me too."

"That's my girl. And Rick, I do owe you an apology for well, you know they way things have been between us. I have to admit that I didn't think you were good enough for Jasmine. But you've been nothing *but* good to her, and I couldn't ask for anything more than that."

"What? Don't tell me the fire-breathing dragon has a heart somewhere in there," Rick teased.

"Don't push it Mr. Wright," Kimara warned.

Rick looked forlornly at his daughter as he prepared to leave, as if he missed her already before he had even left the room. Kimara rubbed his back reassuringly, then ushered him gently toward the door.

Seated alone with baby Faith, Kimara was in awe of how precious life actually was. All the time she had spent confused and depressed seemed like time wasted now, and she felt ashamed of herself. There was a part of her heart that would always belong to Jared because he was the first person that she had ever fallen in love with. She would always hold some regrets about their relationship but she realized now that knowing him had helped her grow in many ways. For that, she was grateful.

Now it was time for her to get on with the business of living. Her fear of making the wrong choices had prevented her from taking a chance on anything worthwhile and she no longer chose to live that way. Fearing the future had kept her entrenched in what she believed to have been the best part of her life—an unattached and uncomplicated youth. But now she understood that the best was indeed yet to come.

Baby Faith kicked her legs into the air again, her tiny fists pumping frantically. It was as if she too, was ready to face life and all of its challenges, kicking butt and taking names. Faith had a hard road ahead of her, but Kimara no longer doubted that she'd make it through. The love Jasmine and Rick held for this baby was enough on its own to make that happen, and Kimara would be on the sidelines pulling for them every step of the way.

You win, I win
You lose, I lose
We walk
Together
You fight, I fight
You give, I give
We stand
Together
So tough the struggle
So long the road
So deep the bond
So pure the love
You live, I live
You die, I die
We are
Together

"Jasmine, this is Jared Porter. How are you?"

"Jared, wow, what a surprise. I'm doing just fine and yourself?" Jasmine asked into the phone, raising a brow at Rick who reciprocated. Rick was sitting on the sofa feeding the baby while Jasmine folded Faith's freshly washed and dried laundry.

Four weeks and three days had passed since Faith had made her startling entrance into the world. The family was now at home, settling into a new routine that had the proud parents deliriously exhausted and enjoying every minute of it.

"I can't complain. And Rick, how's he holding up?"

"Rick's just fine. He's sitting there holding his new baby girl as happy as he wants to be."

"Oh man, you had the baby already? Congratulations!" Jared exclaimed.

"Yeah, she surprised us by coming a little early, but she's doing just fine."

"That's beautiful. I'm so happy for you guys. Give Rick my best, and tell him I'd love to take him out for a celebratory drink some day."

"Thank you, Jared, I will. It's good to hear from you."

There was a pause in the conversation, Jasmine waiting for the real reason for Jared's call and he trying to find the right words to present it.

"How is she?" Jared asked finally, posing the question that he'd been dying to ask from the moment Jasmine had answered the line.

"Is it too hard to say her name?"

"Sometimes. I miss her," Jared admitted.

Jasmine smiled. "She's doing fine Jared and . . . she still misses you too, but if you repeat that, I'll deny it."

"I guess that means she's still the same, huh?"

"Well, she's mellowed a bit, especially since her new goddaughter showed up."

"That's nice. Listen, Jazz, I was thinking . . . uh, do you think she'd see me? Just to talk about things."

Jasmine beamed, the wheels of her meddlesome brain already turning in full gear as she planned Jared and Kimara's reunion. While there was always a small possibility that it would backfire and that Kimara would bite her head off and chew it up for dinner, Jasmine could hardly resist the chance to help her friend find her way back to the love of her life.

Chapter 36

The house lights were off. Kimara, Delphina and Simone held hands as they crossed the stage and took their places. The band was already seated, instruments in hand. Kimara closed her eyes and allowed the tranquility that had conquered a once embattled spirit to flow through her. She looked back in the wings where Jasmine stood and smiled. Her girl, her friend, her sister. So much time had passed since the day they met as little girls with no vision nor hopes past the next day's double-dutch game. Many tears had been cried, many quarrels had surfaced, to be squashed and then resurface again. But through it all, Kimara had been learning lessons and receiving blessings.

Jasmine had arrived shortly after sound check. It was the first time Kimara had seen her in the past three weeks. She looked good, having almost returned to her pre-baby weight. She was wearing a gold pants suit, brown leather boots and a matching brown leather swing coat. Her hair was freshly braided and hung down, framing her glowing face.

"What are you doing here so early?" Kimara asked as she sat at a vanity in the dressing room. She was sniffing the dozen red roses her father had had delivered earlier in the day. "And how's Faith?" Kimara added.

"She's just fine. My mom is at home with her. She's turning into a chubby little thing too. Tipped the scales at six pounds yesterday. The doctors are amazed at how quickly she's growing."

"Must be that mother love." Kimara smiled. "But again, what are you doing here? The show doesn't start until six."

"I came to check on you. You doing all right?" Jasmine asked.

"I'm nervous, you know, but at the same time I feel like I'm exactly where I'm supposed to be, at precisely the right time," Kimara mused wistfully. "It all feels so normal in an abnormal way."

"I'm so happy for you Kimara and . . . I'm so very, very proud."

"Really?" Kimara asked, feeling the tears forming even before they reached the surface.

"I know I give you a hard way to go and sometimes I've been so unfair to you. Part of me is jealous of you, I think."

"That's crazy. You've got so much—with Rick and the baby and teaching those kids. You always seemed like you knew exactly what to do. If anything, I was jealous of you," Kimara admitted shamefacedly.

Jasmine cupped Kimara's chin with two fingers. "Kimara, you've got this spirit that's so free and so unchained it's like watching a butterfly. It lands on a flower, sniffs around and then moves on. It rests near you for a moment and just when you think you can catch and keep it with you forever, it flies away. And you want to chase it but you know that its life is not yours. Part of you is happy for the little butterfly but part of you is afraid that it'll fly away and leave you forever."

"I'd never leave you girl. You're the only real friend

I've ever had. Who else would put up with me?" Kimara joked.

"I know that's right," Jasmine agreed laughing. "But seriously, you are so beautiful and talented, and I'm honored to be able say I know you. I always have been, whether I acted like it or not."

"Oooh, Jazz, stop it. I don't want to start blubbering and ruin my makeup," Kimara warned. The women hugged and they both began crying anyway. After several moments, and a dozen sobs and hiccups, they collected themselves.

"All right now. This is it. Your debut. Do your thing girl," Jasmine said as she stood and prepared to leave.

"You know it," Kimara promised as she dabbed at the mascara beneath her eyes.

"And remember, you've already got a fan club that loves you just for you."

When Kimara took the stage that night, it felt like coming home again. Within herself, she had found a passion that was familiar and comforting, as if she were finally face to face with the true spirit from which she had been trying to run away. The blue and green stage lights rose slowly and rotated across the stage in a slow pattern, illuminating the room. The hushed crowd waited, this time not with impatience but with eager expectation.

"Baby why you gotta make it so hard, when it should be easy?" Kimara asked in a low voice.

The audience erupted as she spoke the lyrics from *In Your Words*, the group's first single which was already burning the airwaves up. Delphina and Simone began singing and it was on. They performed song after song, giving the audience a taste of the mastery to come when the album hit stores the following day.

All three women wore original designs created especially for them and for this night. Kimara's was a micromini strapless dress which accentuated her toned

golden legs. Delphina wore pants and a halter top and
Simone, a form-fitting T-length dress. Their look and
their style was sensuality at its best and the women
worked the stage and the audience mercilessly. They
performed three of the thirteen songs on their new
album and by the time they were done, the crowd was
whooping and hollering, clamoring for more. Harrell
joined the group on stage and let the crowd know that
they could hear more by coming to one of the group's
upcoming concerts. The tour would be kicking off the
following month and the final concert would be in the
city at Madison Square Garden.

An hour later, Kimara left the stage elated. She
floated backstage, filled with a satisfaction that rivaled
almost any feeling she had ever known. As she stepped
backstage, headed for her dressing room, she stopped
midstride. Standing in the wings, an ebony figure as
striking as the first time she'd seen him dressed in his
police uniform, was Jared. In spite of the fact that she'd
believed herself to be over him and cured of the ache
he'd left, seeing him brought it all back. More than that,
it made her realize that she still loved him with the same
ferocity as ever.

He walked over to where she stood unable to move.
"You were amazing," he said.

Kimara looked away from him, the intensity of his
eyes too much for her to face.

"Kimara, I'm proud of you," Jared continued.

"What are you doing here Jared?" Kimara asked
finally.

"I wanted to wish you well on your album release."

"That's lame," Kimara countered, folding her arms
across her chest, her head cocked to one side.

Jared smiled in spite of himself, glad to be in the presence of that fire again and not giving a damn whether
he got burned or not. "Okay, I couldn't stay away. Since
the last time I saw you—"

"Oh, you mean the day I met your fiancée?" Kimara sneered weakly, wanting to hurt him as much as he'd hurt her.

"I've wanted to see you ever since that day."

"For what Jared? I think everything that needed to be said has been said, wouldn't you agree?"

"I ended it with Millicent."

Kimara looked at Jared, trying to read his expression but failing. Was he serious? All kinds of thoughts ran through her mind, colliding and crashing into one another until everything was a jumbled mess.

"What do you mean?" she asked.

"It's over between Millicent and me and to be honest, it never should have started. I can't possibly be happy with someone else when I'm still in love with you," Jared confessed bravely.

Kimara quietly contemplated Jared's words.

"But you proposed to her."

"But I don't love her. I love you."

"You left me Jared. You left me without looking back. How do you think that made me feel?"

"I know. I was wrong. But so were you Kimara. You didn't care enough about me to change—not one little bit. What was I supposed to do?"

"Love me the way I am—just like I loved you."

"I do love you Kimara. I love you so much it hurts. I'm not perfect and I don't expect you to be. I just want to be with somebody who knows all my faults and still accepts me," Jared reasoned.

"Didn't I do that Jared? Did I ever ask you to be something you weren't?"

"No, but for the longest time, Kimara, most of my adult life, I've been afraid to be anything. I couldn't quite be happy, couldn't quite trust you, couldn't quite just be. It was unfair to you for me to bring my issues into our relationship. I see that now. I realize now that by not dealing with my pain over losing my father, I've put up walls around me that even an amazing woman like you couldn't penetrate."

"Jared, this is all . . . this is too much. Right now, I feel like I've finally gotten myself together. I'm out in the world, a part of something big, something creative and wonderful."

"Are you happy?"

"Yes, Jared, I am. I'm very happy."

"Weren't you happy with me? At least a little bit?"

"Jared, I love you. Just as much today as I did when we were together. I . . . just . . . I don't think that I have the right to ask to be any happier than this."

"Yes, you do. And so do I," Jared exploded. "Kimara, we had something real, something potentially fantastic. I refuse to let that slip away."

"Jared, you can't control everything. Haven't you learned that just because you want something to be a certain way, doesn't mean that's what's going to happen?"

Jared silently regarded Kimara, stared into sparkling buttery light brown eyes and he saw the love she held for him shining there. Kimara, always playing the tough-guy role, was this time unable to hide what she really felt inside.

"Why does it always have to be a fight with you?"

"'Cause that's how it is. I am who I am . . . like it or leave it."

"Is it really that simple for you?"

Kimara stayed rooted to her place, although the scared little girl in her wanted to run like gold medal-winner Marion Jones in the two hundred meter dash. She wanted to run so fast and so far that her feelings would lag two days behind. But she knew that eventually it would all catch up to her and she'd still be loving Jared as much as she did right now.

"No, not always," she responded and in an instant found herself in Jared's arms again. The love that lay rooted firmly in his eyes was enough to silence the child in her, allowing the woman she had become to emerge. Kimara had reached a new plateau in her life, on her own terms and at the same time, discovered that she was precisely who she was meant to be.

Their reunion was interrupted by a sudden flash of cameras, lights shining in their faces.

"Kimara, can we ask you a few questions?"

"What predictions do you have for the success of this album?"

"Is this the man in your life Kimara?"

Kimara had become accustomed to this type of scene, but she knew instinctively that Jared would be made uncomfortable. She turned to face him, for the moment ignoring all the commotion around them. She slipped the key to her suite upstairs into his hand and leaned close to whisper in his ear. "Room 1710. Will you wait for me?"

A slow smile spread across Jared's face. He looked down at the beautiful newly famous woman in front of him, feeling like the luckiest man on the face of the Earth.

"I'll wait for you forever," he whispered back, taking the key. He squeezed her hand and then slipped away, leaving Kimara to the adoring crowd.

Speak Easy shook hands, signed autographs and answered questions for over an hour. Her parents fought their way through the crowd to congratulate her.

"You were magnificent," Gena said, her face wet from the tears of joy which she'd been crying all evening.

"Mom, you're going to ruin your makeup," Kimara joked as she dabbed at her mother's eyes.

"That's what I told her," William said, his own eyes full of water.

"You two are a mess," Kimara teased. "Thank you guys for being here tonight. I can't think of what could have made it better."

"I can," Gena said smiling conspiratorially at her husband.

They had run into Jared shortly before the show had started and he'd told them of his intentions. They both wished him luck and hoped that their stubborn daughter would find a way to forgive whatever had happened between them and move on.

Gena excused herself to the ladies room to freshen up. William gave his daughter another tight squeeze and she thanked him again for being there. She had never confronted her father about what her mother had told her. She realized that it was not her place to question what went on between them as husband and wife. She was just glad that they had managed to keep it together, despite the odds. She prayed that twenty-some-odd years from now she'd be able to boast of having done the same thing with Jared.

William knew that Kimara had been told about his transgression. Gena was apologetic about having dug up their past wounds but had felt certain that it was something Kimara needed to hear. He wrestled with broaching the subject with Kimara, but realized that if she needed to hear about it from him, she would ask. He appreciated the fact that she never did and their relationship had not changed in the slightest way by her knowing. His little girl had definitely, and finally, grown up and from now on, he could concentrate on preparing for his and his wife's golden years and needn't worry about her.

The celebratory mood in the ballroom could not hold Kimara's attention as she thought about Jared waiting for her upstairs. She remained on edge and anxious throughout the interviews and champagne toasts. Finally, she found a moment when a great escape was possible, and she seized it. She slipped out of the ballroom, knowing that eventually she would be missed, but not caring in the least. This night of magic had just begun for her, as the man her soul had been calling out to for months waited to reclaim her and she, him.

Kimara arrived on the seventeenth floor and practically ran down the long corridor to her suite. The door was slightly ajar, and she pushed it open hesitantly. Inside, everything was illuminated by a barrage of dinner candles. She stepped into the suite, closing the door behind her.

"Jared," she called out, just as she noticed a trail of yellow rose petals leading from the door into the sitting room. She giggled softly and followed the trail slowly, her heart threatening to jump from her chest in anticipation.

Jared stood near the fireplace waiting for her. He had removed his suit jacket, his dress shirt and his T-shirt. His bare torso with skin flawlessly smooth and even, like the rich darkness of a Hershey's milk chocolate bar, caught her eye first. A nervous smile rested on his face as he picked a small square of dark chocolate from the carton in his hands and offered it to Kimara.

Kimara approached him, placed her hand over his and bit into the rich dark sweet Jared dangled before her. She took a huge chunk of its minty freshness partially into her mouth. Holding it between clenched teeth, she moved her face closer to Jared's. She rubbed the candy slowly and delicately across Jared's lips. He parted them and she inserted the exposed portion of the chocolate into his mouth. He closed his lips over it and over Kimara's sweet lips. Together, they devoured the savory morsel and each other, relishing the stickiness left behind as if it were their last meal.

Jared ran his hands through Kimara's short natural and tugged at the curly roots as he pulled her body to his. Once, he had believed that the only way he would touch her again would be in his dreams. Yet here he was, fully awake, and he wanted to consume her and to be consumed by her. He wanted to stroke every part of her delicious body, inside and out.

Kimara moaned as Jared's tongue lapped at her throat. She, too, was eager to reclaim his body, to make her mark on him. The memory of the heights of pleasure he had once sent her to egged her on. She demanded a repeat performance.

Jared led Kimara along the path of yellow roses to the bathroom. Candles burned brightly, casting alluring shadows across the room. The Jacuzzi whirred softly, bubbles dancing and crashing against one another inside. A bottle of Dom Perignon sat chilling in a bucket of ice, two champagne glasses beside it.

Kimara unbuckled Jared's slacks and let them drop to his knees. She wanted to see all of his magnificence, unencumbered, unveiled. She shoved his boxer shorts south too, and he stepped out of them. Her eyes hungrily roamed his body, taking in everything from his muscular calves to his silky black eyebrows. She rubbed his chiseled chest, the soft fine hair which blanketed it tickling her fingers. She followed the rippling muscles of his abdomen, down to strong hips, finally moving her hands around back to feel the firmness of his tight rear.

He delighted in her touch, felt electrified by it. With eyes that burned with desire, she stared at him as she gingerly felt the steel that was both his pleasure-receiver and giver. She massaged him slowly, applying just enough pressure to tease and tantalize, but not enough to drive him over the edge. Not just yet, for as much as she wanted to satisfy him, she wanted equally to savor this moment, this night of nights and every minute of their reunion.

Jared pushed Kimara away, turning her around so that her back faced him. She leaned against the counter-top, the wall-length mirror taking a picture of them. In the mirror he looked at her, into her soul by way of sparkling eyes. She smiled at him. He unzipped her dress and peeled it from her body. Kimara kicked it away from them with a three-inch heel. Jared cupped her breasts, filled his large hands with them as he kneaded and squeezed them. He released one and ran his thumb across the erect nipple. Kimara inhaled sharply—sucking in air as if she had just remembered to breathe. She turned to face Jared and they kissed for a long time—a sweet surrendering of both a physical and emotional nature. The length of him pressed against her, expressing his need to bury himself within her. He lifted her onto the counter, never breaking the connection their mouths had made. Quickly, as though a second was much too long to wait, Jared retrieved a condom from the wallet in his pants pocket.

Kimara gasped audibly when he entered her, piercing an opening that had seemingly sealed itself for lack of having known his touch for all those months. Her body welcomed him, a roll–out–the–red–carpet type of welcome. Jared grasped the chilled bottle of champagne and poured it slowly down the front of Kimara's nude body, over each nipple and down the center. Kimara screamed once and then again as Jared's tongue traced the cold liquid, making her feel like fire and ice at the same time. She arched her back, leaned against the mirror and moved her hips demandingly against his. Pelvis to pelvis, face to face and eye to eye, they rode one another, over one hill after another, climbing higher and higher until only the blue horizon of ecstasy remained in view.

"Ja-red," Kimara screamed, loving the sound of his name as it bounced off the walls around them as much as she loved the feel of him in her body.

Jared's voice was lost to him. He could only whimper as he fought not to release the life force within him. A valiant fight, but he could not hold back, it was way too good. He climaxed, driving himself as far as he could into her candy-filled walls and his last full-body thrust penetrated her soul and sent her heart, mind and body over the final hill to meet his.

Satiated for the moment, they climbed into the bubble-filled Jacuzzi that awaited them, the water, now cool, feeling good against their sweaty bodies. They sank into the tub, touching and teasing one another, still not believing that the impossible had actually taken place. They were together again, despite how bleak things had seemed, how insurmountable the odds. Neither had any intention of letting what had so beautifully been reconstructed ever be torn apart again.

Chapter 37

Who am I to want more?
when I am owed nothing
Where should I go to find?
what I am looking for
Why should you care?
Because you love me.

The boat swayed gently under the weight of a mild spring wind. Two weeks ago, Kimara had led Jared blindfolded down the pier, having told him that she had a surprise waiting for him on Marco's boat. Only, when she finally removed the blindfold, they stood in front of a thirty-foot miniature yacht. The name on the side read *Horizon*.

Using a portion of her deal money, Kimara had made a sizeable down payment on the boat in Jared's name. He was overcome and unable to react when she handed him the keys and the bill of sale. The look of sheer joy and gratitude on his face made her want to cry herself.

Kimara looked out at the horizon, the tangerine-painted sky as still as a picture in a frame. Jared stood behind her, his arms encircling her body tightly as if to protect her from falling overboard.

"Three months is a long time you know," Jared commented.

He was referring to the three-month tour that Speak Easy was embarking on the very next day. They were co-headliners in a Birch Liquors Virtual Tour which was headed to forty cities across the United States. Tomorrow Kimara would be doing a sound check at the Louisiana Superdome in New Orleans. She looked back longingly at Jared, already missing him.

"I know," she answered solemnly.

"I was thinking that, uh, time might go faster if we were to seal the deal now."

"What do you mean by 'seal the deal'?" Kimara asked.

Jared reached beneath the steering wheel and retrieved a medium-sized silver-wrapped box from a small shelf. A satin ribbon was tied around the perimeter ending in an elaborate bow on the top. Kimara slowly untied the ribbon and timidly removed the box's lid.

She gasped. The inside of the box was filled with red and white rose petals. In the center, perched in a cradle of red velvet sat a two-carat round diamond ring in an intricate white gold setting. Kimara removed the ring from the box and looked from it to Jared.

"It was my mother's ring. My father gave it to her, his mother having worn it and given it to him."

Jared had known about the ring all of his life, having been told that it was a treasure that had been handed down for generations and that it signified a spirit of love and family. He had never considered giving it to Millicent, and although he was not conscious of it at the time, this was probably due to the fact that in his heart he'd always known that she was not the one for him.

"It's beautiful." Kimara looked from the ring to Jared. "Are you sure you want to take me on for life? You might be biting off more than you can chew."

"I've already taken you on for life. You make me smile even when I think I don't have anything to smile about.

For a long time I felt like I didn't have a right to be happy. Maybe that's what made me so uptight all the time, feeling guilty over being joyful. You make me feel like dancing and singing and what's more, I know now that it's okay to want to do those things. And I also know . . . I know in my soul that wherever you go, I want to go. Whatever you need, I want to be the one to give it to you. I don't care what else is going on in the world, as long as I have that pretty smile focused on me, it's all good," Jared said without taking a breath.

Kimara began to cry, the sheer ecstasy of what she felt for Jared too much to contain. She had spent so much time worrying about being trapped by circumstances outside of her control that she almost let true happiness slip through her fingers. Jared's love made her feel freer than she'd ever thought possible.

She slid the ring onto her ring finger. A perfect fit.

"In case you haven't noticed by now, I have a hard time being in relationships. I need to know that if I falter and if I do things that disappoint you, you'll still be here," Kimara said, her eyes questioning him.

"You have my word. And when I stumble or just act like an ass—"

"I'll still be here," Kimara smiled.

She wished that she had a crystal ball with which she could look into the future and see the mistakes she was sure she would make before they happened. She worried that she would not be the kind of partner that Jared deserved, but she loved him too much not to try. Of course, there was no crystal ball nor was she clairvoyant. If she were, she would know that she and Jared would spend the rest of their lives together, in love. She would know that Speak Easy would become a multi-platinum selling group, receiving numerous awards and accolades. She would see that she and Harrell would go on to become partners and launch their own successful record label. She would also know that baby Faith would grow to be a healthy, happy child and that Jasmine's second baby, a son, would be born exactly two weeks before her own son and that these two boys would grow up to be best friends who were more like brothers.

Not knowing any of this, Kimara relied on the love she had in her heart and the hopes and dreams she'd dared to envision, stepping out on faith.

"I love you Jared Porter, and I would be honored to be your wife," she declared.

As easy as summer rain and moonlit nights, frothy waves and bareback horse rides of which Kimara spoke in her music, their love was the purest of melodies. Their hearts sang, and sang, and sang. . . .

Chapter 38

What is Love
Breathe in, breathe out
Free to inhale
Cushioning blades of grass,
the finest carpet beneath my feet
Liquid sun caressing
skin so thirsty, so wanting
Blue blue salt water
lapping hungrily it's kisses icy
Breathe in, breathe out
No restrictions, no constrictions
No titles, no labels
No commands, no demands
This is love.
Breathe in, breathe out
Free to exhale

Dear Reader:

I hope you enjoyed Jared and Kimara's tale. More importantly, I hope that through them you find the courage in your own lives to take chances and seize opportunities.

The best part of writing for me is being able to tell the stories of loving, romantic people who are just like you and me. Like us, Kimara and Jared are trying to find themselves as they make their way through this crazy thing called life. And, just like us, their road is sometimes bumpy, sometimes unsure, but always exciting.

Keep an eye out for my next novel, which promises to sizzle just as much!

Continue reading and loving.

Yours truly,

Kim Shaw

About the Author

Kim Shaw resides in Roselle, New Jersey, with her husband and two children. She works as a high school English teacher, is active in her community, and is currently working on a third novel.

BOOK YOUR PLACE ON OUR WEBSITE AND MAKE THE ARABESQUE ROMANCE CONNECTION!

We've created a customized website just for our very special Arabesque readers, where you can get the inside scoop on everything that's going on with Arabesque romance novels.

When you come online, you'll have the exciting opportunity to:

- View covers of upcoming books

- Learn about our future publishing schedule (listed by publication month and author)

- Find out when your favorite authors will be visiting a city near you

- Search for and order backlist books

- Check out author bios and background information

- Send e-mail to your favorite authors

- Join us in weekly chats with authors, readers and other guests

- Get writing guidelines

- AND MUCH MORE!

Visit our website at
http://www.arabesquebooks.com